PRAISE FOR THE LOVE OF GLITTER

"☆☆☆☆☆☆ "A drama-filled, coming-of-age novel, perfect for older YA who enjoy character-focused, suspense-filled novels. I'm delighted to recommend this novel to 14 - 17-year-olds who enjoy a smartly crafted story populated with complex young characters. I think most readers will enjoy getting to know the full-on personality of Grey and watching how she and Sy develop. All in all, a fab read."

WISHING SHELF REVIEWS

"Young adult readers will find *For the Love of Glitter* a powerful story of love, struggle, and survival that's realistic in its fantasy worlds and hard to put down.

DIANE DONOVAN- DONOVAN'S LITERARY
AND MIDWEST BOOK REVIEW

"It's refreshing to see a teen character who confronts mature situations in realistic and thoughtful ways: first loves, friendships, and family loyalty. Combined with the swashbuckling scene in Bosch, this makes the latest Grey Shima story a compelling adventure."

—EMILY AUERSWALD, SECONDARY
SCHOOL LIBRARIAN

"A captivating and down to Earth sci-fi packed with the complexities of friendship, love, and self-discovery."

—SARAH NEWLAND, AUTHOR OF *EXTANT*

PRAISE FOR OTHER BOSCH ADVENTURES

"Swashbuckling, vengeance and heart - all wrapped up in one heck of a strong woman."

—SALLY ALTASS, AUTHOR OF *THE WITCH LAWS* AND REEDSY.COM REVIEWER FOR *A MERRY LIFE*

"A rollicking page-turner, *North Country* captured my heart and imagination from the very first page. Sarah Branson's storytelling shines with rich, narrative prose and heart-pounding pacing. She crafted a story of resilience and empowerment that kept me on the edge of my seat, turning the pages late into the night."

—HEIDI MCINTYRE, AUTHOR OF *SEA MAGIC*

"I LOVED IT! I don't usually like books but this one really blew me away. I liked Grey as a character and I kinda wish we were friends in real life."

LIA, 14 FOR *UNFURLING THE SAILS: A GREY SHIMA ADVENTURE*

FOR THE LOVE OF GLITTER

A GREY SHIMA ADVENTURE

SARAH BRANSON

SOONER STARTED PRESS

For more information, visit www.sarahbranson.com

Edited by Rebecca Maizel, David Aretha
and Andrea Vanryken
Cover design by The Book Designers:
Ian Koviak and Alan Dino Hebel

ISBN (paperback): 978-1-957774-20-6
ISBN (ebook): 978-1-957774-21-3
Printed in the United States of America

"When the whole world is silent, even one voice becomes powerful."

-MALALA YOUSAFZAI

ARANIA
NORTH COUNTRY
DOBARRI
FAIRNEAU
Toronto
TABONNE
BOSCH
New Lisbon
Haida
New Detroit
OCEANS BAY
Truvale
STATE OF ETERNIA
BELLCOAST
MENIA
NEW CARIBBEAN
Boiling
PARIDA
Seething Swamp
DAKAL
District Ⓘ   Banking, Financial, Theater
Distract Ⓘ   Light Industry, Business
District Ⓘ   Mining (Clay & Glitter)
District Ⓘ   Harbor
District Ⓥ   Mining, Manufacturing (Bricks &
     Glitter) also a developing artist community
District Ⓥ   Agricultural (Grains, Livestock)
District Ⓥ   Agricultural (Vineyards, Orchards)

Toft
Birka
RUTHENIA
CANIA
Burnt Wasteland
RUS
Yakutian Plateau
CHINA
Kiharu
Steppe Infinite
New Beijing
EDO
New Shanghai
Khumi City
Scorching Frontier
Arabia Deserta
w Cairo
Sarapion Grasslands
d Savannah
A Black Flatlands
B BPF (Bosch Pirate Force) Base
C Old airfield
D Residential areas
E Downtown
F Hidden cave (behind Mt. Tamrood)
G Canyon
   Wooded areas
IV
III
V
Saltend
Saltend Harbor
A
B
I
II
E
D
C
Quiet River
F
G
VI
Tamrood River
Mt. Tamrood
VII
BOSCH

CONTENTS

A BRIEF HISTORY OF GLITTER

Excerpt from *Foundations of New Earth: A Boschian Perspective*, First Year Civics and History Edition, 2370

"To understand Bosch is to understand Glitter—not as a vice, but as a vital force."

~Master Commander Emeritus Miles Baldwin-Bosch

Over a century ago, during the Great Sea Escape, a fleet of five ships led by Hizir Bosch made landfall on what would become the independent pirate nation of Bosch. Borne of the Uprising, these now-freed thralls—descendants of the survivors of the Climate Wars, the Great Flooding, and the collapse of Old Earth's governments—sought refuge and renewal. They found it on a rocky island rich in peat bogs, brackish water, and wild opportunity.

While excavating clay from the northern bogs to mold bricks for shelter and defense, early Bosch settlers unearthed a peculiar, iridescent fungus within the peat. Veins of this new fungus shimmered with a glitter-like sheen in sunlight and, when dried and ingested, induced mild euphoria, heightened sensation, and temporary enhanced perception. Dubbed *Glitter* by the early builders, the fungus was at first a curiosity—then a revelation.

Though Bosch culture, founded on strict personal discipline and communal integrity, rejected the use of Glitter among its own people, its economic potential was undeniable. Trade routes soon flourished. Within two generations, Glitter became the planet's most coveted substance—outlawed in some territories, taxed heavily in others, yet always in demand.

Today, Bosch remains the sole producer and exporter of Glitter. Every shipment is monitored and marked, its origin traceable through the bioluminescent markers embedded in the product. Revenues from the Glitter trade fund universal healthcare, education, infrastructure, and a guaranteed basic income for all citizens of Bosch. Despite its controversial nature abroad, at home, Glitter is viewed as a sacred commodity—one not consumed, but honored for what it provides.

Glitter is more than an export. It is the cornerstone of Boschian sovereignty, a symbol of resilience, and a reminder that even in the muck of bogs, something brilliant can grow.

CHAPTER 1
BOARDGAMES AND GLITTER

GREY

"What do you mean, they refused to pay?" Mama's voice cuts sharp from the study, slicing into the living room where Sy and I are deep into the final Skyriders & Serpents battle before school starts.

I usually tune out her work calls—master commander of Bosch, first woman to hold that title, no big deal—but this one snags my attention.

Sy's eyes widen. He mouths, "Glitter?"

A shudder runs through me. I hate that word—Glitter. It always sounds so sparkly and harmless. Before the shipwreck, I used to think so too. But I've seen what it can do. It can lead people to their deaths.

I nod.

We edge closer to the study door, leaning in without making a sound.

"What else?" A pause. "Protesters? Dammit."

I grin. I'll take any anti-Glitter sentiment. Sy gets a silent thumbs-up from me, and he chuckles. We both tune back to the conversation on the door's other side.

"Yeah, we're seeing more of that." A beat. "Ugh. Fucking Bluies. They're the worst."

A low shiver slides down my spine, and my eyes widen. Bluies *are* the worst. Two summers ago, when I was stranded on the Drowned Islands, they tried to use Glitter as a virus bomb and almost got away with it.

"They what?! Was anyone injured?" Mama's voice hardens with every question. "Seriously? Did we fire on them? Sweet New Earth, I can't believe the flight engineer was that careless. Well, they need to understand the price of Glitter." A long inhale. "The FE will face consequences. I'll have Major Holloway handle discipline. And listen—you know I won't have my troopers put at risk just to maintain a relationship with some backwater bigwig who thinks he's above paying for our Glitter." Another pause. "Cut him out. And get Engineering to check the engines." Click.

Sy and I scramble back to the board game, pretending we've been here all along. I shove a handful of dice into place, trying to focus on finding Yvarax, the most dangerous serpent in the game. But the conversation buzzes in my brain like some rogue wasp. Then—*bang*! A red-gold blur barrels toward me.

"Rummy, no—sit, girl!" I yelp, but it's too late. Rummy collides with the ottoman, sending dice, board tiles, and character pieces scattering across the floor. "Dammit! I was about to slay Yvarax!" I groan even as my hands find Rummy's floppy ears, scratching them despite myself.

Sy's already laughing, crawling across the floor to scoop up pieces. "Sorry, Grey. But you know the rules—external forces count!" He flashes a teasing grin. "Looks like next kill's mine."

I stick my tongue out at him. "Traitor."

Sy Mercer. My best friend since second-year advanced maths. I still remember how terrified he looked when I dropped into the only open seat next to him—lanky, thick-rimmed glasses, hair like a permanent windstorm. It hadn't taken long to realize we were basically the same: obsessed with sailing, fantasy stories, and sharp cheese and allergic to dating drama.

With Sy I can be myself even that self is alternately tense, suspicious, and reckless. I mean, Leia and I have been friends since we were little kids, but she doesn't get what it's been like for me the past few years. There's a part of me that never fully relaxes. Not since the summer Abernathy got too close, and I thought I'd lost everything in a single breath. I just call it That Awful July to everyone else. But to me? It was the month I stopped believing that everything would be okay and everyone would always be safe. Even in the warmest of moments, I know this cozy chaos could be ripped away in a heartbeat. So I have to be vigilant. But I don't say that to Mama—she has enough on her plate. Or to Leia because she thinks I'm being overdramatic. But Sy… Sy has been star-sent for me. He listens. He always makes things lighter. Safer.

And two years after me taking that seat, he is still always there for me. Of course, he's taller now, his shoulders a little broader, and I'm… Well, my clothes fit different too. Growing up sucks.

Sy's laughter dies off when Rini, my four-year-old whirlwind of a little sister, toddles over, big brown eyes blinking. "What you doin', Sy?" she lisps.

Sy grins and taps her nose. "Saving Grey's sorry hide from total defeat."

"That Rummy ruined!" I add, shooting Rini a mock stern look.

Her bottom lip trembles. "I sowwy," she whispers, lifting her arms.

I melt, then scoop her up and pepper kisses across her cheeks until she giggles uncontrollably.

"You know I can't stay mad at you." I ruffle Rummy's head too. "Or you either, you fluffy chaos monster."

Mama pokes her head out of the kitchen, smiling at the mess. "Uh-oh. Looks like a Rini and Rummy tornado hit."

"It's okay." I sigh. "We were almost done. I just really wanted my chance to slay that serpent."

"Well, you'll have to wait until after dinner." Mama's gaze shifts to Sy. "You staying? You know you're family."

Sy blushes, fumbling out, "Uh, sure, MC—Ms. Wallace—uh, Kat." He ducks his head, scrambling to gather the last of the game pieces while asking, "Can I do anything to help?"

Mama laughs. "Besides calling me Kat, can you cook the chicken? Just looking at it makes me queasy."

I catch Sy's startled look. He doesn't know yet. Mama's expecting again. Another Wallace–Warner—and sorta Shima— sibling in the works. "I'm on it!" he says quickly, disappearing into the kitchen.

Mama smiles at his retreating back, then turns to me. "I always like it when Silas is over. He's a good one. Now can you go call your brothers in to wash up?"

I grin, setting Rini down. "Yeah, yeah. I'll go gather the boys."

As I head toward the back door, Rini tugging on my hand, a whisper of Mama's words flickers through my mind—Bluies. Protesters. And Glitter—always Glitter. What did Mama say on the comm? *They need to understand the price of Glitter.* I know the price. It's death, destruction, and trouble. The world outside is changing faster than we are ready for.

And Monday, final year begins.

♡

SY

"Daddy home!" Rini called out from her boosted seat at the table.

Sy glanced up from where he was setting the roasted chicken thighs on the table in time to see Grey's mom, Kat Wallace, scoot back from her chair and cross the room to greet her partner, Colonel Matt Warner. Grey always called him her "bonus dad," and from the way he treated her and the twins, it was obvious he thought of them as his own, no different from Rini.

Across from Sy, Grey tucked a stray strand of hair behind her ear before picking up the serving spoon for the potatoes. In his chest, a thrill, like butterflies—a stupid, automatic reaction that he shoved aside before focusing on the food.

"Hi, Colonel Warner," he greeted, nodding as the tall, dark-skinned man with the scar on his cheek stepped inside, slipping off his shoes. He had the kind of presence that made people sit up a little straighter—Sy included.

"Well, Sy! Good to see you," Warner rumbled in his deep voice. "I see you're helping out as usual. Let me get washed up, and I'll be right there."

A few moments later, all seven of them were seated around the table, chatting about their Saturday. The warm smell of roasted chicken and spiced potatoes filled the kitchen, but Sy was barely paying attention to the food. Not with Grey sitting across from him, tilting her head in that thoughtful way she did when she was half-listening, half-lost in her own thoughts. He knew that look. It usually meant she was about to say something that would make people either admire her or argue with her.

Kat—he was okay calling her that in his head, but as usual, when he opened his mouth, his words got muddled—leaned toward the colonel and asked in a low voice, "How was your mission this morning? No problems? No protesters?"

Warner answered casually, scooping another serving of pota-toes onto his plate. "Easy as could be—just a quick Glitter drop on the outskirts of Toronto."

The second the words left his mouth, the table went silent.

Sy barely had time to brace himself before Grey slammed her flatware down. "Ugh! Glitter? Again? Are you serious right now?" Her brow wrinkled, voice rising with each word. "How can Bosch keep selling that stuff? How can *you*, Matt? It's awful. It kills people!"

Here we go.

Her dark eyes flashed, voice full of fire, and Sy knew—*knew*—that there was no stopping her once she got like this. She burned bright, Grey Shima, and he...he'd spent years trying not to stare too long, not to let himself get pulled in.

Her mom, as always, stayed calm. "Grey, I know you have strong feelings about the Glitter trade. And we respect your views. But the views of one person…"

"It's not just one person, Mama!" Grey shot back. Her hands curled into fists on the table, and Sy had this absurd urge to reach across and smooth them out, to calm her even though he knew she didn't want calming. "There are lots of us in Bosch that hate Glitter and what it does."

"Please don't interrupt and lower your voice." Kat's voice was still steady but sharper now. "Glitter was what made it possible for our ancestors to cease marauding. It has been around since before any of us, or even any of your grandparents, were born. The Bosch rely on its sale. It is the backbone of our economy…"

"But—"

Kat held up a hand, cutting her off. "I do not disagree that there are complications and moral gray areas surrounding it…"

"Gray areas?" Grey scoffed, half-rising from her seat. "No. It's wrong and—"

And then, something shifted. Sy felt it before he saw it—the way the air in the room went still, the way even Rini, usually oblivious to adult conversations, stopped moving.

Grey must have felt it too because for the first time in the argument, she hesitated.

Kat wasn't just Grey's mom anymore, or just the woman who always welcomed Sy into their home, who made the best fish stew he'd ever had, who treated him like family. Now she was the master commander of Bosch. And when she spoke again, her voice wasn't that of a mother scolding her child. It was the voice of a leader, sure and unshakable, giving an order, absolute and final.

"Your input and opinion are noted, Ms. Shima. This conversation is now at an end. We can discuss the subject another time."

If she had spoken to him like that, Sy would have wanted to melt into the carpet.

But Grey?

She just exhaled sharply, shaking out her hair as she met her mother's gaze with equal intensity. Sy swallowed, his throat dry. It wasn't the first time he'd watched her take a stand, and it wouldn't be the last. But every time, it made something tighten in his chest—something he couldn't name, something he didn't dare name.

Finally, she pressed her lips together, pushed her chair back, and stood. "Fine. But we *will* have this conversation again." Her voice was measured now, the fire banked but not extinguished. She turned toward the counter. "I'll get the fruit salad."

Sy let out a slow breath and caught the colonel's eye. Warner gave the tiniest shake of his head as if to warn, *Don't get involved.*

Not a problem. Sy wasn't about to step into the crossfire between Grey Shima and Kat Wallace. But he also wasn't about to stop looking at Grey when she wasn't watching.

CHAPTER 2
AND WE'RE BACK AND MOVING FORWARD

GREY

First day of final year. I turn and wave to Mama and Matt, who always drop us off on our first day. A pang of wistfulness hits me as I realize that this is my last drop-off. The wave of emotion surprises me, and I look back as Matt pulls the vehicle out of the drive and heads home. Then I shepherd my brothers to the big front doors. Kik and Mac are starting secondary this year. It's funny, I always think of my brothers as little kids, but they really aren't. Glancing at their faces, I can tell they are scared spitless but trying to play it cool.

Kik has gone full Edoan artist, with close-fitting black trousers and a black knit shirt covered with a stylized Edoan black haori adorned on the back with a golden fox and lotus flowers on the sleeves. Mac, definitely more like me when it comes to clothes, is wearing casual denims and a green tunic—though the tunic has a stylish asymmetrical hem, belted with Papa T's old BPF belt from when he was a new trooper a million years ago. They both look good and really grown up.

"You guys look great," I encourage. "Real storm-stoppers.

You'll have a great day. First-years hang over there." I point to a section at the main hall's far edge, where several equally nervous thirteen-year-olds are milling. I grin at my twin baby brothers. "See you in the halls." I wink and they grin before heading off to see their friends.

I move toward the final-year section of the main hall, and a couple of third-years see me. "Hi, Grey! I like your outfit," one of them calls.

"Thanks. First-day fancy," I answer, and they laugh as if I said something remarkably hysterical. Kids…

I do look nice. I'm wearing a pair of charcoal, very slim-fit, cargo-style pants with a few zip pockets on the thighs. Super comfortable but fitted in all the right places. They already passed the parent test because Mama paused when I wore them downstairs and asked, "I shouldn't be upset by those, right?"

"No, Mama. It's the style. And these are the looser ones," I promised, though her vague hoot of disapproval assured me I had chosen well. I paired the pants with a boat-necked shirt in seafoam with a subtle wave print on it. It's bamboo because September is still quite hot. I finished the outfit with my regular boots and the leather cuff bracelet with a working compass that Sy gave me for my fifteenth birthday.

I find my group and slip in. Sy gives me a soft punch on the arm. "Nice bracelet," he grins.

My best girlfriend, Leia, gives me a hug as she blurts, "It's my Pebble!" That's the nickname she gave me long ago; she says I may be little, but I cause plenty of ripples. "How are you? How was your weekend?"

The question stirs up big feelings as I snort with derision and start to unload my frustration about yesterday, irritation still simmering under my skin. "I had to sit through yet another patented Kat Wallace discourse on how the world isn't just black or white."

Sunday dinner is always for extended family, and usually, I

enjoy the time with my cousins, aunts, and uncles, plus Mama M, my mama's mama; and Jace, her new husband. But today, I'm still fuming—first from the lecture Mama gave me that morning when she warned me not to start a scene, and then from having to sit through my uncles waxing poetic about the "glorious history" of Glitter in Bosch as they laughed over their midday meal. I really had wanted to start a scene then, but I didn't—only because I'd given my word. I could barely choke down my dinner, though it was one of my favorites: braised lamb shanks with rosemary and garlic mashed sweet potatoes.

For years, I wanted to be just like Mama—pilot, pirate, fearless leader—and I mean, years. I remember thinking that way before I even started school. But something about That Awful July made me see Mama a little differently, and ever since I learned what Glitter really costs, all I can think about is how to make Bosch better. Safer. For Rini and for my brothers. For the girl I used to be, the one who didn't know what cruelty looked like up close. But does that mean the Force or something else?

Leia giggles and flips her newly dyed hair, which shimmers in orange and red. "Well, she did name you Grey, Pebs."

Her remark sends a ripple of laughter through the group, starting with Mason—the boy Leia currently "can't live without." They actually are wearing matching armbands with their initials entwined now. I control my eyeroll and make a mental note to ask Leia later when they reached that level of commitment. The ripple passes on to Anya and Paige and their respective generic boyfriends *du jour*—none of whom are wearing matching armbands, though the guys have their hands practically fused onto the girls' bodies, and finally to Gemma and Sadie, who have been banded since second year and so don't need to cling to each other in public.

But the shimmer of amusement dies when it reaches Sy. He doesn't laugh. His expression stays serious; his dark eyes focused on me with concern.

"Did your mom say anything about reducing the Glitter trade this time?" he asks.

It always comes back to Glitter. Why can't I just shut up and eat the lamb like everyone else? I'm sure Mama wishes I would. But I can't. Someone has to care.

I push my irritation at this weekend and Leia's flippant comment just now aside long enough to send Sy a look of gratitude. My thanks are short-lived, though, cut off by Leia's loud scoff.

"Rust and ruin, Pebs—you've got to back off your issues about Glitter. It's like you're obsessed. But you still plan to enlist after graduation, right? You gonna refuse to run Glitter once you're in? That'll be a one-way ticket to discharge." She wears that superior look she gets when she's absolutely sure she's right.

Obsessed? Maybe. Or just awake. Glitter is a problem that denial won't fix. I've seen what denial does. Absolutely zero.

Sadie cuts in before I can snap back. "She's not wrong. You heard about that second-year's brother who got shot in Truevale? I heard it was a Glitter deal gone bad."

This news is like a gut punch. "That's awful. Did he die?" Sadness and anger swirl in me.

"No. But he could've," she replies, and I nod intently.

Leia retorts in her superior tone, "Yeah, that's awful *and* has nothing to do with being in the Force."

Sadie continues to take up my cause. "Well, maybe enlisting in the BPF isn't for her. Even if she thought it was. Did you ever consider that, Leia?"

Leia rolls her big brown eyes. "Let's talk about something else."

Sadie turns to me. "You know, you could go to university. I saw a flyer about an anti-Glitter rally happening at the main campus early next month."

The enlistment-versus-university debate is an ongoing parley among final-years. Leia and I have always planned to enlist right out of secondary—since we were little. After about six months of convincing, Sy decided he would too, with the goal of going on to Officer Training School and becoming a flight engineer, which requires university as well. Sadie and Gemma are definitely university-bound, as is Anya. Paige and Mason are still deciding, and I have no idea what the generic boyfriends' plans are beyond the obvious one of publicly mauling my friends.

I somehow figured Bosch's Glitter trade would be over by the time I enlisted. But it isn't. I told Mama what I'd learned about Glitter over two years ago, and she agreed it was a problem. But she hasn't done anything about it. Two whole years. Yet it's still going strong. Leia's words are an uncomfortable reminder of that fact.

I turn to Sadie instead. "An anti-Glitter rally? I've heard about those in Truevale but not actually in Bosch. Can anyone go? Even if they aren't in uni?"

Sadie shrugs. "I don't know. Let me find another flyer, and you can check."

"Hear that, Leia? A whole rally for anti-Glitter." I let the smugness seep into my voice.

Leia huffs back, "I heard. You think a little rally is going to make the Force say, 'Oops, sorry, never mind, no more Glitter sales for the world?' Hardly."

Mason drapes an arm over Leia's shoulder, twirling a strand of her hair with his fingers. "For the love of Glitter, Shima, why can't you just accept things the way they are? You know, if you'd finally go out with Jonah, maybe you'd stop obsessing over Glitter."

My irritation spikes. I hate that expression. My eyes narrow, my hands clenching.

Jonah is Mason's best friend, and he and Leia have been after us since last spring to go on a double date. I mean, he's not hideous—actually, he's pretty nice-looking and pleasant enough—though kinda all sail and no rudder, but Leia just doesn't get it. I. Don't. Date. My armbands are for me alone. I've seen what happens to people when they get all love-drunk—forgetting their friends, ignoring important things, and worst of all, pawing at each other in the halls like they have no self-respect. Love? No thanks. At least not now. Maybe when I'm way older, like thirty-five.

I used to think Mama and Papa were in love, but then Papa took up with Hayami, and everything fell apart. The divorce was messy, and I'll never go through anything like that. Mama says she was too young when they met, that her head wasn't screwed on right. Maybe that's why she and Matt work—they were old when they got together.

Before I can say anything, though, Sy touches my elbow. "Hey, we're gonna be late for art. We should go."

I exhale sharply through my nose, jabbing a warning finger at Mason before grabbing my schoolbag.

As we head down the hallway, I mutter to Sy, "Thanks. I was ready to punch Mason."

Sy chuckles softly. "I know. And I know it's my job to make sure you don't end up in too many fistfights this year."

SY

Sy hadn't always cared much about Glitter, one way or the other. Its existence and its trade with the larger world of New Earth had just been a fact of life growing up—one his father often summed up with, "*Makes for the comfortable life you get to lead, kid.*" And he wasn't wrong. Glitter profits ensured every citizen of Bosch had a standard income, making sure no one went without basic housing or food. It funded everything—schools from daycare through university, medical expenses through the Glitter Reserve Fund, and even generous grants for research and startups. As a kid, Sy simply accepted that Glitter was interwoven into Bosch society.

Then he met Grey. And Grey… Well, she was amazing—filled with life and passion for things that Sy also loved. But more than that, she opened the world for him. His life was divided into two parts: before Grey, which equaled alone and lonely, and after Grey, which equaled friends, laughter, connection, and love. He would not return to the solitude and dimness of the time before Grey.

So there he stood on a lovely October evening, in line for an anti-Glitter rally.

Next to him, Grey leaned forward, rising onto her tiptoes, craning her neck to see past the dozens of university students queued in front of them.

He glanced down, allowing himself the guilty pleasure of really looking at her. People often said she looked younger than her age, which annoyed her to no end, though he remembered thinking the same thing when she first sat next to him in math. *Who is this girl?* he had thought at the time. *She looks twelve. Why is she talking to me?*

Now, after going on three years of friendship, she looked exactly right to him.

Perfect, in fact.

It was perfect how the late-fall breeze played with her dark waves, how the cool evening air flushed her cheeks pink, blending with the excitement in her face. Her honey-toned skin was all soft curves, and he knew—without ever having stroked her cheek the way he sometimes daydreamed—that it was warm and smooth. He knew because over the years, he'd brushed a stray speck of food off her face during lunch, wiped away a few stray tears.

She was looking toward the doors now, dark eyes—*her* eyes, curved in a way he'd never seen on anyone else—sparkling, flashing, telegraphing every bit of her eagerness.

She was so pretty.

A wholly insufficient word, but the one he always landed on when he let himself really take her in.

Two years ago, he must have thought she was pretty—in a *kid* sort of way—when she first sat next to him. He had thought plenty of girls at school were. But none of them ever spoke to him.

Or if they did—asking for a pen, a piece of paper—he'd become flushed, get tongue-tied, mumble something at the floor. By his first year of secondary, it had become a joke. A girl would come up, ask him something, and when he predictably got flustered, she'd giggle, turn away, and scurry back to her waiting friends, who would dissolve into laughter at his expense.

But Grey was different.

She talked to him like he was just a regular person, not some mumbling scarecrow with glasses. She had come back to her seat beside him every day that first week, asking how his classes were, sharing little details of her day as if it was the most natural thing in the world.

Then came the day Cassie—the popular last-year, the one in all the right clubs—came over to play *embarrass Sy* for the amusement of her friends. Sy had seen Grey's expression shift, the way her dark eyes narrowed, the way her full lips pressed into a thin line. At lunch, he spotted her striding toward the last-years' table, leaning toward Cassie, speaking low and earnestly. The table had gone quiet. Sy could have sworn he saw Cassie swipe at her cheeks before Grey turned and walked away.

Before he'd even processed what was happening, Grey and her friend Leia had appeared at his otherwise empty lunch table. They sat, waving over others in their friend group, which rapidly became Sy's first friend group.

That was the end of the jokes. And the start of what Grey had declared "a beautiful friendship."

He had felt admiration for her that day. The love came later—and was carefully boxed and wrapped, stowed away where it wouldn't disturb the friendship.

"Hey, they're opening the doors!" Grey tugged at his coat sleeve, practically vibrating with anticipation. "I can't wait to hear the speakers."

The crowd surged forward, pulling them along.

He and Grey had debated the place of Glitter in Bosch—and in New Earth—for months after they first became friends. Her arguments were persuasive—she had seen firsthand the damage it could do. He still had reservations about the rising anti-Glitter sentiment that had gripped the city and the island these past couple years, but what harm could come from listening to some university students?

CHAPTER 3
LET'S RALLY

EDMUND

Edmund Sinclair stared into the mirror and wondered, *Will the crowd like what it sees?*

He thought they would. Looks had come easy for him. The face was good. Strong jaw, high cheekbones that set off his eyes—eyes that glowed a deep gold with a rim of dark brown behind sleepy eyelids that experience had taught him gave everyone—men, women, or middles—a small pang of desire. He turned his head this way and that, surveying. His burnished bronze skin was smooth, his lips full, and his teeth white and straight. He smiled at himself and then moved through some orator exercises, opening his mouth wide, stretching his jaw up and down and side to side the way he had seen his father do long ago as a child sitting on the bathroom counter, watching him prepare for some big board presentation.

He remembered how Father had focused only on his own reflection and the upcoming meeting agenda and thus hadn't noticed his little son gazing worshipfully and copying his every move. Father had finished up and left the bathroom, flicking the light off and shutting the door, oblivious to his youngest son. *You were easily overlooked—a little nothing*, he scoffed inwardly. That little boy who cried when he was left forgotten in the dark was now grown and taller than Father by a couple of centimeters. *Taller, younger, sexier, more relevant*, he thought with a stab of resentful glee.

Edmund smoothed his gold-and-red-layered tunic, tightening the deep brown belt before making his way to the wings to peer out at the crowd forming in the auditorium of Hizir Hall. Bigger than last month's. He shook his head while grinning to himself. A bunch of people whose very livelihoods depended on Glitter, yet here they were, rallying against the drug. He knew why—his secondary theater teacher, Mr. Mendez, had told him. "Edmund, you're a good-looking fellow, smart, and your voice commands attention. Those are innate gifts. Now I can teach you how to use those gifts to entrance an audience. You've got star quality. Wield it wisely."

And Mr. Mendez was true to his word because Edmund developed charisma, and the people, except Father and Mother, of course, fell in line, entranced, willing to do anything to be in his sphere. By his last two years of secondary he was reaping the benefits of his gift. Some of which were of a…personal nature, while others moved him forward in the public eye. Despite being slightly disappointed when Edmund dropped drama, Mr. Mendez still happily coached him to become both his class's elected leader and their school's board student rep. By graduation, his peers and most of the adults at school gushed that he was *going places*.

His family barely noticed, too busy with what they termed "adult issues" to be concerned with "how or what little Edmund was playing." To Mother and Father, second place was the same as losing. The small victories Edmund experienced fell below their lofty ideals. Mother had said airily when he started secondary, "Darling, we did our time at school meetings with your brother and sisters. We are far too old to be dragged into a classroom. You'll manage just fine without us showing up all the time." And manage he did, utilizing his gifts as he drummed up satisfactory excuses for his absentee parents during student conferences.

Upon his arrival at university last year, he and his friend Curtis began a search for a movement they could both back and be the faces of. Anti-Glitter had been one of several orphan causes they considered embracing. Further study found it espoused by only a few extremists and niche researchers. No one else seemed interested, making it ripe for the picking. Personally, Edmund didn't really care about the Glitter trade one way or the other, but it was a cause that could be invigorated into a crusade. And that was what he had done.

His name, announced along with those of the other speakers, made him stand straighter as he slipped his thumbs into his belt. He was primed. He flicked on the light inside of himself that illuminated his magnetism. There was a reason they named him luminary. He had prepared talking points and stood ready to work the crowd. Lifting a hand to the cheering masses, he strode onto the stage. Never again would he be left in the dark, an afterthought, sobbing to no one.

GREY

It's not my first time at the university, not even in Hizir Hall, the auditorium where my very first anti-Glitter rally is kicking off. The hall is classic Bosch: brick exterior, sweeping stairs leading to double doors, and inside, dark wood paneling with deep red velvet curtains.

My family and I have come here for concerts before, sinking into the plush seats. But tonight, the seats are gone, folded into the floor to create a vast, open space before the stage. I'd heard they could do that, but seeing it transformed feels like stepping into a different world.

The place is filling fast. I nudge Sy. "I love that all these people are showing up to support the anti-Glitter movement." It makes me feel like maybe together, we can all make Bosch and New Earth safer.

He nods. "It's a good turnout. Though I bet not everyone here's against Glitter. Some are probably just curious. And I'd wager there are a few hecklers too."

Two burly college guys jostle past, knocking my shoulder. Sy immediately shifts behind me like a human shield.

"Thanks, Sy. Nice having a tall friend," I remark, steadying myself. "You really think there'll be hecklers?"

He grins. "Happy to be a buffer for one of the shortest people in the room, Grey." Then with a casual push of his glasses, he adds, "And yeah, there's always opposition at things like this. Let's get closer to the stage—or else I'll have to put you on my shoulders."

We laugh, weaving through the crowd with muttered "Coming throughs" and "Excuse mes" until we reach the front.

Sy leans toward a group camped out ahead of us. "Hey, can my short friend squeeze by? Otherwise, she'll be staring at your back pockets all night."

The group—three men and two women—turns. A girl with long, black hair smiles. "Sure. Come on up, shorty. You'll want to see the speakers as well as hear them."

Ordinarily, a height comment would set me off, but not tonight. Maybe because she says it kindly. Maybe because I'm too buzzed on excitement.

Another girl laughs. "Especially when Edmund takes the stage."

The whole group chuckles and shifts to let me through.

I glance at Sy, impressed. He's never been great with strangers. Back when we first met, he told me he'd rather eat a bucket of nails than talk to someone he didn't know. I guess we're both growing up.

"I'm Grey Shima, and this is Sy Mercer. It's our first rally," I declare, raising my voice over the hum of conversation.

The black-haired girl leans in. "I'm Miranda. Too noisy for full introductions, but we're founding members of the University Anti-Glitter Circle." She gives a warm smile. "It's great to see new, young faces."

My goodwill flickers. New, young faces? Kid faces, she means. I'm about to snap back when Sy, peacemaker as always, jumps in.

"Grey and I are in our last year of secondary," he says smoothly. "She's been all about anti-Glitter since I met her three years ago."

Miranda blinks, impressed. "Wow. That's awesome." She nudges me playfully. "Sorry about the 'kid' thing. You must get that a lot."

I breathe out, letting the tension go. Something about her makes it hard to stay mad.

Before I can answer, the lights dim. The crowd's buzz lowers to a murmur, the speakers are announced, and the crowd cheers. Two men and a woman step from the wings into the spotlight.

I tilt my head up, eager. The woman speaks at the podium first, making a passionate economic argument. An older man follows, mapping the environmental consequences of Glitter extraction. Their arguments are strong, reasoned—and I file them away mentally for the next showdown with Mama.

Then the final speaker steps forward. He doesn't use the microphone. His presence alone stills the crowd. He stands tall, broad-shouldered, his thick, black hair slightly messy, his bronze skin catching the glow of the lights. Confidence rolls off him like a tide as he surveys us.

And then he speaks.

At first, it's just his voice—warm, commanding—but then it's his words, each one sliding into a space inside me I hadn't realized was hollow. It feels like stepping into sunlight after months of rain. His words don't just make sense—they make *me* make sense.

I tear my eyes from him for a moment, glancing at the crowd. Faces are lifted toward him like flowers seeking warmth.

I turn back, breathless. I have to hear more. I have to know him.

♡

SY

Sy watched the way the crowd leaned toward Edmund Sinclair and wondered whether anyone even realized they were doing it.

The first two speakers made strong cases—the woman laying out the economic dangers of relying on Glitter, the older man painting a grim picture of environmental collapse. Their words had been smart. Precise.

But Edmund? Edmund made them feel.

"I speak tonight to the youth of Bosch," he declared, voice like a lit match in a dry field. "Look around you! Who truly profits from the Glitter trade? Not you. Not me. Not your parents. Glitter wealth piles up in the hands of the powerful few while the rest of us are shackled to their scraps. We call it survival. But it's nothing more than chains. And what's it cost us? Across New Earth, our name is whispered in shame. Bosch—the drug capital. Bosch—the poisoners of the world. Is that who we are? Is that the story we leave behind? I refuse to believe it. I refuse to believe we are so weak that we cannot build something better. We are not dealers. We are builders. Creators. Dreamers. Fighters. The time for excuses is over. The time for action is now."

The room erupted. Sy clapped too, mostly to fit in, but something inside him twisted. Not at the words. They were good. Right, even.

No, it twisted when he turned to Grey.

She stood frozen, her face tilted toward Edmund Sinclair like he had pulled the stars down from the sky and offered them to her.

Sy's hands, still warm from clapping, went cold. He flicked his eyes from Grey's enraptured face to the handsome man on stage and felt defeated. For the first time, Sy understood what it meant to lose something you'd never truly had.

He shifted his gaze to his best friend. Her face was glowing. He took a deep inhale and smiled anyway, because some people were worth loving—even if they never looked back.

♡

GREY

Edmund Sinclair's words linger in the air like the last notes of a song I never want to end. I clutch the edge of the stage, half-afraid that if I let go, something inside me will snap.

The applause crashes around me, a wave I'm barely riding. I track him as he turns from the podium—broad shoulders, confident stride—fading into the wings with the other speakers. A ridiculous, reckless part of me wants to follow. Wants to call his name.

I tighten my grip on the stage and force my feet to stay planted. *Get it together, Grey.*

"Hey," someone says, cutting through the thick haze around me. I blink, expecting Sy, but it's Miranda, grinning beside a girl with thick braids.

"So," the braided girl teases, "was I right about Edmund?"

I open my mouth. Nothing comes out. Heat floods my face, and I only nod helplessly.

Miranda laughs, but it's kind, not mocking. She clasps my arm. "Don't stress. Everyone looks like that the first time. Right, Abeni?"

"Definitely." Abeni's eyes twinkle. "He's like a storm you don't see coming—and then suddenly, you're drenched."

"He's devoted to the cause," Miranda adds. "No time for distractions, even if half the campus would gladly throw themselves at his feet."

Their easy humor loosens the knot in my chest. I manage a

shaky breath. "It wasn't just how he looked," I admit. "It's...how he made me feel. Like I've been waiting my whole life to hear someone say those things."

Miranda's smile softens. "That's why we're here. It's not just about words—it's about what they spark in you."

She glances over her shoulder. "We're heading to the after-party. Come meet the Circle. Maybe help us start a junior chapter at your school?"

The thought jolts me into motion. I scan the crowd, spotting Sy hunched over his comm.

"Sy, let's go to the after-party!" I call. "It could really help us...recruit."

He pockets the comm slowly, his shoulders stiffening. "Sure," he says. "Whatever you want."

I wince, sensing the strain under his words, but I can't back down. Not now.

I step closer, giving him a grateful nudge with my elbow. "Thanks. I owe you."

He meets my eyes for a beat longer than usual, something raw flickering in his gaze before he pastes on a smile. "Anything for the cause," he says. But somehow, it doesn't sound like he's talking about Glitter anymore.

CHAPTER 4
EDMUND SINCLAIR

SY STOOD ON THE SMALL BALCONY, THREE FLOORS UP, THE NIGHT AIR cool against his skin. The stars sparkled in the night sky; still clouds loomed on the horizon—tomorrow would be rainy. Out here, in the quiet and the dark, he could breathe.

Through the sliding glass door, the apartment glowed bright, filled with young men and women talking animatedly. His gaze swept the room until it landed on Grey. She stood with Miranda, Abeni, and a few others, her expression relaxed, her laughter easy. At least that Edmund guy wasn't here. Not that it really mattered. He'd already seen the way Grey had looked at him on stage, how her eyes sparkled with emotion.

Sy exhaled, glancing at the door to make sure no one was coming out for a smoke. Then, with practiced care, he unwrapped the sturdy box he kept inside his chest and looked at his love. Turning it over in his hands, he inspected it closely. His most precious belonging. He had worked so hard to keep it safe over the years, but now, as he studied it, he noticed fresh dents and dings.

She'll always be your friend, Mercer.

He'd listened to her rants about how teenage love never lasts, seen firsthand how couples—the friends he'd made through Grey —went from inseparable to strangers, or worse, enemies. He'd never risk that with her. Ever.

His mind drifted, unbidden, to all the things he knew he loved about her—her laughter, that sharp sense of humor. He recalled the first time they'd gone sailing together. His lips quirked into a smile at the memory—her delighted praise of his skill with the lines, the way they had leaned out together through a tack, laughing, perfectly in sync. Grey made him complete in a way he couldn't be without her in his life. In his heart.

He blinked, looking down again. The love in his hands was smooth now, unmarked as if never having been damaged at all. With a quiet sigh, he moved to box it away again—but a sudden roar from inside made him pause.

His head snapped up. Through the dirty glass, he saw the front door swing open, and there Edmund stood, framed in the entrance, greeting his admirers like a conquering hero.

Sy's stomach clenched.

Where was Grey?

He needed to get inside. Now.

He shoved the box closed, hurriedly wrapping it, but in his rush, he left a corner loose.

♡

GREY

Sweet New Earth, he's here.

A cold sweat prickles down my spine, and I fight the humiliating urge to grin like an idiot. *Be calm. Be cool.* I force my attention back to Miranda and Abeni.

"And there's our fearless leader, fashionably late as usual." Miranda's teasing laugh floats between us. She nudges me playfully. "You want to meet him? I promise you won't actually melt into a puddle."

I try for nonchalance. Shrug. Casual smile. My heart hammering a traitorous rhythm under my ribs. "Sure. If it's convenient. Either way."

Abeni gives me a look that says, *Sure, kid. Whatever you say.*

Before I can come up with a snappy comeback, Sy materializes at my side, pulling me slightly away from the conversation.

"Hey, where'd you go?" Miranda asks.

"Needed some air," Sy says, voice tight. He jerks his chin toward the door. "Looks like your guest of honor's here."

There's a weird pause. Like he's waiting for me to say something. My throat locks up, but I croak, "Uh-huh. Let's go meet him. I want to tell him…" *What do I want to tell him, that hearing him speak was like breathing for the first time? Nope, not saying that out loud.* I bite my lip to focus. "…that his speech was really inspiring. For the movement."

Sy exhales slowly, somewhere between amused and resigned. "Good idea. But we should head back soon."

I nod, pretending normalcy as Miranda and Abeni lead us toward the knot of people gathering around Edmund Sinclair. He's mid-conversation, laughing at something, the sound low and rich enough to stir the already-electric air.

Okay. Just a person. Just another activist. Just breathe.

Edmund turns at our approach. The second his eyes land on us, something shifts. He straightens, smile widening as if already drawing us into his orbit.

Abeni does the honors. "Hey, Edmund, these are the secondary students we were telling you about—Grey Shima and Sy Mercer. They came to the rally tonight."

His gaze flicks over Sy—polite, distant. Then settles on me.

And lingers.

"Wonderful," he says, voice as smooth as warmed honey. "I think it's great you both came." He tilts his head slightly, assessing. "What year are you two?"

I open my mouth and let out a stupid, nervous giggle. *Earth, swallow me whole.*

Sy steps in like the true friend he is. "Final year. We plan to enlist after graduation."

Edmund's brow furrows slightly. "An Anti-Glitter trooper? That's a new one." His mouth quirks in an almost-smile. "Those folks are a... special breed." The Circle members around us chuckle knowingly.

Then he turns fully toward me. "But you—" His tone softens into something lightly teasing. "You can't possibly be old enough."

Heat flashes through me—not a flush of embarrassment but of anger. I straighten. "Sixteen. Seventeen in April. Old enough to enlist." I lift my chin, meeting his eyes squarely. *Don't look away.*

There's a pause. Then his smile shifts, less condescending, more interested. "Old enough," he echoes, like he's testing the weight of it.

I seize the moment. "And I think starting Anti-Glitter activism inside the BPF could be key to reaching Bosch's leadership. From the inside. What you've done here is amazing, but we need to do more. Bigger. Make the leadership take notice that we have strength in numbers and in position."

A beat. Something flashes in Edmund's gaze: Surprise? Respect?

Then he laughs, low and genuine. "That's a fascinating idea, from a fascinating person."

The words tumble through me, dizzying. *Fascinating.* I scramble for something equally brilliant to say, but before I can, he leans in slightly, voice pitched for just us.

"Your looks... They're unique for Bosch. You weren't born here?"

I flush but keep my voice steady. "Born in Edo. Moved here when I was little."

He smiles thoughtfully, like filing away a puzzle piece. "Really?

Wait…" His brow furrows, recognition sparking. "Are you related to that massive Edoan man who's always at the markets? The one who looks like he could level a house with a sneeze?"

A laugh bursts from me, bright and unexpected. "That's Riki. He's like family but not my dad. More like an honorary uncle and a dear friend. My real papa's a diplomat, and my bonus dad is Bosch."

Something shifts. A whisper, a name passed into Edmund's ear by one of his followers. His expression flickers. Surprise, calculation. Then returns to me, a new sharpness behind his smile as he extends his arm. "Grey Shima, you say?"

I reach forward instinctively, my much smaller hand and arm swallowed by his.

He leans in, voice silkier now. "Curtis tells me our illustrious Master Commander Wallace has half-Edoan children with a diplomat." His smile sharpens. "You wouldn't happen to be *her* daughter, would you?"

Silence stretches. The air thickens. I squeeze his arm once before releasing it and stepping back. "I am." My chin lifts. "But I'm here because of what I believe, not what she believes. She knows I'm here, though."

The room holds its breath.

"And," I add, my voice clear, "I don't need her permission to fight for what's right."

For a heartbeat, Edmund simply studies me. Then he laughs. Big, rolling, delighted.

He slings an arm around my shoulders in one easy motion, raising his free hand to the crowd. "Listen up, Circle! Bosch's finest just joined us. Welcome, Grey Shima!"

A cheer goes up around the room. People clap me on the back, beam smiles at me.

It should feel like a victory. And it does. But where's…? My eyes find Sy across the room.

He's standing stiffly, arms folded tight across his chest, face shadowed with something that feels dangerously close to heartbreak.

♡

SY

Across the crowded room, Sy watched Grey laugh—bright, bold, unforgettable—as Edmund Sinclair slung an arm around her shoulders like they were old friends, like she belonged there. Like she belonged *with him*.

Sy's stomach twisted painfully. He knew that laugh. It had rescued him from loneliness. He had spent years delighting in it, pulling it from her—the way she threw her head back just a little, the way her eyes crinkled at their edges and her shoulders raised the tiniest bit toward her perfect ears. But tonight, it wasn't for him.

The applause rose, filling the air, but it all sounded muffled in Sy's ears. Like he was underwater, sinking. Sy folded his arms across his chest, willing himself to look casual, invisible. Trying not to look like a fool with his heart laid bare.

Grey glanced around, her smile still wide and brilliant, and for the briefest moment—*the briefest*—her gaze caught his. Something flickered there. A small, uncertain tether between them. And then it was gone, swallowed by the lights, noise, and the way Edmund leaned in, whispering something that made her laugh that laugh again. For the first time, Sy understood something he had tried not to face: You could love someone with everything you were— and still have to let them go.

But maybe, just maybe, someday...she would look for him, and he knew he would be there.

With a deep inhale, Sy decided not to wait for the speeches to end or the music to swell again. Instead, he simply slipped through the crowd and back to the patio unnoticed, his hands shoved deep into his jacket pockets. Outside, the night air hit him like a slap—cold and sharp, the way truth often was.

Above the city, stars pricked the darkness, distant and indifferent. Sy tilted his head back, breathing them in. Maybe he should have felt like a fool. But he didn't. Maybe he should have been angry, even resentful. But he wasn't. Maybe Grey would never see him the way he saw her. Or maybe she would. Either way, he would keep moving forward, carrying the piece of her that had always been his, even if she never knew it.

CHAPTER 5
FALLING

GREY

"THIS IS GOING TO BE GREAT, DON'T YOU THINK?" I LEAN AGAINST the chill window of the public transport, not really seeing anything beyond the glass. I don't wait for an answer—my nerves have my mouth running. "I wonder if we'll get to be part of the next protest. I hope so. Mama probably wouldn't like it, but it's what we believe, so she can't be upset about that." I pause, then shift gears. "What did you think about Miranda? She seemed really stellar. Abeni too. Maybe we should invite Leia next time."

Finally, I glance over at Sy. He's grinning at me, and I realize I haven't seen that expression much this past week.

"What?"

"For a girl who's sailed across the Great Sea, been ship-wrecked, and escaped Formosan pirates, you seem pretty nervous about making posters with a bunch of uni students." His eyebrows lift, and his shoulders shake with silent laughter. "Makes me wonder if there isn't something else you're nervous about."

I scoff. "No." I turn back to the window, watching the buildings blur past. Edmund's face flickers in my mind. "Maybe."

"Figured as much." Sy's tone shifts, more serious now. "Miranda and Abeni said he doesn't date."

"Neither do I," I snap a little too fast, my chest tightening at the reminder.

Sy bumps my shoulder lightly. "Hey, I'm just looking out for my friend."

My irritation cools into a sigh. "I know." I sink back into my seat, hugging my arms across my chest. "It's just...weird. These feelings. They're not what I expected. They're...bigger."

"I get it."

I shake my head. "I don't think you do. It's like..." I hesitate, searching for the right word. "It's like I'm standing on the edge of something, and part of me wants to jump, but the other part knows it's crazy."

Sy cuts in, quick and firm. "Don't say you're in love with him."

I huff out a breath. "I'm not." I bite my lip. "At least...not yet. You can't be in love with someone you barely know, right?"

Sy doesn't answer. His eyes are closed, the easy grin gone, his head tipped back against the seat. "No, you can't," he says softly.

I poke him in the belly, making him jolt upright. "Hey!"

I grin, letting the moment lighten. "Tell you what, Sy—I'll get to know him first. Then I'll get back to you."

The transport slows, and I pop up from my seat as we arrive at the university stop, heart racing for reasons I don't want to admit yet.

♡

EDMUND

Edmund scanned the library's meeting room, watching as members of the Circle hunched over posterboards with thick markers, slogans blooming under their hands. They were there because he created the Circle. He was their leader, their luminary.

This was the work. The mission. And of course, he cared about it —he planned on impacting Bosch's future and making a name for himself.

But now he found himself eager to spot one particular girl in the crowd. Why? *Because she has the passion you lack for this, Sinclair.*

Grey. Her name was Grey.

He scowled at himself and moved toward a corner table where Curtis and Abeni were setting up. Just as he leaned in to offer a suggestion, he heard it—a laugh, light and clear, threading through the clatter of conversation. His head snapped up before he could think.

Abeni followed his gaze, smirking. "Uh-oh. Looks like the cause may have some competition."

Curtis snorted. "Competition from the girl next door. Or...next door to China."

Edmund's eyes narrowed, and Abeni's smile flattened into something sharp.

Curtis threw up his hands. "I didn't mean it like that. Edo's near China, right? Look at a globe." He shrugged and bent over his poster.

Edmund let it go—for now. But the taste of irritation stayed in his mouth as he drifted toward the table where Grey sat, her tall, gangly friend at her side. Sam? No—Sy. That was it. Not that it mattered. It was Grey he wanted to see.

"Mind if I join you?" Edmund asked, dragging a chair around to face them.

Grey looked up—and smiled. Not polite, not forced. Bright and real. For a second, it lit up the whole dreary room. "Sure," she said. "We're happy to share, right, Sy?"

Sy's face said otherwise, but Edmund kept his smile neutral as he sat down.

Grey slid a poster sheet and a list of slogans across to him, already turning back to her work.

Edmund picked up a marker but found himself watching her

instead—the quick, sure way she moved her hands, the tiny crease of concentration between her brows. When she bit the corner of her lip, her tongue's tip peeking out for just a second as she adjusted the lettering, he caught himself smiling.

It wasn't about how pretty she was, though she was in an earnest, unpolished way. It was something else. Something that tugged at him just below the surface. He wondered, suddenly, what else there was to learn about Grey Shima.

And he realized he very much wanted to find out.

♡

EDMUND

Edmund spun his marker slowly between his fingers, watching Grey out of the corner of his eye. She was outlining bold letters, brow furrowed in concentration. *Say something, idiot. Anything.* He cleared his throat. "That's…good work."

Grey glanced up, confused. "The slogan?"

"No." He caught himself too late. "I mean, yes. The slogan's great. Very…impactful."

Her mouth quirked a little like she wasn't sure whether she was being complimented or teased. "Thanks. I guess."

He cursed silently. *Smooth, Sinclair. Real smooth.* Determined not to look like a complete fool, he leaned closer and pointed. "You're outlining it wrong."

Grey blinked. "What?"

He tapped a spot near the bottom where her "S" curled a little wider than the others. "The spacing's off. See? It'll look crooked from a distance."

She frowned, then leaned back to study it. "I like it," she said firmly and went back to shading in the letters without changing a thing.

Edmund sat back, watching her brush a loose curl behind her ear, unfazed by his "correction." He smiled—this time for real.

She wasn't the type to bend for anyone. Not even him. And somehow, he liked her even more for it.

♡

GREY

Accidents happen. I know that. Life is full of coincidences that spin into full-blown adventures. Maybe it's chance that Edmund ended up across from me, chatting as I outline letters and exclamation points in bright, eye-catching colors. And maybe it's just serendipity that every time I sneak a glance at him, I find his eyes on me.

The first time, we both look away, laughing softly, pretending we hadn't noticed. The second time, he holds my gaze, and something electric buzzes in the air between us until I break, ducking my head, my face burning.

I press harder into shading my poster, but eventually, curiosity wins out. I look again. Edmund is hunched over his work, dark hair falling into his eyes, mouth tugged into a thoughtful frown. Then, almost imperceptibly, his head tilts, and his gaze cuts to mine.

I don't look away this time. Instead, I tuck a stray curl behind my ear, clearing the view between us.

His expression shifts, first surprised, then something warmer like a slow-blooming sunrise. His brows lift slightly, a silent invitation.

I answer with a tiny smile.

He pushes his chair back, stands, and holds out a hand toward me. "I need to stretch my legs. Walk with me?"

My heart skips like a pebble across water, but I manage a steady "Sounds like a fine idea" and take his hand. His palm is warm against mine. Sy looks up sharply from the table, his mouth half-open like he wants to object. Instead, he snaps it shut and returns to his poster with ferocious focus.

"We'll bring back some tea," I say, trying to sound casual. Sy nods without looking my way.

Edmund releases my hand as we step into the hall. The silence between us is filled with unspoken words and nervous energy.

We walk in that liminal space for a moment, then he asks, "Final-year, huh? So that'd make you…?"

"Sixteen. Seventeen in April," I answer. Leia had been a tiny bit scandalized when I told her that the first guy I was interested in was already in uni, but I don't think that's any different than when she was a second-year while dating a final-year.

He gives a little shrug. "I'm eighteen. Nineteen in December."

Silence again. Then we both speak at once, our voices tangling together, which prompts nervous laughter from us. "You go ahead," I offer.

"I was just asking about the rest of your family. I mean, I know who your mom is, but who else is in it?"

"I have two brothers and a sister, plus my bonus dad, Matt Warner, at Mama's house, which is where I am mostly. At my Papa's there's his wife, Hayami, and my little half-sister and half-brother. I see them mostly in Edo, but they do have a place here."

His face brightens. "I have two brothers and a sister as well. They're way older than me, though. I was sort of an oops to my folks." A bitter look flashes across his face, rapidly replaced by a curious one. "Is it weird having two houses to go to?"

I shrug. "Not really. My papa was gone so much when I was little—even before he and Mama divorced—that it's sort of always been that way."

"So which place is your favorite?"

"That's easy. Bosch. I love Edo, of course, especially the village near where I was born and the mountain where we lived for a few years when I was little, but Bosch is home."

"That's stellar," Edmund comments. "I've traveled with my folks to the Eastern Continent but never the Western. I'd like to see Edo someday."

I grin. "Well, now that you know me, you'll have a place to

stay and a tour guide." As the words leave my mouth, I kick myself in my head. *You're assuming an awful lot.*

Edmund isn't uncomfortable, though. "That is a great offer. I may take you up on it." He pauses in whatever hallway we have wandered into and looks at me with those amazing eyes. "Listen, I'm glad you came tonight," he reveals. "It's easy to show up for a rally. Harder to stay when real work needs doing."

"I'm not afraid of work," I say. "I'm just glad there are people willing to fight for the future."

He smiles a real smile at that. "Okay, I always forget which one..." He searches around the hall, peeking through closed doors, until "This is the one." He opens it, and before us awaits a narrow, fairly steep stairwell. He turns and reaches for my hand, which I give happily. Four flights up later, he pushes open a heavy door, and cool night air rushes over us.

"Here," he tells me. "I love this place."

The rooftop patio stretches out, framed by a brick railing. The city beyond shimmers with scattered lights, mirroring the stars overhead.

"It's beautiful," I breathe.

He leans against the railing, studying the view—then looks back to study me. "It is, and I wanted to show it to you. But it's not the only reason I brought you up here."

I face him, heart hammering in my chest. "Oh?"

"I...sort of... Well, I want to be alone with you," he admits with a sheepish tip of his head. "You're different, Grey. You make me wonder what else I'm missing while I'm so busy planning out the future." He laughs, a self-deprecating sound. "You've completely thrown me off course—and I think I like it."

I laugh, startled and giddy. "At least you have one. I'm still figuring out my course. But I didn't mean to throw anything anywhere."

"Maybe not." His voice softens. "But I'm glad you did."

He steps closer, hesitates—giving me space, a choice. And I don't step away.

He then bridges the distance, forehead resting gently against mine as he whispers, "Would you let me get to know you?"

I breathe back, "Yes."

I rise onto my toes, my eyelids fluttering shut, and meet his mouth with mine.

The kiss, my first, is tentative to start—new and wondering—and then deepens slightly as if we're both realizing, together, that this is something different.

Something real.

CHAPTER 6
I'M HERE FOR YOU

SY

SY PUSHED THE SPORTY RED VEHICLE MASON HAD LENT HIM, URGING it just a bit faster through the November drizzle. The roads in this part of Bosch were narrow and winding, forcing him to ease off the speed he wished he could maintain. Grey's house was in a neighborhood not far from the base, a good distance from the secondary school. Sy's home lay a couple of kilometers past hers, and for the past three years, they had walked to school together whenever the weather was nice, only resorting to the school transport on cold or rainy days like the current one.

But Grey hadn't been on the transport that morning. He remembered the bitter thought that had crossed his mind— Edmund had probably driven her in again, giving them yet another opportunity to wrap their arms around each other and kiss goodbye for everyone's viewing pleasure.

Up ahead, a small, blue vehicle crawled along the meandering road, testing his patience. *Come on, I have to get there…*

Leia had practically ambushed him the moment he'd walked through the school doors, grabbing his arm before classes began. "Did you hear?" she'd asked, voice urgent.

He frowned at her, perplexed. "Hear what?"

"She didn't call you?" Leia's serious expression tightened a new knot in Sy's stomach.

Grey's calls had dropped off dramatically over the past month as she became more involved with the anti-Glitter Circle. And with Edmund.

"Are you talking about Grey?" He'd grabbed Leia's elbow, panic edging into his voice. "Did something happen to Grey?"

Leia had shaken her head. "No—her mom. Pebs called me crying this morning to say she wouldn't be at school, but she didn't say anything else."

"Oh, shit," Sy had breathed. "I need to get over there."

"Take my vehicle, man."

Mason's voice had startled him—Sy hadn't even registered him standing there.

He'd turned to Mason, grateful, as the brown-haired boy dug into his pockets for his keys and handed them over.

"Thanks, I—"

Mason had shrugged. "Hey, don't worry about it. I'll let Ms. Randolph know you had to leave. Just tell Grey we're thinking about her and her mom."

♡

SY

Sy spent so much time at Grey's house that her parents had eventually told him there was no point in knocking. So, as always, he let himself in, pushing open the cobalt-blue front door.

Grey sat curled on the sofa, a comm pressed to her ear, clutching a throw pillow against her stomach. Her little black cat, Jerome, lay on the sofa back near her shoulder. Grey's red, puffy eyes were shadowed by dark circles.

Sy only caught part of what she was saying to whoever was listening on the other end of her comm device. "I know you have class. I just wish…" She looked up as Sy slipped off his shoes. "Sy!"

Her comm slipped to the floor with a quiet *thump* as she launched herself at him, arms wrapping tightly around his neck. Sy froze for the briefest moment before returning the embrace, feeling her dissolve into sobs against his shoulder. "I'm here, Grey. What can I do?"

Her weeping continued for a few moments before she pulled back, eyes darting to the comm on the floor. "Oh, no," she breathed, hiccupping as she scrambled to retrieve it. "Edmund? Are you still there? Yeah, Sy's here. Yeah…" She turned to him with a wan smile, her nose running along with her tears. "He *is* a good friend." A pause. "Are you sure? Of course, you can come over now." Another pause. "Okay. See you soon."

She pocketed the comm before turning fully to Sy, her lower lip trembling. "Mama lost the baby…" she whispered mournfully.

Sy felt like he'd been punched in the gut. The whole family had been so excited for the new arrival. Hell, he'd been excited too. "Oh, no, Grey…" He reached for her, but she held up a hand as her face moved from sad to stricken.

"I guess there were complications, and they took her into surgery, and…" Her voice cracked as fresh sobs overtook her.

Sy's thoughts went to the darkest place. He reached out, rubbing her back in slow, gentle circles. Grey inhaled a shaky breath. "Matt says she'll be okay, but I've never heard him sound so scared. And Mama M just said, 'The doctors are doing every-thing they can, and she's where she needs to be.' Which terrifies me."

"Your grandma will make sure they treat her right." The words felt hollow, but he said them anyway. Miss Miriam—Mama M to Grey—had been a midwife for years. He hoped she'd make sure things were okay. "Where are your brothers and Rini?"

Grey wiped at her face, looking utterly exhausted. "Oh, Sy, I'm so glad you came. I meant to call, but everything was so…" She trailed off, misery carved into her lovely face. It was almost more than Sy could bear.

"The boys are upstairs, and Matt's mom, Mae, took Rini to school before heading to the hospital. Matt said not to tell Rini yet, that she should go to school like normal, and he'd be back soon, but that was hours ago. What if…?" Her eyes begged him to tell her the worst wasn't possible.

He gave her the best reassurance he could. "Your mom is the second-strongest person I know. She'll fight hard to be okay. You know that, right?"

In what had to be an attempt to regain some composure, Grey swallowed a sob and rubbed her hands over her face, smearing the tears and snot. Sy watched her back straighten the tiniest bit and kept his smile to himself as he admired the strongest person he knew. She took a deep breath and replied in a small voice, "You're right. She'll be fine."

Glancing around, he softened his voice. "Tell you what—go splash some water on your face, then curl up on the sofa. I'll make some tea and breakfast for you and Kik and Mac."

♡

GREY

The cool water feels good against my skin, a brief relief from the heaviness pressing down on me. I pat my face dry with a small towel and glance at my reflection. A pale, washed-out version of myself stares back. Edmund will be here soon, so I reach for my toiletry bag and swipe on some cheek stain, adding a hint of color to my face. Better.

He bought the cheek stain for me. And the lash tint. And a few other cosmetics after our first date the week after the rally.

"Here, I got you something." He handed me a box wrapped in gold paper, tied with a shimmering ribbon—one I still have tucked away with my precious things.

I remember how he watched me open it, eyes bright with excitement. *"But I don't have a gift for you,"* I protested.

"Just getting to see you is a gift for me," he said, *"although this gift is sort of for us both."*

My eyebrows lifted at that, but I was too flustered by his attention to do more than smile. *"Okay then, let's see."*

Inside the box, sleek tubes and containers nestled in delicate packaging—makeup. And not the cheap kind, either. I hesitated, searching for the right words, not wanting to sound ungrateful. *"How very thoughtful of you,"* I finally replied, eyeing the collection. *"I've never worn any of this stuff before."*

Edmund smiled that slow, knowing smile of his and brushed his fingers over my cheek. My pulse fluttered. *"I know. I think it will help you look more sophisticated and polished."*

Sophistication. That's something Edmund carries with effortless ease. He's eighteen—nineteen in December—but somehow, he's always seemed older, his confidence so natural, so refined. Meanwhile, I have all the poise of a skiff in a gale. The Bosch saying flits through my mind, and I laughed then, teasing, *"So, maybe if I wear this, I won't look so much like a thirteen-year-old?"*

He chuckled too. But he didn't disagree.

Now, standing in front of the mirror, I finish applying the lash tint and lipstick. I suppose more crying is off the table unless I want a streaky mess. Running a brush through my hair, I take a steadying breath and head out to help Sy.

♡

EDMUND

Edmund exhaled sharply as he guided his vehicle toward the neighborhood near the Bosch Pirate Force base, where nearly every house—if not all—had been bought with Glitter profits. *Bought-and-Paid Force, more like it,* he thought, smirking at his cleverness.

This would be the first time since he had started seeing Grey after the rally a month ago that he planned on stepping inside her house—owned and occupied by the chief Glitter hound herself. If someone had told him before the rally that he'd willingly cross that threshold, he would have been ready to throw hands. But then Grey had appeared in his life, all youthful beauty and burning passion against Glitter.

He hadn't planned on taking on a girlfriend. Not that the opportunity hadn't presented itself. In university, just as in secondary, there had been plenty of girls, and even some guys and middles, who had made their interest clear. But unlike in secondary—where he had gleefully sampled the entire buffet of available people—his focus now, outside of his coursework, was to be *somebody*. Somebody that everyone—his parents included— saw as consequential. And he was building toward just that. Already the Circle saw him that way. It was just a matter of time and effort for him to become the one to end Glitter's hold in Bosch. So, no time for romance.

And yet, Grey Shima had caught not only his eye but also his interest. Someone in her position—oh so close to the center of Bosch's power—would be a good asset to the Circle. But that wasn't what really intrigued him. Her passion about anti-Glitter was palpable, not performative. He reflected a bit guiltily that his leaned toward the latter. But there was more. He couldn't stop thinking about her—the way she carried herself, how her hair cascaded over her shoulders in soft waves, how she had stood up for herself, eyes flashing when he voiced his initial suspicions of her presence due to her mother's position. She was striking, articulate, intelligent—and he wanted to know her.

He smiled as he maneuvered his little green vehicle, recalling their first kiss. As soon as their lips had parted, he leaned in to taste her again, but she stopped him.

"Not yet. I need a minute," she had whispered, dropping her head and turning slightly away.

His brows had furrowed. "What? I'm sorry… I thought you wanted me to kiss you." He began to pull away.

Her head had snapped up, eyes searching his. "I did… I do…" Earnest. Hesitant. "It's just… Oh, I feel silly." She had let her cheek rest against his chest.

She had felt tiny in his arms. He could have propped his chin on the crown of her head. "Why silly?" he murmured.

A pause. Then: "You'll think I'm a baby. That was the first time I've ever kissed someone. I mean…like that. And I wanted to really remember it before moving on to another kiss."

He had been more than a little surprised by this admission. And delighted. "That's big, Grey. I'm glad I didn't know that before. Was it everything you hoped it would be?"

She had tilted her face up, a playful smile dancing on those lovely lips. "I think so…but I'm not sure. Maybe I need to review?" Then she reached up, fingers curling at the back of his neck, and kissed him again.

He lingered in the memory for a moment before shaking it off to return to the present. This wasn't a visit to meet her family—far too soon for something that serious. But her mother was in the hospital, and Grey needed support. *That's not why you jumped in the vehicle, Sinclair,* he chided himself. No. He was here because Silas was also. The best friend. The boy who watched her with quiet longing whenever she was near. Edmund had seen it. He knew the type—always lingering, always waiting, available.

That friendship could gain no further traction.

Pulling off the road, he parked beside the white picket fence, straightened his cuffs, and muttered under his breath, "Step back, Mr. Mercer. A real man is here now."

SY

Sy walked downstairs after taking a tray of food to Grey's fraternal twin brothers, Kik and Mac. Rummy, the red-gold retriever, padded alongside him, ears perked and tail swishing in anticipation. Sy had offered to take her out so the boys could eat in peace, figuring he and Grey might walk and talk a bit now that the drizzle had subsided.

He expected to find her curled up on the sofa, but the room was empty. She must still be in the bathroom, pulling herself together. He poured two cups of tea, set one aside for her, then knelt to fit Rummy's harness. She, however, had other ideas. Sensing the tension in the house, she nosed and licked at him, determined to fix what she didn't understand.

"Hold still, Rum," he murmured, fumbling with the straps. A knock at the door startled them both. Rummy's ears perked, and she bolted from his grasp, wiggling excitedly toward the entrance.

"Dang it, Rum. Come back here." Sy scrambled after her and swung the door open—only to find himself face to face with Edmund Sinclair, luminary of the University Circle.

Edmund's expectant smile faltered as he registered Sy's presence. "Silas. How kind of you to attend to Grey before I could get here." His gaze flicked to the harness Sy still gripped before settling on the overenthusiastic retriever wriggling at his feet. His expression cooled. "They have a dog?" Edmund asked as if it were an unfortunate revelation.

Sy opened his mouth, but before he could respond, Grey appeared beside him.

"Edmund!" She practically flew into his arms, tilting her face up as he bent to kiss her.

Sy knew he should look away—manners dictated as much—but something about her made it impossible. Her cheeks were unnaturally pink, her eyelids shaded, her lashes darker, longer. Her lips—what little of them could be seen between Edmund's— were outlined and accentuated.

She didn't look bad. That wasn't possible. But she looked… different.

Grey pulled back with a sigh, and Edmund lifted her chin, appraising her with a satisfied smile. "Look how lovely and sophisticated you look." Then, as if just remembering Sy's presence, he added, "But I imagine we're making your friend uncomfortable. We mustn't be rude, no matter how much we care about each other."

Grey turned, eyes sparkling. "Oh, Sy, I'm sorry. I didn't mean to be rude."

Sy barely had time to shake his head before Edmund smoothly interjected, "Silas was just about to take your lovely pet for a walk. Sadly, I can't help as I'm terribly allergic."

Grey's expression shifted to concern. "You are? Oh, dear, we can put Rummy in another room or outside when you're here." She turned to Sy with an apologetic smile. "Thank you so much for taking her out. You are the best."

Sy pressed his lips together, forcing the corners upward. "I love Rummy. You know that. C'mon, girl."

He stepped onto the front stoop, leading Rummy toward the gate. He pushed it open, moved through, then turned to pull it shut while looking up. At the open door, he saw them. Edmund stood with one arm snugly around Grey, the other lifting a cup of tea—the one Sy had poured for himself. Grey leaned into his chest, speaking softly.

Edmund, however, was silent.

He met Sy's gaze across the yard, a slow, smug smile spreading across his face as he raised the cup in mock salute—then shut the door.

CHAPTER 7
THE LAMB

CURTIS

The sun was sinking below the horizon as Curtis and his father pulled up to a modest house in District Four, several blocks from the ocean and Saltend Harbor. Unusual for Bosch, the place looked abandoned—curtains drawn, no lights visible, weeds creeping through cracks along the walkway. His father approached the door, glancing left over his shoulder, then right.

Curtis stood behind him and rubbed his thumbs against his fingers, eyes slightly wider than usual as he contended with the knot in his stomach. His father rapped on the door—once, then three times, then twice more.

The door swung open to reveal a woman in a blue cloak. Curtis hadn't expected a woman and quickly ran through the hierarchy of the Bluest in his mind. *She must be a Daughter of Devotion.* She motioned them inside and shut the door behind them, leaving all three standing in the dim foyer.

A small light flickered in her hand as she murmured, "The Earth Remade, the Path Revealed."

Curtis' father nodded. "And the Chosen walk it true."

The woman bowed her head in acknowledgment, then handed Curtis' father a folded blue cloak of rough material. He accepted it, pressed a reverent kiss to the fabric, then shook it out and draped it over his shoulders, concealing his business clothes.

"This is my son. I was asked to bring him to the Visicomm meeting."

"He is not yet of the Chosen and may not wear our garment." She withdrew a small blue ribbon and pinned it to the shoulder of Curtis' shirt. "But he shall be marked." She stepped aside. "Please follow me."

Curtis had known for almost a year that his father had joined the Chosen of New Earth. As he followed behind, he mulled over everything his father had taught him about the CNE. The group, considered borderline illegal in Bosch, was also known as the Bluest—a reference to the robes they wore, their varied hues marking rank within the church. He silently recited in his head the five tenets, unsure whether he'd be called upon to intone them:

1 Honor the Divine Order: A man is ordained to lead, and a woman finds her highest fulfillment in service. No other union is righteous.

2 Multiply the Faithful: Reject the corruption of herbs and chemicals that hinder the birth of new Faithful. To bear children is to serve God.

3 Accept the Sacred Hierarchy: God has established ranks among the Faithful: leaders, followers, and thralls. Each must embrace their rightful place with humility.

4 Reject Worldly Corruptions: Shun the poisons that cloud the mind, the falsehood of equality, and the deception of democracy.

5 Expand the Dominion of the CNE: Spread the Holy Word and bring all nations under its divine rule.

They descended a staircase into a large open room where half a dozen robed figures stood.

One of them turned toward Curtis' father. "Welcome, Faithful.

The Visicomm connection is about to begin." His gaze shifted to Curtis. "Welcome, young one. Perhaps tonight, you may earn a robe."

Curtis fought the urge to grin and instead kept his expression neutral as he recited the response his father had taught him. "If it be God's will, I will be Chosen."

A murmur of approval passed through the gathered Faithful. The man who had spoken bowed his head. "Your Path will be Revealed." He checked the timepiece on his wrist, then turned toward a large screen mounted on the far wall. "Let us welcome the archminister of the Central Continent."

The screen flickered to life, revealing a man in a familiar blue robe seated in a high-backed upholstered chair. His face was visible—blond hair, a darker beard, light eyes. Curtis estimated him at about his father's age, perhaps a little older.

The man on the screen spoke. "The Earth Remade, the Path Revealed."

The assembled responded in unison. "And the Chosen walk it true."

A pleased smile touched the archminister's lips. "It is heartening to see the Faithful grow, even in the heart of Bosch's corruption." His voice carried a reverent weight. "You are the Thrice-Blessed, the Keepers of the Path, bravely bringing the Truth to the misguided, as one would bring water to the thirsty. May your numbers continue to grow."

The congregation chorused, "May God and the Patricians bless our work."

Then the archminister's expression sharpened as his gaze landed on Curtis. "You, boy—Curtis, correct?"

Curtis straightened.

"Your father tells us you have intelligence that may aid in revealing the Path in Bosch." The blond man leaned forward expectantly.

Curtis glanced hesitantly at his father, who gave a slight nod of encouragement. "Yes, Your Grace. I…" He swallowed, his throat dry. "I am part of the anti-Glitter Circle at the university. Our luminary is Edmund Sinclair. Last month, we held a rally, and two final-year secondary students attended. One of them was a girl Edmund has begun seeing socially."

The archminister's brows drew together. "I fail to see how the social life of university students is relevant to our goals."

Curtis' stomach twisted. "No, sir—I mean, yes, Your Grace. It's just…the girl he is seeing happens to be Grey Shima, the eldest daughter of the master commander of Bosch, MC Wallace."

Silence. Curtis' face burned as he realized his information was insignificant. Had his father truly brought him here just to humiliate him? He fought the urge to glare at him.

The archminister said nothing, only stroked his beard, pale eyes fixed on Curtis. Curtis wanted to disappear. Sink into the floor. But then, at last, the man spoke.

"The daughter, you say? At an anti-Glitter rally?"

Curtis barely found his voice. "Yes, Your Grace."

"I see." The severe man leaned back, staring toward the ceiling as if calculating unseen variables. Curtis' heart pounded so hard, he was sure the others could hear it. Finally, the man's gaze moved back to him. "Daughter, fetch a supplicant robe for the newest member of the Bosch Bluest community," he boomed, apparently speaking to another member of the congregation.

Curtis blinked. Had he heard that right?

The archminister continued, "With this insight, you have earned the right to step onto the Path. Your next task is to bring the luminary who courts the child of that woman…" His tone dripped with disdain. "…onto the Path."

Curtis barely breathed.

"Submit a dossier on the luminary to your father in two days. I expect him here at the next Visicomm in one month."

Curtis just stared, too stunned to speak until his father nudged him sharply in the ribs. "I am but a humble servant before you, Your Grace," he stammered.

"Very good." The archminister's attention returned to the group. "Walk in the Light of the Remade Earth, and may your service glorify the Path."

In perfect unity, the congregation responded, "The Earth Remade, the Path Revealed. I serve with humility and faith."

The Visicomm screen went dark.

CHAPTER 8
LOVE IS STUPID

The last day before winter break. Exams were done and papers turned in. The air in the slackbay practically hummed with that weightless anticipation that came with feeling so close to freedom. Bits of snow whirled in the December air outside the large windows.

"Can you believe when we come back, it'll be the year we graduate?" Leia's eyes widened as she spoke, disbelief and giddy excitement mixed in her voice.

Mason's fingers lazily tangled in her hair, playing with a strand as they lounged on the couches reserved for final-years. He looked half-asleep, half done with everything. "Earth, I'm ready to be done and move on," he said with a dramatic sigh, the words edged with conviction.

Leia pouted, furrowing her brow. "Oh, real nice."

"I didn't mean from you—you know that," Mason replied, mirroring her pout with a touch of exaggeration. Leia burst into giggles, and he grinned like he'd won something. "So...what's everybody doing tonight? Wanna try Barton's?"

That got a few raised brows. Barton's was known for two things: decent food and a floor crawling with BPF officers.

Sy shook his head. "Anyone can get in there. But if you're thinking you'll get a drink, forget it. Between Leia's mom and Grey's family? They know exactly who we are. Exactly how old too."

Mason groaned. "I gotta get off this little island. I bet they'd serve me in Truevale."

Leia smacked his arm. "Again with the leaving me."

Sy's eyes drifted to where Grey sat angled just slightly away from the group, thumbs flying over her comm. She hadn't looked up once. He tilted his head. "Hey, Shima, what are you up to tonight? Sounds like we're heading out—likely to watch Mason humiliate himself in public again."

Mason offered a playful growl and a wounded "Hey, now."

Grey didn't respond, still messaging Edmund—Edmund, now referred to as *Ed-Dumb* in Sy's head. He was trying not to let it slip, but the nickname had bubbled up more and more lately in his head, descending closer to his lips with every word he spoke in their group.

"Earth to Shima…" He nudged her leg gently with his foot.

Grey jumped. "What? Oh, sorry. I was just messaging with—"

"Edmund!" Leia and Mason sang in unison, dragging out the name like a spell they could mock-evoke. They added kissing sounds for effect.

Grey rolled her eyes, set the comm down, and finally turned their way. "You guys are so immature."

"And what's the sophisticated university crowd doing tonight?" Sy asked, trying to keep it light even as something in his chest pinched. He missed spending weekends with her. School nights weren't enough. Not since the rally. Not since…everything changed.

Grey tossed her hair back, cool as ever. "We're going to a pub in the city."

Mason perked up. "Now that's an idea. They won't know us there."

"No way," Grey said instantly.

Leia narrowed her eyes, faux-suspicious. "What's wrong, Pebs, afraid we'll embarrass you in front of your uni friends? Remind them you're still in secondary?"

To Sy's surprise, Grey laughed. "Can you blame me? First time Edmund and I went out to dinner, the server asked if he was babysitting."

Leia's gasp turned into laughter. "That's awful!"

"Tell me about it. I was mortified. But Edmund said not to worry. That's when he got me the makeup. And…yeah, it helps."

Ah, that explained it. The reason for the subtle liner and contour she only wore when she was with him. Sy had known it was about Edmund, and that knowing had sat like a pebble in his shoe ever since.

"So how come you never wear it to school?" The question passed through his lips before he could stop it.

Grey looked a little confused. "What? Makeup?" At his nod, she shrugged and replied dismissively, "I don't need it around you guys. You know how old I am. It's a hassle. I don't get why anyone would wear it every day."

Sy wanted to say, *Maybe you should stick with people who don't want you to be something you're not.* He wanted to tell her she was perfect—radiant—without a thing on her face.

Instead, he heard his mom in his head, quoting that old Bosch saying she loved: *Costs the same breath to bless as to bruise.*

So he blessed inwardly, then said while studying her, "Well, you certainly don't need it. But the few times I've seen you with it, it looks great. Makes you look older. I bet that helps when you're out."

Grey smiled, and the sight made something warm and achy settle deep in his ribs. But then her comm buzzed again, and just like that, her attention was swept away—back to that other life. The one that didn't include him.

She's your friend, he reminded himself. And she was. Even if it didn't feel like enough.

Leia reached over and squeezed his arm, a gentle, wordless comfort. Mason gave him a look too—half-pity, half-brotherly support. Sy forced a shrug like it didn't matter, like the box that held his feelings for Grey hadn't started coming undone since that stupid rally.

"C'mon." Sy scooped up his books and then hers, like always. "We're gonna be late for languages. Last class of the year."

Grey stood without a word, still focused on her comm, still texting Ed-Dumb. Sy tossed a "See ya," to Mason and Leia as they waved, not remotely concerned over their own lateness.

They walked in near silence, Sy steering them through the crowds while Grey typed furiously. *Huff. Tap. Groan. Tap.* He slowed their pace as her frustration grew, and finally, with a quiet "Fine," she shoved the comm into her bag.

She worked her face into something meant as nonchalance. But Sy knew her well. Her posture was tight, her breath uneven.

"You wanna talk about it?" he asked softly.

She glanced up at him, and his heart cracked. Her eyes were glassy, her voice raw as she forced out, "He has a meeting in District Four tonight. With Curtis. He promised he'd go." She swallowed hard. "I'm disappointed, sure. But what really sucks is, I won't even see him until after Winter Gifting. He's leaving for Truevale tomorrow with his family." She sniffed and wiped at her eyes. "Love is stupid."

And as much as it hurt hearing her use that word—*love*—in terms of someone else, Sy couldn't disagree.

"You can say that again."

CHAPTER 9
THE BLUEST

The wind off the harbor was bitter, carrying shards of icy rain that stung Edmund's face as he yanked up his anorak's hood. A motion that did nothing to improve his mood. The last damn day of first semester finals, and instead of hoisting a drink in a warm pub with his arm around Grey, he was trudging through the cold to some meeting he had no desire to attend.

He cut off his silent grousing as the house Curtis and his father had led him to came into view. What the—? The place was more than just rundown; it teetered on the edge of ruin. A couple of shutters banged back and forth in the salt-laced gusts, barely clinging to their hinges. The pavers leading to the door were uneven, some lifted, others swallowed by creeping weeds. Shingles were missing, leaving dark, jagged gaps, while years' worth of leaves, branches, and pine needles had settled thick in the roof's angles. It wasn't just neglected; it was also an eyesore on a street of otherwise modest but well-kept homes.

Edmund scoffed inwardly. If they thought letting the place go to seed would make it inconspicuous, they were fools. That might work in the poorer neighborhoods of Truevale, but in Bosch? It was a beacon.

Still, he shrugged off the thought and picked up his pace to catch up to Curtis. One night. That's all this was. Curtis had insisted it would be worth his time, promising it would "help the cause." He'd been irritatingly vague about who exactly Edmund would be meeting, only offering, "It's a worldwide organization. Very influential. Lots of power."

Influence. Power. A planetwide reach. Too tempting to ignore. And Curtis had proven himself a loyal part of the Circle, so there Edmund was, standing on a sagging porch while Curtis' father rapped several times on the door.

It swung open, revealing a woman in a light blue robe.

Bluies. Edmund's stomach tightened, though his expression remained smooth. He knew who they were—The Chosen of New Earth, or the Bluest, a religious-political group intent on spreading their ultra-conservative views through proselytizing and brute force. Most people in Bosch reviled them, thus their pejorative nickname, Bluies. But elsewhere on New Earth, they held undeniable power. Though their influence in the Federal Alliance of Nations—the largest and most dominant coalition on the planet—had waned in recent years, they had regrouped and stood poised to triumph in the coming elections in Eternia, the heart of the FA.

Edmund exhaled slowly, steeling himself. He didn't care for their views, but any willingness to support the anti-Glitter agenda could make them useful allies.

He offered the woman a polite nod and pleasant smile as introductions were made, carefully concealing his distaste when she pinned a small blue ribbon to his shirt. Then, without hesitation, he followed her—along with Curtis and his friend's father—down a dimly lit staircase into the basement.

This should be an interesting night.

♡

EDMUND

The archminister's image loomed large on the Visicomm screen. He looked calm—*too calm*, Edmund thought—as he reclined in a plush chair, hands draped over the arms like a man with nothing to prove. His robe shimmered a deeper, richer blue than the faded cloaks worn by the ten figures flanking Edmund in the basement. Unlike them, the archminister wore no hood. His pale face, framed by ash-blond hair and a neatly trimmed beard streaked with silver, was completely visible. Clear, blue eyes swept over the group with practiced ease.

As those eyes narrowed, Edmund heard a collective inhale from the hooded assembly around him. The air snapped taut with unspoken expectation.

He shifted slightly, catching Curtis' eye. His friend stood silent beside him, nearly swallowed by the oversized robe. Even his breath seemed held.

Then came the archminister's voice—quiet but steady. "The Earth Remade, the Path Revealed."

As one, the others answered, "And the Chosen walk it true."

Something in Edmund twisted, giving rise to a whisper from deep inside him: *Be careful. These people hide themselves for a reason.*

The archminister's eyes sparkled as though he'd heard the thought. "I imagine our guest is unsettled," he said with a dry smile, "to find fellow islanders—people who claim to share his vision for a better, stronger, more moral Bosch—unwilling to show their faces. Let's remedy that."

The screen figure gave a small nod toward Curtis. "Our young supplicant assures me Mr. Sinclair is more than aligned with our goals. He may very well be a future leader—not just in the anti-Glitter movement but also within the CNE itself."

The room shifted. The words hung heavy, impossible to ignore. Something flickered in Edmund—pride, cautious and coiled.

Then, without hesitation, the others dropped their hoods and stepped forward. One by one, they clasped Edmund's elbow in the formal greeting, murmuring "Welcome" or "We're glad you're here."

He returned each with a nod and a polite, practiced smile—masking the recognition that struck him like a blow. These were not just islanders. These were some of the most powerful men in Bosch.

The archminister's eyes gleamed with satisfaction. "Better," he said softly like a grandfather indulging his favorite child. "Chosen, please step upstairs. I'd like a private word with Mr. Sinclair. We'll reconvene afterward."

Edmund watched, half in awe and half in scorn, as these titans of Bosch politics obediently filed up the wooden stairs without protest. Like children excused from the table.

The screen's attention returned to him. "Discipline, Mr. Sinclair," explained the archminister. "It is the cornerstone of our order. Every voice is valued, but there must be order. I suspect you've learned that in your anti-Glitter efforts. And no doubt as the youngest Sinclair, you've had discipline drilled into you since childhood."

He knows more about you than you know about him. Edmund straightened. "Indeed. Discipline is important," he replied smoothly. *Keep it noncommittal, safe.*

The archminister's smile never wavered. "Quite so. I believe there's a chair in the corner. Please bring it closer. Let's speak comfortably."

Edmund found the straight-backed chair tucked in the shadows, brushed it off, and returned to sit before the screen. He kept his posture relaxed yet alert.

"If we were meeting in person," the archminister said warmly, "you'd be offered something stronger than dusty furniture. Perhaps next week, when your family visits Truevale, you could spare a few minutes for me?"

The words hit Edmund like cold water. Of course, he knew about the family trip. *I should be with Grey,* he thought bitterly. Her curls haunted him—dark brown at first glance but kissed with streaks of gold and ink in the right light.

He exhaled through his nose. "That's twice now you've mentioned digging into my life, Archminister. Should I take it as a compliment or a threat?"

A chuckle rolled through the speakers. "As expected, intelligent, charismatic...no-nonsense. We don't play games with outsiders. I had to know if you were worth the risk. And I believe you are. We share a goal: to end the reign of Glitter over Bosch."

Edmund sat forward, interest sparking in his chest. "We need support. Our Circle is growing, but most Bosch citizens still see Glitter as either a necessary evil or a cultural cornerstone."

The archminister nodded. "You've mobilized students well. But to change Bosch, you must sway both the young and the old. Only then will that...female commander listen to reason."

His mouth curled in distaste as common ground opened between the two men. "She will," Edmund promised, his tone suddenly alive. "Her daughter—Grey Shima—has already joined the Circle."

"Aha!" The archminister leaned in. "A fortunate twist. Perhaps you could deepen a friendship with this child."

"Grey isn't a child." Edmund's words tumbled out before he could rein them in. "She's—she's extraordinary. We've been seeing each other."

The archminister froze, then steepled his fingers in thought. "Ah. I see. Thank you for your honesty. Of course, I'd never suggest manipulating a romantic connection for political gain. Perhaps...someone else could reach out instead?"

Edmund blinked, startled. He was the luminary. *He* led the cause. "Sir, Grey is as committed to the cause as I am." *She actually believes in it,* he thought ruefully. "Maybe more. If she's willing to help, we should let her."

The archminister stood abruptly and retreated off-screen, returning several seconds later with a steaming cup in hand. "It's troubling," he remarked after sitting and taking a leisurely sip as if deliberating carefully over current events. "This is why we don't encourage women in leadership. Their gifts lie in nurturing, not rational thought."

Edmund bit his tongue so hard he tasted blood.

The man continued, calm and certain. "Still, I believe you are a gift from the Lord, Mr. Sinclair. Come see me next week. My secretary will arrange it. For now, please send the Chosen back. Wait upstairs. You are not yet one of the Faithful."

The call clicked off before Edmund could reply. He stared at the blank screen, adrenaline humming through his limbs. His emotions had been tossed about—wanted, disregarded, elevated, excluded.

He climbed the stairs slowly, jaw clenched and unclenching as possibilities swam in his mind. He would meet the archminister— and he would show him and Bosch that he was a leader who could change everything.

Grey's face swam into his mind's eye. And he wouldn't do it alone.

CHAPTER 10
OH, WHAT A NIGHT

GREY

"Hey, baby, Matty and I are going to play cards after he gets Rini to sleep. Want to join us?" Mama's voice cuts through my wool-gathering (good Bosch wool, ha!) as I stare out the front window.

I shake my head, turning to look at her curled up on the sofa, one of Mama M's bright patchwork quilts wrapped around her. She's been home from the hospital for a month now and went back to work almost immediately because, as she put it, "Bosch's issues don't stop just because I had a personal problem." Personal problem. She hardly ever talks about the baby or the fact that she almost died. Matt says that's just how she copes. Even Papa agreed, telling me, "Give her time, Grey. Your mama's emotions are complicated." But she still looks pale, and I can't help but worry.

"Sure, that sounds fun," I say, though without much enthusiasm. My gaze drifts back to the window, where half-frozen rain blurs the streetlights—a typical December night in Bosch.

Mama's voice is light. "Where's your young man tonight?

Feels like you've been seeing him nearly every weekend since that rally."

I know where this is going and try to sound casual. "Oh, he had a meeting over in District Four with a friend."

"Mmm." A pause. "So…"

Here it comes.

"I'd really like to meet this Edmund. Beyond just a nod at the door when he picks you up or drops you home."

She's sincere, no edge to her voice—yet. I exhale, my breath fogging the window for a second. "I know, Mama. You've said this before. It's just…weird. He's the luminary of the anti-Glitter Circle, and you… Well, you run the whole Glitter operation."

A beat of silence. Then a quiet, clipped, "I'd like to think my job is a bit more than that."

There's the edge.

I spin around. "Of course, it is! I get it, Mama. You're *so* important, and you expect my boyfriend to come grovel at the Great Woman's feet." I mean for it to be a venomous jab, but the last words break on a sob, and suddenly, tears I've been holding back spill over. "Well, you'll have to wait because I won't even see him until after Winter Gifting and the new year. He's leaving for Truevale tomorrow with his family."

Before I can brace myself, Mama is up in a flash and pulling me into her arms. "Oh, my baby." She smooths my hair, rocking me slightly. "It's hard to be apart from the people we care about. I'm sorry he'll be gone so long."

We fight a lot, but right now, I need this hug. I let myself sink into it.

"Oh, Mama, I feel so stupid getting upset over him being away for a few weeks."

She keeps swaying like she does with Rini—like she did with me and the boys when we were little. Then I realize she's on her feet, and worry floods in, pushing past my sadness. "Mama, you shouldn't be up. You need to rest. You've been working all week, and you still look so pale."

She squeezes me gently. "Shh. I'm fine. I'm your mama—it's my joy to take care of you. But if it'll make you feel better, we can sit on the sofa together. You can tell me a little more about Edmund—why you like him so much—and I'll braid your hair. One of those fancy braids like when you were a little girl." She presses a kiss to my temple. "I've missed out on a few conversations these past weeks. I'd like to catch up."

I hiccup back my tears and nod. "I'd like that."

She braids my hair while we talk and laugh more than we have in weeks, and little by little, I start to feel lighter. Like maybe things are going to be okay after all. As she listens without trying to tell me what to do, something inside me settles—and I decide. "Mama, could I skip cards and go over to Barton's? Sy and Leia and Mason are there tonight."

If she's disappointed, she hides it well. "I think that's a fine idea. The storm's blowing in from the coast, so how about you let Matt drive you over?"

"That would be great," I say, already feeling the pull of it. A night out with friends. I could use that.

Just something normal.

♡

GREY

The night is chill and damp as I pull the door to Barton's open. A rush of warm air wraps around me, the smells of frying oil and fresh bread chasing off the December cold. I turn and lift a hand toward the street—a part-wave, part-signal to Matt that no brigands have ambushed me between curb and door.

Matt sits in the vehicle, headlights still on, watching like a hawk. He and Mama have gotten even more protective since the baby died. They want to know exactly where I go, who I'm with. It took hours of convincing to even get permission for my first date with Edmund. Even now, I have to be home at a ridiculously early hour. I mean, I get it. They've had more than their share of worry over the years. But honestly? Nothing ever really happens in Bosch. It's one of the safest (read: most boring) places on New Earth. Years ago, I complained to Emily, my therapist, about their worrying, and she just shrugged and said, "Parents are gonna parent."

Matt raises a hand back at me and swings the vehicle around, heading home. I've got three hours before he's back to pick me up, so I push into the restaurant, scanning the booths. Sy, Mason, and Leia sit against the far wall. There's someone else, too, sitting next to Sy, but the dim light blurs their face.

Weaving between tables, I head over. Mason's in the middle of spinning some story, but Leia spots me first. Her smile freezes. "Pebble! You came.... You're...here!" She sounds happy enough, but there's the tiniest undertone of panic in her voice. Her eyes flick from me to Sy—then to the person sitting beside him. Who is it? I glance over and see a tall girl with a thick, black braid.

Lorraine. Her name pops into my head like a trivia answer. One year behind us. Writer for WER-Bosch, the student radio station. Works the lights for theater productions. Reputation for being...well, mostly invisible. Since when did she start hanging out with Leia?

I hang my rain jacket on a hook and slide into the booth next to Sy, who still hasn't said a word. Instead, his mouth hangs open like he's caught mid-thought. Mason, on the other hand, looks like all his birthdays just came at once. He lets out a bark of delighted laughter.

I reach over, steal a fried potato finger from Sy's plate, dunk it into the spicy sauce we both love, and pop it into my mouth. "I decided not to sit home and sulk. To tell the truth, Mama and I had a good talk, and she told me to 'get my butt over to Barton's and have some fun.' So here I am!" I lean around Sy to grin at the tall girl. "Hi, Lorraine. Didn't expect to see you tonight."

Lorraine isn't smiling. Her voice is clipped as she replies, "Same."

Whoa. Okay. What did I ever do to her? No wonder she doesn't get out much.

I glance down—and that's when I notice it. Lorraine and Sy are sitting very, very close. Like, thighs-brushing, shoulder-bumping close. My brain, usually as keen as my sailor's compass, tries to piece it together...but it's like dragging through mud.

"Sy?" I manage, pouring every confused question into his name.

Sy clears his throat, a flush creeping up his neck. "Hey, Grey. Thought you said you were staying in tonight, so..."

Lorraine leans forward, fixing me with a pointed stare as she finishes for him: "So we are on a double date."

Double. Date. Sy. On a date. With tall, glowering Lorraine.

I glance at Leia, desperate for confirmation. She nods almost imperceptibly, wincing a little.

"Oh. shit. A date. That'd make me..." A thousand words flash through my brain—third wheel, outsider, spare tire, anchor dragging behind the boat—but Mason beats me to it.

"Hilarious," he crows, pounding the table with his fist. "It makes you hilarious."

Leia smacks his shoulder with the back of her hand, and he exclaims, "Ow! What was that for?"

"You're not helping," she hisses through gritted teeth.

I scramble to my feet. "I should go."

Sy's voice, more natural now, breaks through the confusion. "No, don't go—"

"Yeah, don't go, Shima!" Mason pipes up, grinning wickedly. "Perfect time to call Jonah. Finally get you two on that date." He pulls his comm from his pocket, waving it around like it's a magic wand.

"Oh, hell, no." I'm already heading toward the door. I push it open, and the cold rain slaps me in the face. My jacket's still inside, but there's no way in New Earth I'm going back for it.

"Grey, wait!" It's Sy, jacket in hand. Rain wets his curls, darkening them even more.

I hover near the front walk, torn between bolting and facing him.

He holds the jacket out. "You forgot this."

I grab it, awkward. "Thanks. Um...sorry. I didn't..."

"I didn't really either." His smile is small and sheepish. "Until I got here. So...there's that."

His lopsided grin, all nervous energy and familiarity, I know better than my own. "You're getting soaked," I inform him. "And you're on a date, you dog. Get back in there and have fun." I make my voice bright, light, like it doesn't matter at all. Like it doesn't sting. Though I'm not sure why it does.

"You could stay," Sy offers, his voice low, earnest.

I shake my head. "No. I just stopped by. Matt's coming soon anyway." The lie tastes sour in my mouth.

"You sure?"

"Absolutely. Get back in there. Tell me all about it later." It's the right thing to say. But really, I don't want to hear a single word about Lorraine.

"Okay. Talk later?" he asks.

"Yep."

I watch through the window as he returns to the booth, sliding back in beside Lorraine—close, too close—and then I turn away. I duck my head against the rain, walking fast, letting the night swallow me as I head home.

EDMUND

It was already late when they headed back toward the university from District Four. Curtis slept in the front seat, and his father drove in silence, ever the taciturn man. The dark road slid past in endless monotony. Edmund sat in the back, wide awake, his mind circling like a restless hawk.

He couldn't believe he'd been summoned to speak directly

with a leader of the Bluies. No—he had to start thinking of them properly. Not Bluies, not that sneering nickname. The Chosen: the strongest anti-Glitter allies on New Earth.

Still, the encounter looped in his mind, the archminister's words repeating like a chant he couldn't quite decipher. He needed to talk it out. Needed someone who would listen without judgment.

And he knew exactly who he wanted to see. He pulled out his comm and typed.

> Hey, are you up?

The answer appeared on the screen immediately:

> Hey! I am. Well, sorta. Not asleep.

> I really need to talk to you.

> Okay. Talk.

> No. Not on comms. In person.

A pause. Edmund waited. Then:

> When?

> We're headed back now. I could meet you around two bells.

Another pause. Finally:

> There's no way Mama will let me wander out at two bells.

> Grey. I need you. It's important.

Longer hesitation this time. His pulse sped up.

> Okay. But not my house. Rummy would bark. I'll meet you at the park.

> Perfect. I'll message when I leave my dorm.

> Okay.

> Grey. This is huge. For us. And for the movement. Thank you.

> I understand. You know I'm all in. For the movement. And for us.

He tapped out the words: *I love you.* For a beat, he stared at what he'd typed on the screen, then deleted them. Too soon. Too serious. Too…everything. Instead, he wrote:

> I know. Me too.

And pocketed his comm.

GREY

I pull down the coiled length of purple rope from its peg on my wall and consider it. I've used it as a mooring line before when Sy and I went sailing. My mind darkens a little as I think about Sy and Lorraine. It's not that I mind him finally having a date. Of course not. It's just…I don't think she's his type. Too quiet. I shove the thought away. Tonight isn't about what I can't fix. It's about who I want to be with.

I need to get to Edmund. I look at my second-story window, then at the rope in my hand. Mama gave it to me for my birthday last April. She had said it got her out of several tight spots back when she ran missions, and she knew I'd have use for it.

I don't think sneaking out of the house in the wee hours of the morning was quite what she had in mind, but here we are. I tie it off with a sailor's knot on my bed frame, inch my window open, then shimmy down the purple rope, boots hitting the wet ground with a soft thud.

I tug my jacket tight, hop the fence—no way I'm risking the squeaky gate—and head down the street toward the park, my body buzzing. Part of it's the thrill of sneaking out—something I've never dared before. Most of it is Edmund.

I slip through the night like a secret, the whole city hushed under the storm. When I reach the park, I spot his vehicle immediately, low and dark against the curb. As I approach, the door pops open, and he moves toward me, pulling me into his arms without hesitation.

"Grey," he murmurs into the hood of my jacket, voice thick with relief. "You really snuck out for me? You're amazing."

I smile against his chest, nerves and excitement tangling inside me. He steers me around to the back of the vehicle, lifting the hatch to reveal a secret nest of blankets and pillows, tucked like a hidden promise against the storm.

"I figured you'd be cold," he says. "And... I need to hold you while I talk."

I hesitate. Cozy was one thing. This looks daring, almost dangerous.

"I don't know..." I start, heart skipping. "You know I'm not ready..."

His hand brushes mine, reassuring. His voice is soft and certain. "I know. Nothing like that. Just talking. Holding you. That's all." He pauses. "Well, and kissing you."

I giggle. "Well, of course, kissing is a given." The rain taps harder against the car roof. I bite my lip, consider, and then nod. "Okay."

He helps me out of my soaked jacket, tossing it over the front seat, and I climb into the little haven he's made. He follows a second later, his warmth curling around me, and suddenly the world outside feels impossibly far away. For a moment, we just sit there, breathing each other in.

"Now," he says in a low voice, brushing a lock of damp hair from my forehead, "I can actually see you."

He kisses me then—slow, deep, utterly patient—and every nerve ending in my body lights up. Our mouths meet and part, then meet again, a rhythm older than thought.

He trails kisses down my jaw, along my neck, murmuring between them, "You are so beautiful, Grey."

I whisper his name against his ear, feeling him shudder. His hands find my waist, sliding under my sweater, warm and strong. I freeze instinctively—but he stops immediately, pulling back to search my face.

"May I?" he asks, voice hoarse with restraint.

The trust between us is its own kind of magic. "Yes," I whisper. "But just that. For tonight."

His answering smile is devastating and tender at once. "Just that."

Carefully, reverently, he helps me lift my sweater off, leaving me in my blue lace tank.

He exhales slowly. "You are..." He shakes his head. "Magnificent."

I laugh—nervous, shy, thrilled all at once. "Turnabout's fair play," I tease, tugging at his sweater.

He grins and pulls it over his head, revealing muscled arms and a strong chest that looks like it was carved by the sea winds themselves. He leans closer, eyes dark with something raw and real.

I hesitate—then, heart hammering, I pull my tank over my head too, baring myself completely.

For a long moment, he simply stares at me. Not like I'm a thing to be devoured but something sacred.

"I wish you could see yourself the way I do," he says, voice breaking slightly.

When he touches me—tracing slow, warm circles around my breasts—I gasp, the sensation ricocheting through me like lightning. My fingers dig into his arms. I tip my head back, breathing hard, wanting more.

He takes his time—stroking, teasing—each flick of his thumb over my nipples sending bright shocks of pleasure through my body. I arch toward him, half-desperate.

He takes the cue, his mouth pressing hot kisses along my throat, across my collarbones. Then lower, until his lips close over a nipple, and something between a gasp and moan slips from my lips.

I can feel him, hard against my leg. I feel myself, aching and molten inside. Part of me thrills at the proof of how much he wants me. Another part grows dizzy with how much *I* want him. So much, it terrifies me.

Maybe it does him too because suddenly Edmund pulls back, chest heaving. He grabs my discarded tank, presses it to his face for a moment like he needs the scent of me to survive—and then hands it back, voice hoarse. "Put this back on," he says gently. "If we don't stop...we won't stop." He yanks on his own sweater and throws open the hatch, stepping into the rain to cool off.

He is right, of course. I take the shirt and pull it on. Something primal inside me keens its disappointment. *Patience*, I tell it. Some things—the best things—are worth waiting for.

When he returns, soaked but steadier, he offers me his hand, and I leave this nest of desire. He strokes my cheek and kisses my forehead. "Let's sit up front. I need to tell you what happened in District Four tonight." His voice is serious, more luminary than lover now.

I slide into the passenger side. The rain is shifting to sleet that pings off the vehicle, and a rumble of thunder foreshadows more rough weather; still, I believe our course to be steady. I feel certainty inside of me, and when I look at Edmund's profile as he takes his place beside me, I see courage. Whatever's coming, we'll face it together.

CHAPTER 11
THERE IS DEFINITELY A MORNING AFTER

GREY

My comm vibrates near my head. I fumble under my pillow, desperate to silence the buzzing. One sleepy swipe of my thumb and blessed quiet returns. I start to drift back to dreaming until the smart part of my brain kicks me hard. I bolt upright and my breath catches as the events of last night rush back like a flooding tidal wave.

Flood. That is exactly right. I kick my feet over the side of the bed and survey my room. The rug under my window is soaked, and tell-tale muddy smears from my boots darken the sill. The trusty purple rope is drenched as well and oozing dampness onto the floor, where it lays sprawled underneath a heap of damp clothes. It's not quite five bells. Less than an hour since I collapsed in bed. My warm blankets and soft pillow whisper promises of comfort, but I force myself to put my feet on the floor.

This mess isn't going to clean itself. As I gather wet clothes and mop at the rug, my mind replays everything Edmund told me.

The drive out to District Four. The ramshackle house and knock on the door. The woman in a blue robe—Bluies. My stomach flips even now.

"Those are bad people, Edmund," I said, my voice sharper than I meant. The memory of that tiny tropical island flashes hot and bright—the Formosan pirates, the fear, the Bluies' appearance, ready to pay for chaos.

He looked surprised. "You've heard of them? On the Obi or something?"

Or something, I thought grimly, remembering what they'd wrought on the island two years earlier. "They're extremists," I warned. Which is putting it mildly, to be sure. They want nothing less than complete control over…well, over everything.

His brow crinkled and he shrugged, casual. "I don't know, Grey. I mean, of course you'd have been taught that. The Force resents any of the other powerful groups on New Earth."

His easy dismissal of my concerns and grasp of Bosch politics stung. I knew a lot. I follow Bosch and world politics like some kids follow footy scores. While Anya could tell you the latest Truevale fashion trends, and Mason could rattle off every game stat, I track elections, political movements, rising alliances. There's a reason I'm top of my class in history. But this was not the time to parade out my credentials. "Are they trying to convert you?" I asked instead, heart thudding.

He shook his head. "I don't think so. The archminister…"

"Archminister? Of what? Not of the Central Continent?" My voice pitched higher in alarm.

"I guess? I don't really know their hierarchy." He offered a sheepish smile. "Sounds like you must've studied more than me. But it doesn't matter what his title is, Grey. It's what he's offering that counts." He leaned closer, folding my hand between his. "He wants to help us. To eliminate Glitter. For Bosch. For us."

For a moment, I said nothing, my brain spinning. Eliminating Glitter is what we want. It's good. But trusting Bluies—terrifying. Still, I wanted to hear him out. "How?" I asked.

He hesitated. "Not sure yet. I'm meeting him again over Winter Gifting, when I'm in Truevale visiting my sister."

"Oh, Edmund," I breathed. "Be careful. Don't trust them."

At that, something changed. His mouth tightened, his expression shifting from warmth to the faint condescension I remembered from the after-party. "Really, Grey. I'm not the child here." His voice began to escalate into the rally's fervor now. "Bosch cannot stay isolated forever, clinging to drug profits while the world moves on. We may not agree with the Chosen on everything, but they're willing to help us change things."

Don't ask me why I didn't clap back at him. I certainly would have with anyone else. But my feelings for him were so new to me, so intense, I bit back my urge to dispute.

"I... guess." I managed a weak smile, though my shoulders stayed stiff. He was older. Wiser. Luminary of the Circle. If he believed this, maybe he was right. But then why did it feel wrong? "I just worry," I added softly. "I want you to be safe."

His face softened, and he cupped my cheek in his palm. "That's my girl," he said, voice low. "We have to work together. I'll handle the Chosen. You can be in charge of the base."

That snapped me back. If I could get Mama and Edmund together, maybe he could convince her to stop the Glitter trade. And she *did* want to meet him. "Mama said you should come to dinner!" I blurted, excitement bubbling.

"No." The word, sharp and immediate, landed on me like a slap.

I blinked. "No?"

He sighed and rubbed the back of his neck. "Grey...your mother, Colonel Warner, the BPF leadership and I are on two separate sides of a vast divide. About Glitter, to be sure, but also about the direction Bosch should move. They are the old guard, protecting the old ways. We are the future; we see the value in connecting with the larger world. Until they are willing to build some bridges, I cannot in good conscience socialize with them."

But you can socialize with Bluies, I thought bitterly but kept uncharacteristically silent. I could fix this. I *would*. But how? The solution sprang from my lips without me stopping to assess it.

"Then I'll get you a meeting with the master commander," I promised. "I'll make her see reason."

And just like that, Edmund's whole face lit up. "That's perfect."

He kissed me then, soft at first, then deeper, hotter. I matched him, the heat of his mouth chasing away every doubt for a moment. When we pulled apart, laughing breathlessly, I thought, *Together, we can do anything.*

I find myself now standing in my room, looping my soggy purple rope around my elbow, heart still hammering at the memory of those kisses.

Our love won't be some tragedy like Romeo and Juliet, I promise myself fiercely. *We'll write a new ending—one where we win.*

♡

EDMUND

Edmund sighed heavily as his sister gestured to the Grayson Yang Gallery sign, leading the family through the Sunset Yard District of Truevale. It would be the third art gallery she had schlepped them through that morning, and Edmund wondered whether this one would be another temple to NeoDecay—all mold, moss, and mood lighting—or more Crystallax monstrosities pretending to be sustainable, though everyone knew the so-called recycled plastics were really imported polymers from China.

"Edmund," his father snapped, slicing through his thoughts. "You need to keep up. Your indulged, youngest antics don't fly at home, nor will they here. You are not excused from the expectations we have as a family."

"Yessir." Edmund bit back the dozen retorts that sprang to mind. The "indulged, youngest" bit irked him every time he heard it, which was often. Yes, he was twelve years younger than his next oldest sibling. But that status did not equal indulged. If anything, he'd practically raised himself with siblings who were more like chilly, aloof aunts and uncles than sisters and brothers, whose parents had used up all their parenting chops a decade earlier and figured their late-in-life surprise could pull himself together and behave like an adult once the diapers were dispensed with.

He held the gallery door open, letting the family file past: parents, two brothers, their wives, his sister, and her husband. No nieces or nephews, thankfully. At least there was the nanny, and he'd escaped being tasked with babysitting. Edmund slipped in behind them.

The gallery was cool and airy, the soft strains of an orchestral sailor's hornpipe floating through the space. No rusted relics or post-industrial nightmares. Just clean, white walls tinged faintly blue, and art that felt...real. Familiar. The first room held a series of seascapes—calm harbors, storm-tossed waves, fog-bound dawns—each with a tiny, white sailboat tucked subtly into a corner. He didn't know why, but that sailboat caught his attention.

He moved deeper into the gallery, where portraits took over. Politicians and celebrities from Truevale. Then ordinary faces: a sandy-haired, freckled young man on a beach wearing a sad expression, a laughing waitress, a grim-faced enforcer leaning on a tree, a street-dweller with haunted eyes. Each one vibrated an uncanny presence, like they might blink or sigh at any moment.

He was almost at the back of the gallery when he saw her. A close-up image of that same white sailboat, bobbing on a cerulean sea. A girl sat at the tiller, laughing, wind in her dark waves of hair. He took in her delicate features, her determined jaw, those unmistakable Edoan eyes. It could have been Grey's twin.

His breath caught. Was it Grey? He leaned in to inspect the face, heart thudding.

"That one's not for sale," said a voice beside him.

Edmund flinched. A tall man with a ponytail and trimmed beard stood at his elbow, dressed in a white shirt and loose linen pants—Bohemian but clean, confident.

"It's already spoken for," the man continued.

"The girl..." Edmund began. "Who is she?" He hoped he didn't sound like one of those guys who thought all Edoan girls looked the same. The face was so familiar. It had to be her. But how? Why?

The man touched a red, leather pouch at his neck. "Friend of the artist. Not local. From Bosch."

Edmund blinked. The jealousy came fast and sharp. "And the artist?" He turned, scanning the painting's corner for a name. There it was: Ash Grey. Grey? Like his Grey? The possessive flare startled him—he hadn't meant to think of her that way, not exactly—but there it was, blooming hot in his chest.

"Who is this Ash person?" Edmund demanded, attempting the same clipped tone his father used on assistants.

Unruffled by the posturing, the man smiled easily and held out a hand. "I am. And you are?"

Edmund hesitated a beat before blurting out, "That girl... She looks like my girlfriend. I think she is."

Now a broad smile spread over the artist's face. "Well, that must make you…" He paused for moment, his eyes sliding left as if retrieving information from that direction. "…Edmund, right?" As he said this, the man clapped Edmund on his shoulder and gave it a friendly squeeze. "How delightful you are here. Grey mentioned you and your family would be in the city over the holidays."

"I… How… Who?" Edmund could barely get his thoughts in line. "Who are you?"

Ash Grey's eyebrows came up. "Grey hasn't mentioned me?" He moved his hand to his chest dramatically, then threw his head back slightly, his growing smile showing that his despair was feigned. "I am mortally wounded." He turned to look at his painting. "Well, I'm sure she's told you the story of the shipwreck, and *Noëlani*, and the Formosan pirates." The artist's hands came up in a gesture of relaxed confidence. "That was me."

Edmund had no idea what this man was saying, but he was

not about to admit he knew nothing about the referenced story. "Ah, yes. So that was you. I see now."

"I would be dead if it wasn't for Miss Grey Shima." The man's eyes took on a faraway cast before he refocused on Edmund. "Now you mustn't tell her about the painting. It's her holiday gift. We're heading up Bosch to see my sister and Grey around New Year's. Will you be back by then? I'd love to take you both out."

"Wait, you're from Bosch? And who's your sister?" Edmund's head was spinning.

"No. I am not Bosch. Don't know that they'd take me even if I wanted to move there. But my sister immigrated and enlisted a few years back." Ash Grey's pleasant expression remained, but his eyes narrowed slightly. "Grey has a rich past. She will share it on her own terms." The man brought up a finger and pointed at Edmund. "You are a fortunate fellow to have captured her interest and heart. See that you are careful with it."

Then, with a wink and wave, Ash moved off, walking with the shadow of a limp to greet a couple examining the waitress portrait.

"And watch out for her kicks," he called back cheerfully. "They're debilitating."

Edmund's jaw hung open slightly as he just stood there staring, frozen in place. Then he pulled out his comm and began to tap on it in earnest.

♡

GREY

The winter air, clear and chill, bites at my nose and cheeks as I jog across the backyard from the workout shed toward the warmth of the house. My face is flushed, breath still heavy. With Circle activities, school, and dating Edmund, my workout routine has slipped more than I'd like. Usually I get in a run, weights, conditioning, and some time with the heavy bag. Now that enlistment's just five months off, I'm getting back on it—especially after Matt reminded me about the fitness test. I still don't know whether the Force is my future, but I want the option.

The sweat-damp tendrils of my hair cling to my face, already cooling. Next week when I'm in Kiharu—Papa's village in Edo, where I was born—these strands will turn to icicles. Papa doesn't even *have* a heavy bag. Calls anything "proto-violent" a moral failing. It's honestly amazing that he and Mama lasted as long as they did. Weirdly, the thought of *marriage* makes me think of Edmund, which is both delightful and…alarming. I don't even know whether I want to get married. If I ever do, it won't be until I'm, like, thirty. Definitely not to someone like Papa, no way. If Edmund and I marry—*if*—it will be more like Mama and Matt, all adventure and honesty and zero "What's for dinner?" monotony.

He and I want the same things: Glitter gone. Bosch connected to the rest of New Earth. Those are our big dreams—but we also have little ones: laughing when the world's too serious, singing songs together. I miss him so much, it aches. Our one-comm-a-day plan? Not nearly enough. I hope it's not enough for him either.

Back in my room, I toss my sweaty workout clothes into a corner and rummage through drawers, starting a messy pile for Edo. My comm sits on the desk. I sent "I miss you" before my workout. Still unread. I sigh. *Touring Truevale*, I remind myself. I pick up my whittling knife instead—something I haven't touched in two chimes. Edmund raised an eyebrow the first time I told him I whittle. "That's kind of an odd hobby for a girl your age." We'll see what he says when I give him his Winter Gifting present.

My comm buzzes, startling me. I glance up, a flicker of hope in my chest. *Edmund?*

Buzz. Buzz. Buzz. Three more messages in rapid succession.

My pulse kicks up. I toss the knife onto the desk, unfinished wood creatures spilling around it. Snatching up the comm, I unlock it quickly, already smiling. And then, just as quickly, my smile falters. The first line doesn't say "Miss you back." Or "You're amazing." Or anything even remotely like him. Just:

> I just met Ash Grey.

Wait. Ash? My mind whirls. Did he go to the gallery? I move to his next message.

> You know, I thought I was a little old to be seeing someone your age, but he's like thirty or more.

My stomach does a slow, sour roll.

> You said I was your first boyfriend. I guess I should've asked about old man-friends.

My breath catches in my throat.

> He said something about a shipwreck. What else haven't you told me?

My hand tightens around the comm. My shoulders stiffen, and I want to hit something. These aren't messages from someone missing me. They're accusations, judgments, jealous jabs. Not the kind of messages you get from someone who cares about you. The kind you get from someone who wants to hurt you. Well, they worked.

Shocked laughter or tears—my body can't decide. But my emotions settle fast, coalescing into one reaction: rage. *Who does he think he is?* I start typing. Stop. Mama's voice echoes: "Never send a message when you're sad, mad, or full of wine." Two out of three. Okay, fine. I take a breath, pull out paper instead, and write:

Here's your answers, jerk: He's my friend. He turned thirty-one on November 12. So not ancient. You are my first boyfriend. Ash is like my big brother. And if you're insinuating anything else, that's just gross—and you should be ashamed. Also, he's a demigod, so tread lightly.

Yeah, there was a shipwreck. It was awful. I still have nightmares. I go to therapy. All things you don't know. And maybe if our conversa-tions weren't all about your glorious plans, you'd know some things about my life too. Maybe, if you'd ever asked.

Ink smears where my angry tears fall. The comm buzzes, once, twice. I try to ignore it, but I can't resist looking.

Shit Grey. I just read what I wrote. I'm a jackass.
A jealous jackass.

No kidding.

Are you there? Can you take a comm now?

I smear at my eyes and sniff, tapping:

Yeah, sure.

The comm springs to loud life. I let it ring three times on purpose and then push the answer button without a word.

"Grey?" Edmund's voice floats into my room—a room he's never seen in a house he refuses to enter.

"I'm here," I answer flatly, forcing my voice not to reveal my tears.

"Storms, Grey. That was stupid of me to write things like that. I… I'm sorry. It's just…"

"Here's something else you don't know about me, Edmund: I know that when giving an apology, you don't follow it with 'but' or 'It's just.'"

The comm is silent for a moment. When Edmund finally speaks, his voice is thick with emotion. "You're right. I'm sorry… Full stop. Please tell me I haven't ruined everything."

My eyes drift to the framed sketch of Ash and me on *Noēlani*. I think of how much I hated Ash at first. It taught me to give people time to show me who they are. I rummage through my feelings for Edmund, and one thing is clear: It would take so much more than those few messages from him to quench what I feel for this man.

"I'm mad," I say. "You were kind of a dick in those messages. But no—you didn't ruin everything." I pause. "It's actually kind of cool you met Ash. He's dear to me. Like a big brother. Also, there's a better than average chance I wouldn't be alive if it wasn't for him."

"That's what he said about you." A breath. "He also said to be nice to you. Which I guess I ignored. Shit. Oh, and that your kicks are…debilitating."

I laugh. "They are. So be nice." My voice softens. "Edmund… why did you say those things?"

"Hang on, I need to move." He covers the comm, says something muffled. Then the sounds of wind, traffic, and the hum of the city slip through the comm as he returns. "Listen, I really don't want to say this on a comm…but…"

My stomach flips. This sounds ominous. He didn't ruin things, but did I? I hold my breath.

"The thing is, Grey, I… I love you. And I guess I got stupid jealous and possessive, and I'm sorry."

For years, I have made fun of stupid movie and romance book characters who swoon when told they are loved. Like, duh? Everybody watching or reading already knew it. The other characters knew it. Hell, even the main characters sometimes knew it before the words were spoken. I always wondered how three words could make otherwise reasonable people act so dotty. But now my heart is in my throat, tears are sliding down my cheeks, and my smile is bigger than any ever on my lips, and I finally get it.

"Grey, are you there?"

"I'm here." I take a breath. "Edmund…I love you too."

EDMUND

Edmund adjusted his collar in the mirrored windows of the Chosen of New Earth's headquarters, flicking a stray dark hair from his sweater. The creamy Bosch wool was a strategic choice—a nod to the island's growing, legitimate exports—but the subtle blue stripes at the hem were a calculated flourish, a diplomatic wink, flattery without surrender.

He straightened the sweater again, smoothing invisible wrinkles and suppressing a tight smile. In just a few hours, he'd sidestepped another morning of babysitting, avoided his squalling siblings, and dodged his mother's needling questions. Now he stood on the threshold of something that could change everything —for Bosch, the Circle…and himself.

Soon, they'd all see. He wasn't just the indulged or even the ignored youngest. He was the future.

A young man dressed in a blue tunic and leggings addressed him. "Mr. Sinclair? Edmund Sinclair? I have your ID and will escort you to the archminister's office."

The lift hummed to the fifteenth floor, depositing Edmund in a gleaming suite bathed in rich blues and polished wood. Sunlight streamed through floor-to-ceiling windows. Against one wall, five golden-captioned lithographs depicted the tenets of the Chosen— all beams of heavenly light, obedient masses, and robed men gazing sternly from towers.

Edmund moved closer, drawn in despite himself. *Accept the Sacred Hierarchy* showed pale-faced, blue-robed men clustered high in a tower while a mass of brown and black laborers toiled below in shabby, blue work clothes. The light barely touched their faces. A trick of the artist, perhaps. Or maybe not.

"A most excellent depiction of our Holy Beliefs, wouldn't you agree?" The archminister's voice made Edmund jump. "Did I startle you, my boy? My apologies."

Edmund jerked back from the wall, heart hammering. He turned to find the archminister—taller than expected, and broader too, with a solemn grace—smiling genially beneath heavy brows. "It's fine, sir. I was just…captivated by the illustrations."

"Art softens the heart when words fail," the archminister said, gesturing toward a deep-blue velvet sofa. "Let us sit, my boy. I believe we have a shared vision for making New Earth a better place."

A better place. That was it. What Edmund wanted. "Yes, Your Grace," he said quickly, seating himself. "The Circle wants to eliminate Glitter—its mining, refinement, trade. We believe that will loosen its grip on Bosch, making New Earth a better place."

"Excellent. So, tell me, Mr. Sinclair, how do you see the Chosen assisting in this endeavor?" The archminister tipped his head ever so slightly to one side, awaiting an answer.

Edmund froze. The Circle created posters, hosted rallies, gave campus speeches. But beyond that… "I'm afraid I'm unsure," he admitted, dropping his eyes, shame creeping up his neck. He braced for correction, a sharp dismissal as he would have received from his parents.

Edmund heard a warm chuckle instead. "Excellent. I admire a man willing to learn. Perhaps you'll indulge me as I relate a little history?"

Edmund blinked. "Yessir, please."

A broad smile spread across the man's face. "Then allow me to offer some context. We all know the story of Old Earth's collapse —but the Chosen understand what truly lies beneath it." He folded his hands. "Yes, scientists blame climate disasters, soil depletion, pandemics. And they're not wrong, technically. But the deeper truth is this: The Lord willed the cleansing of that broken world. He right-sized the planet so that His Chosen might inherit a land purged of sin."

The man paused. Glanced at the table. His watch. The door.

It opened exactly then.

Edmund stiffened. *Did he just…?* No. Couldn't have.

The same young Bluie from earlier entered carrying a silver tray: porcelain cups, cream and sugar, a pot of steaming tea, and a plate of Truevale's traditional sweet biscuits. Without a word, the acolyte arranged the service, poured both cups, and bowed. The archminister lifted his hand—half-benediction, half-dismissal—and the young man retreated, as silent as a shadow.

"As I was saying, it is the Lord's plan to offer a world free of sin to the Chosen, but He does ask us to be part of the cleansing." He handed Edmund a cup of tea with a biscuit on the side. "Help yourself to cream and sugar."

"Thank you." Edmund accepted the cup. "What do you mean by cleansing?"

"A thoughtful question. I assume you follow global politics?" He didn't wait for a reply. "We've seen what happens when nations scramble for dwindling resources, the chaos bred by competing faiths carried over from Old Earth. Politics and faith cannot be separated. That's why we've placed Chosen loyalists throughout the League of States, the African Federation, Rus, Northern Europe, and Bharat. With spring elections ahead, our candidates are poised to gain a seat in every FA region—save Edo —and we are positioned to win the FA presidency and vice presidency." He nibbled on a biscuit, some stray crumbs dropping onto his beard. "God has decreed that through us He shall unite the planet, and the holy Divine Order He established at the beginning of time shall be restored." The archminister's voice soared as he pronounced the last sentence.

Edmund chose his next words carefully. "Those are bold plans, Your Grace. Will eliminating Glitter assist in them?"

"Indeed. Bosch's independence, its isolationism and reliance on Glitter—all are threats. And now, with a mere woman in charge, the time to act is ripe. The Divine Order is clear: Women are to nurture, to anchor the home like a harbor from the storm."

"On Bosch, men and women share leadership," Edmund pointed out. "And caregiving."

The archminister smiled indulgently. "Yes, egalitarian ideals can be seductive. But in the end, they lead to heartbreak. Your master commander lost a child recently, didn't she? Isn't that a sign her body is not built for the labors of a man's work?"

Edmund shifted uneasily. Certainly, he disapproved of the BPF's leadership when it came to Glitter, and he had heard his father and father's friends making occasional jibes about the first woman master commander, but was she actually too weak to lead? He'd never thought of Kat Wallace that way. "Grey did say her mother was drained when she came home from the hospital…"

"Ah, yes. You're involved with the daughter." The archminister stroked his beard. "May I offer some fatherly advice—on leadership and on women?"

"Yes, please, Your Grace."

"Exert your authority. Men lead. Women follow. As men we must show our women the way, for they need guidance. They look to us to bring stability to their disordered minds. It is the natural order. As luminary, you cannot be part of the Circle. You must lead from outside it—because you see the big picture. And in your personal life—choose a helpmeet who supports your mission, one who reveres your leadership, not one who challenges it."

Edmund's first instinct was to balk. Grey was not one to follow, and part of him loved that about her. He never thought of her mind as disordered, but she was headstrong, and that could lead to conflict. Exert his authority… Whether it was the natural order or not, if it advanced the cause, perhaps she would come to see the rightness of it. Perhaps.

He shook the thought away. "Thank you for the advice, Your Grace. Now about the anti-Glitter movement…"

The archminister laughed. "Very good, Mr. Sinclair. Refocus the old man."

"I meant no disrespect."

"None taken, my boy. So, Mr. Sinclair… May I call you Edmund?"

"Uh, yes, that would be fine."

"Since we are going to be working together, let us dispense with the 'Your Grace' title. The name my parents gave me was Simon Bolt, but we shed our worldly identity upon elevation. However, for this undertaking, you may call me Mr. Bolt."

"Mr. Bolt, then."

"The path to break Glitter's hold on Bosch must start with a single step. The first step is simple. Prove your resolve. Take your petition directly to the master commander's office. Have one of your followers record the interaction. Once that is done, we shall talk strategy—and funding."

Edmund inhaled deeply, controlling his excitement at the word *funding*. "I believe we can do that, Mr. Bolt. And in a timely manner."

The archminister stood. "Excellent. I look forward to working with you. My assistant will give you my direct comm code." He waited for Edmund to rise and walked him to the door, murmuring instructions to the assistant who waited just outside.

As Edmund exited the building and stepped out into the crisp Truevale air, he allowed a smile. Grey had already promised to get him a meeting with her mother. Step one was as good as done. And he was ready for step two. Glitter was on its way out. So why was there unease prickling at the base of his spine?

ARCHMINISTER

INTERNAL MEMORANDUM: LEVEL 7 CLEARANCE REQUIRED

From: Office of the Archminister, Central Continent Division

To: Office of His Holiness, the Patrician of Dominion

Date: 23 December 2371 | Time Stamp: 1200

Subject: Status Update: Operation Dominion Rising (DR-2371)

In accordance with Strategic Directive 7B, this report outlines current progress on Operation *Dominion Rising*:

Primary Agent Placement:

Subject Sinclair (Edmund) has been activated and positioned. Subject exhibits high suggestibility and ambition indices, confirming initial psychological profiling. Loyalty consolidation remains underway; projected 94% compliance post-first success milestone.

Stage One: Penetration of Bosch Leadership:

Initial access to Master Commander Wallace is projected within one fortnight. Subject believes access results from his own ingenuity; no known counterinfluence from local authorities detected.

Resource Acquisition Projection:

Following control of Glitter production and infrastructure, projected revenue stream will meet or exceed targets set forth in Asset Recovery Plan 5F. Estimated surplus: 36.3 billion markers over initial five-year period, pending market stabilization post-occupation.

Population Management Forecast:

Preliminary cultural compliance rates indicate expected religious assimilation at 62% by second annum post-annexation. Standard Thralldom Protocols authorized for non-compliant sectors as needed. Attached: Behavioral Adjustment Contingency Charts.

Next Authorization Required:

Pending confirmation of successful first access event, request approval to initiate Subversion Stage Two (SS2), including critical personnel reassignment and targeted infrastructure disruptions.

No external detection anticipated. Operation remains classified under full Dominion Seal.

Prepared in Service of the Divine Order,

Archminister, Central Continent

Chosen of New Earth

CHAPTER 12
DON'T KNOW MUCH

SY

SY HAD STOPPED BY THE LITTLE WHITE HOUSE WITH THE COBALT-BLUE front door to see whether Grey wanted to do something that afternoon and, if he was being honest, find a way to hide from Lorraine.

Somehow—though he wasn't entirely clear how—they were "in a relationship." At least according to Lorraine. In the past two weeks, they had gone on five dates after the Leia and Mason sneak-attack blind date the night before winter break. And though he was annoyed about being ambushed, Sy had to admit...it was nice. Nice to have someone pay attention to him, especially after Grey had practically sprinted out of Barton's that night.

Lorraine had been kind, flashing him a warm smile and asking, "Is she okay? I hope I didn't make her feel awkward." Her genuine concern helped Sy relax and even enjoy what turned out to be his first real date. Lorraine was easy to talk to and interesting.

Later, as she'd driven him home, a war broke out inside his head:

Shit, Mercer, she's going to expect you to kiss her.

But I've never kissed anybody except Mom and Aunt Joan. How do they do it in the books and the movies?

You mean, the history books about Old Earth and the science fiction space movies you like? They don't.

If they hadn't just sprung this on me, I could have done some research.

Well, it's too damn late for that now. You'll have to just wing it.

"Is this your house?" Lorraine's voice had snapped him back to reality.

"Um…yeah. Right here." He pointed unnecessarily at the building directly in front of them, the war in his mind renewing.

Just open the door and run for it!

No way. Kiss the girl and get it over with.

You'll make a fool of yourself.

That ship has sailed. Now shut up. "Hey, it was real nice to get to know you better, Lorraine." That sounded okay.

She smiled shyly, giggling. "I probably shouldn't tell you this, but…I've always wanted to talk to you more. I just get so embarrassed. You and Grey are always together…" She glanced up. "When I heard she was dating a university guy… Well, I asked Leia, who said you two were just friends."

Just friends. The words hit harder than expected—all his hope, frustration, jealousy, loneliness tangled together. "Yeah," he said gruffly. "Just friends." Without giving himself time to think, Sy leaned in, closed his eyes, and kissed Lorraine. Right on her nose. After a millisecond to regroup, and an assist from Lorraine, who tipped her head slightly up, his lips found their mark, and Sy Mercer finally had his first kiss.

It wasn't at all what he had imagined. It was wet and kinda weird, and their teeth bumped together. He had no idea what to do with his hands, which just flailed until he convinced them to settle on her shoulders. His glasses were pushed askew, and he realized his nose was running a little.

When they had pulled apart, Lorraine blinked, then grinned.

Sy rubbed the back of his neck and laughed in sheer disbelief, and Lorraine did too.

"Good night, Lorraine." He opened the car door and leaned away.

A pause. "Good night, Sy. Wanna go see a movie tomorrow?"

He hesitated, one foot already out the door. She was pretty. And nice. But she wasn't Grey. But then, he wasn't Ed-Dumb either. "Sure."

"I'll pick you up at ten bells, and we'll get lunch first."

"Okay."

And that was how it had gone ever since. Dates, kisses (which, to be fair, improved after the third try), Lorraine setting the schedule, and Sy doing his best to keep up. By date three, she had used the word *relationship* twice and *we* a lot.

He wanted to talk to someone about it. Grey was the friend he'd always chosen—but this wasn't something he could tell her. Especially since she had been in Edo with her brothers for ten days. Now she was back in Bosch. And last night Lorraine had asked whether he thought they'd have sex soon.

Sy gulped just remembering it.

Which was why he was now trudging to Grey's door, hoping for a lifeline—and maybe, just maybe, a conversation with Colonel Warner. Because honestly? Sy had no clue what the hell he was doing anymore.

SY

Sy hovered at the kitchen doorway, reluctant to interrupt Colonel Warner while he was brewing coffee but needing to talk.

"Sy! How are you? I've missed seeing you this break." The big man's voice was hearty and welcoming.

"Um...well, Grey's been gone, and I've been..." Sy coughed into his hand. "It looks like I sort of have a... girlfriend."

The colonel didn't even pause in his grinding and brewing of the drink, precious and scarce yet always seemingly available in the Warner–Wallace home. "Is that so? Well, she's a lucky girl. You're a fine young man, Sy."

"Umm...yeah. Thanks. About that... Can I talk to you? I've never had a girl... I mean, this is my first time dating anyone. And I have questions," Sy rushed, desperate to get the request over with.

Now the colonel did look up, eyebrows raised. "Shouldn't you be talking to your dad about this?"

Sy had anticipated the question. "Well, see, my folks got married forty years ago and never planned on having a kid. I just sorta happened when my mom was almost fifty and Dad was nearly sixty. Dad always says Mom was the only woman he was ever interested in. Honestly, I don't think he remembers being seventeen, and I know he didn't have a..." Sy swallowed. "...girlfriend then."

He hesitated, then added, "And I've heard you and the MC talk, and it sounds like you've had girlfriends before the two of you..."

Matt Warner chuckled. "I had one or two...or so." He walked over to the kitchen door and peered into the living room. "Grey on her comm with that elusive mystery boy of hers?"

"Yessir. Edmund."

"You've met him, haven't you?" The colonel's face was thoughtful.

"Yessir."

The large man took down two mugs. "Sy, you've been coming over here for what, three, four years now? You know where the dishes go. You're one of the three people Rini lets do her hair. And I know how you take your coffee."

Sy watched as the colonel dropped two sugar cubes and a splash of cream into one of the cups before filling them both with steaming, fragrant brew.

"Let's take our coffees and walk Rummy. I'll answer your questions on two and a half conditions."

"Absolutely, Colonel," Sy agreed eagerly, then hesitated. "I mean...what conditions, sir?"

"Smart move. Always know the parameters before you agree to a deal," the tall man advised with a laugh.

Sy thought ruefully that if he'd done that with Lorraine, he might not be in this fix. He waited.

"Condition one," Matt counted off, holding up a finger. "Stop calling me 'sir' and 'colonel' unless you enlist, and then only on base or during a mission. My name is Matt. You're like family to me."

Sy grinned sheepishly. "I'll try...Matt. My family's pretty formal, so it's hard not to use 'ma'am' and 'sir.'"

"I get it. Just appreciate the effort." Matt grabbed Rummy's leash and jingled it, summoning the dog.

"What's the second and the half condition?" Sy asked, scratching the dog's ears.

"Second: You need to at least tell your dad you have a girlfriend."

"I can do that. And the half?" Sy prompted as they both slipped on their winter jackets and headed out the door.

Matt waited until they'd closed the gate behind them. "I'd like your impressions of this boy Grey is seeing. She doesn't seem willing to bring him around, and her mother's ready to explode. Anything you can tell me might keep the family engines from flaming out."

Sy didn't hesitate. "Oh, I'm happy to tell you what I think."

Matt gave him a sideways glance. "I figured as much."

SY

Matt listened without interruption as Sy laid it all out—his uncertainties, fears, and total confusion about the whole Lorraine situation.

"It's just all happened so fast." Sy kicked a clump of frozen leaves off the path. "Two weeks ago, I'd never even kissed a girl. Never been on a date. Now I have a girlfriend. Am I supposed to talk to her every day? See her every day?" He huffed out a frustrated breath. "And last night she said it's time to take things to the next level. I asked what that meant...and she said sex."

Matt didn't say anything. Just kept walking, the faint jingle of Rummy's leash the only sound between them.

"Don't get me wrong," Sy pressed, "my body thinks that's a brilliant idea. But what my body thinks it can do and what I'm actually ready for are two totally different things." He stooped to scoop up Rummy's latest deposit, knotting the bag with a yank. "Remember last spring when Grey and I played footy with you and Major Morton and the twins at the park? I whiffed the ball, like, nine times outta ten."

Matt's voice was level. "I remember."

Sy sighed. "Well, this is not something I want to whiff." He shook his head. "I mean, I just figured out what to do with my hands when we kiss. Felt like a major accomplishment moving them from her shoulders to her hair and back without looking like a complete moron. But I don't want to look stupid. Or like a kid. And except for worrying about what the hell I'm doing twenty-three out of twenty-four bells, I do like Lorraine. I don't want to disappoint her."

More silence. Just their boots crunching frost-bitten leaves. Finally, Matt said, "Let me repeat what I'm hearing to make sure I've got it right."

Sy nodded.

"You got set up on a surprise date with Lorraine."

"Yep. Leia's and Mason's grand idea."

"That led to your first kiss, which led to a second date, then a third...and now she's talking about sex."

"Exactly."

Matt's pace slowed a little. "Okay. Let me ask you something: If a friend—say, Grey—came to you and said her boyfriend wanted to have sex and she wasn't ready...what would you tell her?"

Sy didn't even hesitate. A flush of protective anger surged through him. "I'd tell her to kick the guy in his smug, stupid, oh-so-handsome face and tell him to go to hell." The heat in his voice surprised even him.

Matt's eyebrow ticked up slightly, but he kept his tone steady. "Well, there's your answer then. Minus the kicking." He gave Sy a look. "You have every right to set a boundary. Tell Lorraine you like her—you *do*—but you want to slow down. Enjoy where you are. No need to rush."

Sy nodded, shoving his hands deeper into his jacket pockets. *Why does everything have to be so complicated?* He thought of Grey, how easy everything used to feel. Before that stupid rally. Before Edmund. A stab of annoyance shot through his belly.

Matt asked quietly, "Are you enjoying your time with Lorraine?"

Sy hesitated. "Yeah. Sure. I just wish..." He swallowed down the truth. "Yeah. I am." *You've got a girlfriend*, he reminded himself. *A nice, pretty girl who wants you. Any other seventeen-year-old would be celebrating.* But all Sy could think about was Grey Shima. Way out of reach, smiling into her comm at some other guy.

They reached the park. Matt unclipped Rummy from her leash and handed Sy a ball. Sy threw it hard, watching the red-gold retriever race after it. For a few minutes, they stood in companionable silence.

"You know," Matt remarked, "Grey's mom and I were best friends for a long time before we ever got together."

Sy blinked. He hadn't known that.

Matt continued, voice low. "Truth be told, I had feelings for her from the outset, but she was married with a family, and for me that meant off limits. Even after she and Grey's dad split, I was hesitant. She needed time to heal, and I did not want to do anything to endanger our friendship." He gave a wry chuckle. "But those feelings were still there, which made dating other women…awkward. Maybe even unfair."

Sy tossed the ball again for Rummy. Matt's words landed heavily inside him as if the man could see what Sy had thought he'd hidden so well.

"Is that all true?" Sy asked quietly.

"Every word."

Sy's voice was small. "Do you think I'm being unfair to Lorraine?"

Matt's answer was gentle. "I think you're new to all this. And you've been thrown off the bow into deep waters before you even had your sea legs." He paused. "But yeah. Fairness matters. To her. To you."

Sy stared out across the empty park.

"You've gotta figure out what you want, Sy," Matt said. "Who you want to be dating. What cost each choice has. Because every choice comes with a price."

Sy whispered almost to himself, "But she's got a boyfriend."

Matt just said, "First boyfriend. First everything. I'd imagine Grey's as mystified by all this as you are." He smiled a little. "Maybe that's one more thing you have in common."

Sy chuckled, a soft, rueful sound. "Maybe."

Matt clapped a warm hand on Sy's shoulder. "Best friendships weather rough seas, son. You might each sail your own ship for a while. You might drift. But if you keep pulling the same lines, crewing together? You'll end up in the same harbor." He squeezed Sy's shoulder. "Bottom line: You've gotta talk it out."

Sy let out a long, low sigh. "Yessir. I sure do."

GREY

I have to say something to break the silence sitting heavy between Sy and me. "So... sounds like you stayed busy while I was gone." I wince inwardly. *Ugh, that sounds so stupid.*

Sy bobs his head, then runs a hand through his hair—his tell for discomfort. "Yeah. Busy. And it sounds like Edo was good. Snowy. Did you go boarding?"

"Yeah. Once or twice. The twins went more." *Why is this so awkward?*

Our conversations usually bounce from deep to hilarious without even trying. I always leave feeling full, like I've feasted at some grand banquet. This? This is a stale snack left out too long.

We're best friends. Best friends who haven't seen each other since the night I crashed his first date. Stars, that was weird. I mean, I'm happy he's dating someone...but Lorraine? She doesn't seem like his match.

I decide to just ask: "So what do you like about Lorraine?" I glance down at my comm, checking whether Edmund's messaged me.

Sy sits cross-legged near the fireplace, a merry blaze warming the living room on this cold December day. He stares into the flames. "Well...I like...umm. She has nice hair."

My fingers twist a lock of my hair. "Two weeks and all those dates, and that's it?" I laugh—but it comes out wrong, too sharp.

He turns toward me, and I expect him to be laughing too. But he's not. His eyes are narrowed, his brow furrowed, and when he speaks, his voice rises with every word. "Well, what do you want me to say? That she acts like she actually likes me. That she makes time for me. That she treats me like I'm the most important person in her life. Honestly, Grey." He huffs out a breath and turns back to the fire.

I should leave it alone. I *know* I should. Instead, irritation flares and I jab back, "You don't have to yell. Besides, that's how she treats you. I asked what you like about her. Maybe dig a little deeper." Even I hear the snotty edge to my voice, but somehow it doesn't stop me from piling on. "You know, see if there's actually something there."

Sy's on his feet in an instant. "You know, I don't grill you about Ed-Dumb the luminary." His voice spikes. "Did you ever think some things ought to be personal? Or do those rules only apply to Madame I-Date-A-University-Guy Shima and not her sad, awkward sidekick Silas?" He actually kicks the ottoman. "You wanna know what I like about Lorraine?" His voice climbs higher. "She knows what she wants. And what she wants is me. Which is pretty goddamn refreshing." He grabs his jacket from the floor. "I gotta go. Talk to you later."

The door slams behind him. I sit there, mouth hanging open, brain racing to catch up. What the hell just happened? One word keeps circling my mind, flashing like a warning beacon: *Ed-Dumb*?

♡

SY

Sy stomped down the street, fists jammed into his jacket pockets, head bowed against the cold, late December gusts blowing in another storm. A pinecone rolled into his path. He gave it a vicious kick into the road. His shoulders were tight, his jaw ached from clenching, and his chest felt like a fully loaded vessel was parked on it. *What are you so mad about, Mercer?* A faint echo inside corrected him: Who *are you so mad at, Mercer?*

He stopped, tipped his head back, and sucked in a deep breath of biting air before blowing it out slowly in a steamy cloud. A small, brown squirrel sat high in a leafless oak, chittering down at him. Was it scolding him for his foolishness or accusing him of being a coward? Sy squinted up toward the creature. "I hear you. But is it her fault? I never told her how I feel. So who's the villain here—her or me?" He paused, then added under his breath, "Or

Ed-Dumb." Yeah. That felt better—blaming that suave, charming intruder.

He flashed back to their full conversation. When Sy had first arrived back at Grey's house after talking with Matt, he'd been ready to finally reveal that he loved her and always had. He'd sat by the fire, heart hammering, courage barely stitched together—and then opened his mouth, took a deep breath, and blurted out: "So did you have fun in Edo?"

Grey had glanced up from her comm. "Uh-huh. Hang on, let me finish this message to Edmund... Okay, hey, did I tell you he ran into Ash in Truevale?"

Sy had forced a polite smile. He admired Ash Grey. Hearing about Ed-Dumb meeting someone *Sy* respected had felt like yet another punch to the gut. "Did he? That's a coincidence." He stared back at the flames, fumbling for better words. "So... umm...how was the weather at your dad's?" *Pathetic.*

There'd been a pause. "Regular for December. Snowy, cold. What did you do during break?"

Sy swallowed down the real answer and tossed her a casual one. "Lorraine and I did a bunch of stuff—movies, nine-pin, lunches..."

"Mmm-hm," Grey murmured, barely listening, smiling into her comm. Probably sending another love message to her glorious university boyfriend. *Face it, Mercer. She doesn't love you. She barely even wants to talk to you.* The voice inside stabbed deeper.

Then she asked about Lorraine. Laughed at his answer. And all his frustration and anger exploded. He never yelled at Grey. Sure, they bickered sometimes, but this? This had been a real fight. He'd bolted before he said something unforgivable.

Now he stood under a bare oak, a squirrel chattering judgment down on him. He was explaining himself to a squirrel. *Yeah, Mercer. It really doesn't get much more pathetic than this.*

CHAPTER 13
NEW YEAR'S

GREY

My emotions careen from stunned to confused to furious as I replay Sy's ridiculous tantrum. *What is his problem, anyway?* I pick up my comm and start to put his number in, thinking, *He can't just walk off in the middle of a fight.* Then I stop. What am I comming him for? He's the one who should be comming me. Instead, I punch in Leia's number.

She picks up on the third ring. "Grey Shima." Not Pebble, not Pebs. "So you're not dead, huh?"

That's a weird way to answer a comm. "No, I was in Edo."

Leia's laugh bubbles through the comm. "Oh, right. Comms don't work there. No worries. What's going on? You're home?"

"Yeah. We got in last night." I grimace at my comm. I was busy in Edo. And Papa is all kinds of strict about comm usage, so I had to save my allotted time to talk with Edmund. Sy's voice echoes: *Ed-Dumb.* "Hey, what the hell is wrong with Sy?"

"What do you mean?"

"He was just here, and he blew up at me just because I laughed about that Lorraine girl."

"You mean his girlfriend?" She accents the last word.

I pull the comm from my ear to give it a disgusted look. *Girlfriend? That's...absurd. Isn't it?* "Girlfriend? I doubt that. I mean, we're talking about Sy Mercer here."

"Right. Sy Mercer and Lorraine Collins—new couple. Probably gonna do the deed, if you believe Lorraine." There's something weird about Leia's voice as she says this.

"They've only been going out for a couple weeks. That's hardly a relationship."

Leia hoots. "Oooh, look who's an expert on relationships and timing now. How long did it take for you to decide you and Ed-Dumb were an official thing? Like, an hour?"

My ire is on the rise. "What is your problem, Leia?" Then my brain registers what she just said. "What did you call Edmund?"

"Oh, oops." Leia sounds anything but contrite. "That's just what we call him."

Astonishment keeps my anger from bubbling over. "We? Who's we?"

Leia's voice is smooth as she reveals, "We. All the old secondary friends you used to hang out with before you became far too sophisticated for us."

"That's not fair. I see all of you all the time." I realize I am yelling.

"At school. When it's convenient." Leia doesn't sound angry or upset, which stokes both emotions in me. "But settle down. What you do or don't do doesn't even shake the compass. You and Mr. Luminary are a thing. But life goes on with the rest of us, whether you notice or not. We get together for study sessions. We went to the Winter Dance and hang out at Barton's. All the things you used to do but don't anymore. Anyway, Mason just got here. You know, the guy who doesn't vanish between terms. Later." And the comm goes silent.

Tears of anger and hurt well in my eyes. Fine. Maybe she's right. I did skip the stupid dance, even though it was really great last year. And I haven't kept our regular study dates. I feel regret creeping in and swat it away. I don't need them. I have Edmund. *I can't believe they call him that other name.* And there's the Circle… although I really only talk to them when I'm out with Edmund. But Edmund loves me, and I love him. I let my wrath peak. To hell with Leia and Sy. I snuffle back my nose drip and wipe my eyes as I punch Edmund's number into my comm.

♡

EDMUND

Edmund grinned as he saw Grey's comm come through. They had spoken earlier and had messaged throughout the day, making plans. Picking it up after the first ring, he said, "It's my beautiful girl. I can't wait to see you."

A tiny pause, and then he heard Grey erupt into sobs. "Hey, now, what's wrong?" A ripple of worry rolled through him. The only other time he had heard Grey cry was when her mother was in the hospital.

A stuttering gasp and a swallow came through the comm and then, "I'm sorry, Edmund. It's just…I just got off the comm with Leia, who was really awful to me…"

Edmund's brows came down in consternation. He had never met this Leia but knew she had been Grey's friend since child-hood. Grey continued, "And before that, Sy and I had a huge fight."

At this a smile grew on Edmund's face. The farther the Mercer kid was from his Grey, the happier he would be. He chuckled inwardly over the cause of Grey's distress and heard the archminister's words in his head: *Women need guidance.* Maybe he was right; he needed to exert his authority. Using his best cajoling voice: "Now then, sweet Grey, I'm on my way over. I'll meet you at your gate, and I'll wipe your tears and take care of you."

Grey snuffled and he could hear a small smile in her voice. "Oh, Edmund," she breathed, "you always know just what to say." She paused. "I… I really need you right now."

Edmund stood a bit straighter. "You are always there to support me, Grey. I will always take care of you."

"I know you will. I do love you."

He started to say he loved her back. But paused, thinking of what Mr. Bolt had advised—better to keep her reaching, keep her just a little off-balance. "Okay. See you in a bit." He prepared to click off the comm.

"Edmund." Grey's rushed voice held a worried edge. "Thank you…for everything. I'm going to go right now and pull myself together, wash my face, and put on some makeup. I can't wait to hold you."

Edmund grinned. "I'll be there before you know it. Bye."

"Bye."

Edmund tucked his comm into his pocket. Maybe the arch-minister was right. Some girls needed structure to feel safe. Grey did. And he would provide it.

♡

GREY

"Matt? When is Mama getting home?" I call from the bathroom, carefully lining my eyes in black. Edmund says it accentuates their natural shape and makes them even sexier. I giggle. No one's ever called me sexy before—it makes me quivery inside.

Then *sexier* morphs into *sex*, and suddenly I hear Leia's voice again: *Sy and Lorraine—they're thinking about doing the deed.* I scowl.

Matt's voice floats up the stairs. "Not for a few hours. She's helping Aunt Carisa. What's up?"

Actually, I realize, *this might work out.* Even better—Matt's way more lenient than Mama. "Umm…I was going to ask her if I could stay out late, 'til, like, two bells tonight? It's New Year's."

Usually, I have to be home—and alone—by twenty-three bells. I hear footsteps on the stairs. Matt appears in the doorway. He takes in my half-done cat eyes, the smear of shimmer on one lid, and the chaos of products scattered across the counter. One eyebrow arches, but he says nothing.

"You know the curfew is just to keep you safe, Grey."

Safe from what? It's not like there are roving bands of robbers in Bosch. Then I think, *But there are Blues. I wonder if Mama knows that.* "I know. But I am safe. I can take care of myself, and I'll just be with Edmund." I throw in the name fast—he and Mama both get edgy about me being alone with Edmund. "We were talking about going to hear Kestrel & Coil at The Aerie. See in the new year there." *That's the way—appeal to Matt's musical nature.*

"Kestrel & Coil, huh?" Matt nods. "They're good. And The Aerie's top shelf. Maybe I should take your mama there tonight."

I whirl around, horrified. "Maaaat." I drag his name out and lob a tube of lip gloss at him.

He catches it, grinning. "What? Could be a double date."

"You are *awful*, Matt Warner." I toss my hair, but I'm smiling. "So…can I?"

He shrugs. "It's New Year's. That's a nice venue. I don't see why not." Inwardly, I pop the cork on my New Year's champagne. But he continues, "You know…" He leans casually against the doorframe. "Maybe you could invite Sy and that girl he's been seeing?"

What, is Sy Mercer's love life public news now? "I don't think so," I declare, voice flat. "We had an argument."

Matt grunts. "Mmm." Then, more gently, "Friends argue. I know you've got new people now—like the enigmatic Edmund— but don't cut off your old crew. They matter too."

My stomach twists, but I keep my tone cool. "I'm not the one doing the cutting."

He watches me a moment longer, like he's choosing whether to push, then just states, "No later than two bells."

I grin. "Promise. Thanks!"

GREY

I look amazing—a total dawn-stopper.

Yeah, that sounds stuck-up, but it's true. I twist back and forth in the mirror of Edmund's tiny dorm bathroom, watching sequins flicker like bioluminescent plankton. I'm wearing my Winter Gifting present from Edmund—a dress he brought me from True-vale, deep teal with almost no fabric and even less modesty, and it fits like it was grown on me. Off-the-shoulder neckline, a dip in the back that skims my waist, and a flirty, fluttering hem that stops dangerously high on my thighs. Definitely not boat wear. But for dancing? Perfect.

I'd felt practically naked slipping it on. But now I look...like someone older, sharper. A girl stepping into womanhood with a silver heel and a killer twirl. My hair falls loose around my shoulders, tucked behind my ears to show off cheekbones and bare collarbones. Around my neck rests the damascene butterfly pendant that once belonged to my obaasan. I haven't worn it since she died. Putting it on feels like forgiveness—of her, of the things she did and those she didn't. I take a breath and open the door.

Edmund turns. In his fitted black suit with a hint of golden-age pirate flair—stand-up collar, gold buttons—he looks like someone out of one of Mama's Old Days movies. His smile falters when he sees me, then drops altogether.

I panic. "Too much?" I start to duck back inside.

"Grey Shima," he breathes, "you are the most beautiful woman I've ever seen."

Heat flares in my cheeks. *Woman!* My heart wants to explode with happiness. I spin twice, skirt flashing light. "Look what it does."

He laughs, then steps close. "I am the luckiest man on New Earth." His kiss lands hot and deep. His hands find my waist and tug me closer—and I feel him harden against me. I draw back, breathless.

"We should go."

"Yes," he growls, "if only so I can show you off. Welcome the year that everything changes."

His hand slides down, guiding mine to his bulge. My breath catches, and I don't pull away. Instead, I trace the outline gently, and desire pools low in my belly. He groans. "Remember through the night how much I want you."

I bite my lip; his desire for me is heady and makes me feel powerful and weak in the knees at the same time. "I will. And I'll remember how much I want you, Edmund."

Another kiss, this one deeper, needier. Then he pulls away with effort, breath rushing out. "Well, then." He extends his arm. "Shall we?"

"No." My smile is mischievous.

His eyebrows lifts. "No?"

"No. I have something for you first." From my backpack, I pull out the gift I made for him for Winter Gifting—two parts, both carved in Edo. The first is a simple arc of wood on a base. He unwraps it, smiles, and sets it down. Then comes the second: a lantern, hand-carved on each side with dozens of stars and a crescent moon.

"Grey," he breathes, turning it gently. "This is…incredible."

"Made with love," I say, rubbing the callouses on my thumb and forefinger. I pull out a candle and lighter, show him how to open the tiny door. When the flame glows inside, I switch off the light. Sparkling stars dance across the room, their warm light reminding me of the sequins on my dress.

Edmund stares, silent for a long beat. "I don't know what to say."

I wrap my arms around his strong shoulders from behind as I whisper, "You don't have to say a word. You are my Luminary who lights the way to a better future."

CHAPTER 14
POLITICS AND PROTESTS

EDMUND

Edmund had never been on base before.

Growing up in District One, he had seen troopers serving as local law enforcement, patrolling the streets and serving as a deterrent to all but the most minor crimes. Since none of his siblings, either of his parents, or anyone else in his extended family except for a distant great-uncle had ever enlisted, the base had remained tangential to his life. It existed but meant very little to his day-to-day life. Vaguely, he recalled an episode involving a primary school field trip to tour the base that his father had refused to sign permission for, keeping him home for the day instead.

Now as he glanced about him, it wasn't at all what he expected. He had expected a landscape ripe with machines of war and ranks of troopers, heavily armed, drilling and marching about, doing whatever it was they did. Instead, men and women dressed in black and red winter jackets milled, chatting pleasantly as they hustled across the winter-brown yard and ducked in and out of various stately brick buildings.

Grey had come through on her promise to secure their

meeting with the master commander, and together with Miranda, Abeni, and Curtis, they were on their way to what Edmund had begun to refer to as step one in Ending the Glitter Scourge. He wasn't sure what step two would look like, but Mr. Bolt had assured him it would be decisive once Edmund sent evidence of today's meeting. He looked over at his friends. Curtis had his hands shoved in his pockets and his head down, stoic and silent. Edmund knew that his friend's loyalties had shifted now that he was involved with the secret Bluest chapter in Bosch. He was anti-Glitter, to be sure, but whenever the two of them had a private moment, Curtis urged Edmund to come to the next meeting, to accept the Chosen's god and the tenets of the faith. He had even gone as far as warning Edmund that the women of the Circle should be replaced with devout men. Edmund had cut him off, stating, "I will take the steps I deem necessary with counsel from the archminister." And to his surprise, Curtis had demurred, murmuring, "You know best, Luminary." Maybe there was something to this natural order thing.

Grey, on the other hand, was full of life, as usual, her pale cheeks pink from the January cold, face animated as she chatted with the girls. She wore a red wool coat with a brown knit scarf wrapped about her neck and over her head. He thought she looked like a ripe summer berry, and thinking of what lay under the coat and clothes below lit a familiar fire within him. He smiled to himself; there would be time for that sort of celebration later.

Grey was definitely the major asset in this outing. Edmund had known she'd made the appointment with the master commander, but he hadn't realized just how at home she was on base. That became clear the moment they arrived. Abeni had driven the university squad with plans to meet Grey there. As they pulled up to the gatehouse, a tall, broad-shouldered man with a large weapon approached.

"Good morning. IDs, please. What's your base business?" His tone was polite, but his eyes swept the car, assessing for any risk.

Before anyone could answer, Grey jogged up. "Hadi, it's okay. They're with me."

The man's posture eased immediately. "Well, hey there, Grey. Taking these folks to see your mom?"

"Yep. Betsy put me on the calendar." As he tapped at the gate console, she added, "How's your sister?"

"She's better—no more throwing up and her belly's out to here!" He mimed the shape with a grin, nudging his weapon aside.

"That's so exciting," Grey breathed with a delighted squeal. "That baby is going to be so loved."

The guard chuckled and handed back the IDs and base passes. "Park over there. Grey knows the place better than I do."

As they exited the vehicle, Abeni asked, "Don't you need a sticker?"

Grey tugged a lanyard from under her coat. "Base brat. Besides, they all know me."

Edmund had thought that was just her usual confidence talking—until nearly everyone they passed greeted her by name. She moved through the base like she belonged there. It rattled him a little. He was the one with the vision. But there she was— connected, confident, and unmistakably respected. Asset, indeed.

After several minutes of walking, they arrived at a three-story brick building surrounded on three sides by landscaped trees and shrubs and on the fourth side by a large, open, grassy area criss-crossed with walking paths. "This is the parade grounds, and that statue over there…" Grey pointed to a man on a pedestal with hands on his hips and what appeared to be a ratty, three-cornered, too-small hat on his head. "…is my Papa T. Teddy Bosch, master commander emeritus."

"Really? He was your grandpa? My grandad loves to talk about his time in the Force, and it's always Teddy Bosch this and Teddy Bosch that!" Miranda exclaimed.

Grey laughed. "Yep, Mama has some wild stories about the two of them as well."

They made their way into the three-story building, Bosch Hall, with Grey once again greeting the young, well-armed woman who stood guard just inside the door. She chatted briefly with Grey and glanced at the temporary IDs stuck on the Circle members' coats before offering, "Have a good meeting," and then waving them in and pointing to the stairs. Three flights up, and Grey escorted them into an open door, beyond which an older woman sat at a desk working on a device.

The woman looked up the moment they crossed the threshold. "Well, now, Grey, what have we here?"

"Hi, Betsy, these are some of my friends: Miranda, Abeni, Curtis, and Edmund. This is Betsy. Mama says she runs the whole base." Edmund noticed that Grey looked a little abashed as she made the introductions.

The woman, Betsy, smiled warmly at each of them and greeted them by name. "It's lovely to meet each of you. I'll let the master commander know you are here." Then she looked at Grey and said sweetly, "I'm sure it will be a birthday surprise for her."

"I'm going to take her to get empanadas after my friends have had a chance to meet her. My treat," Grey replied earnestly.

Betsy nodded. "Well, won't that be nice." She walked with brisk steps over to a large, ornately carved wooden door, then opened it and disappeared inside, closing it behind her. When she reappeared a few moments later, she announced, "The MC will be ready to see you in five minutes. Please have a seat." She gestured to several comfortable chairs. "I have some cookies in my desk. Let me get them."

A few minutes and two cookies later the wooden door opened, and the master commander of Bosch stepped out. "Well, hello." She moved to give Grey a kiss on the cheek. "Let's go into my office, and you can introduce me to your friends, Grey. This is a group I haven't met." Her voice sounded upbeat to Edmund. He surveyed the woman. Of course, he had seen pictures of her, but those were all carefully posed. Her skin was pale, and she was about ten centimeters taller than Grey, with short, curly, light brown hair. She wore the black tunic of the Force with an ornate vest covered in ribbons and medals that fit her very closely about her midsection. Except for the vest, she looked very…ordinary? He wondered how someone like this had risen to the top office in Bosch.

Once they were in her office, she indicated for them to sit in the somewhat comfortable chairs arrayed in front of a large mahogany desk. Walking around the desk to her chair, she didn't sit so much as assume command of the room. Her eyes landed on Edmund and held, cool and appraising. Not hostile. Not friendly. Just…measuring. "You must be Edmund. As delighted as I am to finally meet you, I wasn't anticipating a parlay with the university's anti-Glitter coalition, but here we are. You have five minutes to explain your position and why I should hear you out beyond that."

"Yes, ma'am." He was definitely nervous but remembered what he needed to do. "This is Abeni, Miranda, and Curtis. Obviously, Grey needs no introduction. May Abeni record the first five minutes of our talk?"

The master commander sat back with a half-smile. "A photo op, huh? I understand. Abeni, you may record, but only visual, no audio. You'll be able to pull some good stills from that. And I'll want you to send me a copy before you leave the building."

Edmund was surprised over how easy the request was granted, and it buoyed him to say more. He waited for a moment as Abeni took out her camera and made some adjustments. When she nodded, he decided to start off strong. "Yes, ma'am, we are part of the anti-Glitter Circle at the university in District One. But we are not the only ones. There are Circles at each university across the island, and we are expanding beyond university students to secondary students. Please know this is a movement. Master Commander, you have to understand, the youth of Bosch do not desire to be the drug dealers of New Earth."

Edmund felt a thrill as the words spilled out, polished, powerful, perfectly staged. He could already picture the clip on the

Circle's site and the acclaim it would gain. Mr. Bolt would be duly impressed. Step one was complete. Now for step two.

EDMUND

"Well done, Edmund." Mr. Bolt's voice came smooth as polished stone through the screen. He watched the video again, each frame seeming to capture more meaning than the last—at least to him.

Edmund tried to keep his expression calm. "Thank you, sir. We felt it went well. The master commander asked some good questions—"

Bolt waved that comment away with a flick of his hand. "Don't waste thought on that woman's questions. She's an obstacle. She will be removed."

Removed. The word snagged. Did he mean politically? Figuratively? Or literally? A chill crept across Edmund's scalp. He opened his mouth, then closed it. *This isn't the time. Stay focused. Remember the cause.* He forced a nod. "Understood. Shall we move to step two?"

"Indeed," Bolt said as if the moment of ice hadn't happened. "Now, the council elections are in the fall, yes?"

"Yes, sir. But—"

Bolt cut him off gently. "Let me explain the path ahead. Voters rarely rally *for* something. But they *always* rally *against.* You and your Circle will give them a villain: Glitter. With the right agitation, the public will lose faith in the old regime. Doubt will rot the roots of power. And the Chosen will sweep the elections."

Edmund swallowed. It made strategic sense. Of course it did.

"Once we hold the council," Bolt continued, "we'll secure the BPF. After that, the rest is…not your concern."

Edmund stiffened but said nothing.

"For now," Bolt went on, "you'll organize several large, vocal, disruptive protests."

That made Edmund blink. "Sir, our rallies have always been peaceful—"

"You live among pirates, Edmund." Bolt's voice never rose, but it filled the room. "You want to move people? You must sound the trumpet of reckoning." He leaned in, his face crowding the screen. "We have data. Experience. The Lord's favor. So, I ask you, Luminary—are you the man to lead this?"

The words echoed like prophecy. Edmund felt his breath catch. Doubt flickered—then fled. "Yes, Mr. Bolt. We can make noise."

Bolt's smile returned, warm and paternal. "That's my boy. Begin with a university protest next weekend. Let it build. I'll provide funds—just give me the account. And this time, record it properly. Visual and audio." The screen went black.

Edmund sat for a long moment, his face's dark reflection staring back. The Circle had always held the moral high ground. They were calm, united, ethical. But what had it earned them? The Chosen had momentum, support, power. And now a plan that included him.

He reached for his device and began drafting the protest announcement. *You can't change the world without raising your voice.* Even if you had to shout over your conscience.

GREY

"I don't know, Edmund. People don't listen better just because someone shouts." I wrinkle my brow, gnawing my lip as I weigh his plan for a loud, disruptive protest.

"I get it, Grey. I had reservations too, but Mr. Bolt—"

I cut him off. "This Mr. Bolt is a Bluie. He can't be trusted. None of them can. Remember what I told you happened on the island?"

Edmund inhales sharply, his expression tightening. I brace myself for another round of the only arguments we ever truly have—always about Bluies. But instead of biting back, he pulls me into his arms.

"Oh, Grey," he murmurs. "I wish I'd been there to protect you." His voice is soothing, his embrace even more so. "I know how you feel about the Chosen. But Mr. Bolt has been a good ally. He wants what we want—an end to the Glitter trade. That doesn't make us Bluies. We're using their expertise. We're using them, not the other way round. When we've won, they'll be nothing more than a footnote."

I want to argue, to tell him I don't need protecting, but his arms are warm, strong, reassuring. I swallow my irritation and soften against him. "Fine," I mumble. "I'll be there." I press my cheek to his chest, syncing my breath to his, willing myself to trust. "I can't promise I'll be loud, but I'll support you. And the Circle."

He kisses the top of my head. "That's my girl. Your strength, your calm—you ground me. I'm lucky to have you."

Maybe he's right. The protest might not be the whole solution, but it's a start. And I do want Glitter gone. No harm in trying something new—right?

♡

GREY

"Glitter has to go now!" The chant pulses through the crowd. Around me, voices rise in unison as we march, waving bright cloth banners with slogans that shout: *Pirates Aren't Pushers*, *Glitter Kills*, or *Say No To Dealing*. The energy is electric.

At first, I feel awkward—stiff with doubt, my voice barely a whisper. But as we march through the multitude that lines our route, the crowd's enthusiasm becomes contagious. Each cheer feeds mine, and soon I'm shouting, fist raised, matching their rhythm. This isn't just noise—it's momentum.

We're confined to campus today, but Edmund says this is only the beginning. There'll be more. Bigger. Louder. We reach the main green where a podium stands at the base of the library steps. It's time. Edmund grips my hand, and I smile, squeezing back. He surprises me by pulling me onto the dais beside him. My heart pounds—not from nerves but anticipation. He lifts his voice. "Glitter has to—"

"Go now!" the crowd answers, echoing him again and again. I join in, swept up in the rhythm. My voice soars. My arms lift higher. I've never felt so alive.

Edmund raises his hands. Silence falls like a held breath. He starts to speak, slow and deliberate. "We are Bosch. We know right from wrong. We honor our past, but we must not be enslaved by it."

He lets the words settle before continuing, voice soaring. "The Glitter trade has run its course. It is time for its elimination. We need your voices. Your passion. Your resolve. We will bring our demands to leadership. They cannot ignore us forever."

His voice booms deeper, volume spiking. "We are the moral. They are the corrupt. We are the just. They are the immoral. Join us—end the chokehold Glitter has on our past, our present, and our future!"

The crowd erupts, roaring approval. "Glitter has to go now!" The chant returns, louder than ever. Edmund stands tall and triumphant, and I want to join in—but something prickles beneath my skin. If the Bosch leadership is corrupt…then Mama is corrupt. And if she's immoral, what does that make me, her daughter, standing beside the boy who just condemned her?

The dais feels like it's tilting, the way a becalmed sailboat might with no one at the tiller. I grip for the edge, dizzy. But then Edmund's hand finds mine. He wraps an arm around me and leans in, whispering, "Listen to them, my love. It's happening. Everything we dreamed."

I nod and wrap my arm around his waist. I push the ugly words far away and steady myself in his warmth. I'm on his side. No matter what.

CHAPTER 15
ANOTHER YEAR, ANOTHER CONSEQUENCE

SY

Sy scrolled through the textbook, lips moving silently. The exam for his History of the Apocalypse class was Monday, and it counted for half their grade—which annoyed him. He liked the topic, but the teacher seemed like a holdover from Old Earth, insisting they memorize dates and events.

He had switched out of his Contemporary Politics class after the new year to avoid seeing Grey in every class. Ms. Anderson's course was the only one with room. He sighed. They hadn't fought again, but they also hadn't said much to each other. Just drifted. Grey was polite and smiled when she was with the friend group, but not at him. Or Leia or Lorraine. Losing that smile stung more than he'd care to admit.

He glanced across the table at Lorraine. She twirled a lock of hair between her fingers as she read, lips pursed in focus. Sy grinned. He liked those lips—a lot. After Colonel Warner's talk, he'd told Lorraine they should slow things down. He'd braced for her to argue or be hurt. Instead, she'd hugged him. "I'm glad," she'd whispered. "I like you so much, but I'm not ready either. I guess I just thought if we did that…it would make what we have special."

He'd kissed her then, grateful and kind of amazed. "I think it's already special."

Now, he nudged her under the table. "You're really pretty, you know that?"

She smiled, but before she could reply, both their comms pinged. "It's from Leia," she said.

Sy tapped the link—and froze. A crowd. Chants. The library steps. Grey on a stage, yelling, pumping her fists. Ed-Dumb holding the podium and preaching like he owned the island. Sy's pulse thudded. "What the hell?"

"Hang on." Lorraine scrolled to another clip. Sy leaned in beside her, fingers brushing her hair. Edmund's voice rang out—condemning Glitter and the leadership of Bosch. Sy was stunned. Did Grey even hear what he was saying? Did she even care? "Oh, boy," Lorraine murmured. "My folks would ground me forever if I was at something like this."

"Same," Sy said. "And if MC Wallace sees this? No way that ends well."

"I don't think that's an *if* but a when." Lorraine stood, comm still in her hand, looking unsure about something. "You've never said what happened between you and Grey…but you did call her your best friend. Maybe you should talk to her, be there for her when the fallout hits."

She looked up at him, uncertain and kind, and Sy's chest swelled. "You're one of the nicest people I know, Lorraine." And finally, he leaned in and kissed her on her lovely lips.

GREY

I have Edmund drop me off a block from home. January is a

deeply cold month here, but I'm well-bundled in my red wool coat.

I told Mama I was going to study at Leia's because when I took her to get empanadas after Edmund and the Circle met with her last week, she said, "That's a very fervent group you are involved with, and that Edmund seems particularly intense."

I frowned. "*That* Edmund? Really, Mama."

She shrugged. "Okay, Edmund." Then she gave me the look that means she wants the whole story. "Just how involved are the two of you? Because he seems pretty…passionate."

I knew exactly what she was asking, which infuriated me. I growled, "You mean, are we having sex? I don't think that's any of your business." We aren't, but she doesn't need to know that.

"Baby…"

"My name is Grey. I'm not a baby. I'll be seventeen in less than three months." I may have stomped my foot. I doubt that helped my case.

To her credit, she just responded, "Fine, Grey. I'm just looking out for you. You *are* almost seventeen and an adult, but you're still my child." Then came the part about not getting swept away, how I had my whole life to fall in love. I stopped listening. She still wants him to come to dinner, but that's not going to happen. Between her lecture and her pushing a dinner invitation, I haven't said much about Edmund to the family. It's just easier if she thinks I'm with my secondary friends. She would never have let me go to a full-blown protest, so I didn't mention it.

Now, post-protest, I open the blue front door and step in, grateful for the warmth of the house. I pull off my boots and coat. Matt is holding a bundled-up Rini, and when he sees me, he picks up the vehicle keys and calls, "Boys, let's go."

I start to ask where they're going when I see Mama on the sofa, unsmiling, watching me. My brothers come downstairs laughing —and freeze when they spot me. Matt gives me a quick look of concern, then ushers them all out. The door clicks shut. The house is silent, the air heavy.

"I'm going upstairs to change," I say, already turning.

Mama's voice stops me. "Come sit with me, Grey." Even, measured. Alarm bells are now clanging in my head. I am in trouble.

I walk slowly to the sofa, heart thudding, and sit on the far end, perched near the edge.

"Scoot closer. I have something to show you." No wiggle room in her tone. I move closer, then closer still. Her eyes flick to the device in her lap.

She holds it up. A still of my face fills the screen. A tap, and the video plays. My voice chants. The crowd roars.

"Mama, I…" I want to explain, but seeing what's on the screen leaves me speechless.

"The show's not over." She clicks again. Edmund's voice booms from the speakers, denouncing the Bosch leadership. Another tap: a news anchor, my face in the corner. "Trouble is brewing in Bosch as the master commander's daughter calls her mother corrupt." Another: a man sneering as he declares, "If she don't like Glitter, she should go back to the Western Continent."

What have I done…? "Enough." My voice cracks. "I get it."

"Do you?" Her eyes search my face, then skim over my body.

I shrink. "What are you looking for?"

"Honestly? To see if you've started wearing blue." The words land like a punch. *I am not like them,* I want to scream. But I'm in enough trouble as it is, so I bite my tongue.

She exhales sharply. "Maybe this felt like fun and games until now, but there is real harm in what, and possibly who, you're aligning yourself with. You started out with a lie—you weren't at Leia's. Instead, you're standing on a stage, looking different than most Bosch, shouting that your own mother is immoral. That's all some people need to turn your message into something else entirely."

"I didn't know," I whisper. But I did know. And I did it anyway.

She sighs, drops her head back. "Grey, when I said Edmund

was passionate, I didn't just mean emotionally. I meant politically. You're smart, and you have good judgment—I hope you're using it. Because this isn't just about Glitter. It's about power. Control. And maybe about who gets blamed next."

I say nothing. My throat is tight.

She sits up. "I want you to take some time to think. Two weeks. Focus on you and what is going on inside you. Not on Glitter, Edmund, or the Circle or protests."

I nod. "Okay." I don't tell her I'm not sure I actually can think about something other than Edmund and the Circle. She'll figure that out when she eventually sees my grades, which have dropped from my usual high marks to...something more mediocre.

"You'll go to school and come home. We'll revisit this after two weeks."

It takes a second to register. "Wait. I can't see Edmund?" Panic rises. *She can't do this. It's not fair.* I scream this in my mind but am not foolish enough to say it aloud. Because I know—she can do this. I blink fast to keep the tears at bay.

"You need space to clear your head. So yes, no Edmund. And I need your comm." She puts her hand out.

That is more than my good judgment can handle, and I wail, "No! That's not fair! You can't!"

Her voice escalates the tiniest bit. "You pointed out to me recently that you are *almost* an adult. Almost. I am still your mother. And you, my daughter, are confined to home for two weeks. Actions have consequences. End of conversation."

I slam my comm onto the sofa cushion, then head to my room, brushing past her without even a glance. *End of conversation? We'll see about that,* I think, my fury building like a wave.

SY

Sy knocked on the blue door, stomach tight. It had been nearly a month since the fight and the last time he stood on this porch. While the Wallace–Warner house had always felt like home, today, something was different. He reminded himself, *Okay, Mercer, Kat, and Matt—not MC and colonel.*

The door opened. "Uh, hi, uh, Kat. Is Grey around?"

The MC looked drawn and tired. "Sy. Where've you been hiding? Come in."

He stepped inside, unsure whether to feel relieved or more nervous.

"Grey's upstairs." Kat glanced toward the steps. "But..."

"She's grounded?" Sy figured there was no point pretending.

Kat nodded. "You've seen it as well? I guess everyone will soon enough." She rubbed at the knuckles of both hands. "Grounded, yes. And under siege if the comment threads are any sign. Go on up. She could use a loyal voice right now."

"Yes'm. I'd like that." Sy didn't know whether his was truly a loyal voice. But he did want to talk to Grey.

Sy stood in front of Grey's closed door and knocked. No way was he barging in like the old days.

A muffled voice called, "What do you want? I hate you, and I don't want to see you. Go away. I mean it."

Tempting, he thought, but opened the door anyway. "I don't believe you hate me. Or your mom."

A pause and sharp sniff. Then she turned and her tear-streaked, defiant expression crumpled. "Oh, Sy...it's you. Sy, what have I done?" She stood in the middle of the room, covered her face with her hands, and began to sob.

Without a second thought, Sy moved to his best friend, pulling her close as she wept on his shoulder. He held her, scanning the room: A new Ash Grey painting on the wall—hadn't seen that one yet; it was really good. Her purple rope was on the floor, whittling kit half-buried under sweaters, a half-packed rucksack on her bed. "Grey," he whispered, "are you planning to run away?"

She pulled back, snuffling. "Yes...but no. Because, you know..."

He gave a lopsided grin. "Because we live on an island?" It had been a joke they shared through the years whenever one of them was annoyed enough with family to want to break free. *We could run away, but where would we go? That's the damn hazard of living on an island.*

"Exactly."

They shared a breath of old warmth. Then her face turned bitter. "Of course, the master commander would hunt me down and drag me back home since she thinks she can control everything I do." She glared at the doorway before swinging her eyes back to Sy. "I don't like fighting with you, Sy Mercer, but I'm still mad over that name you and Leia call Edmund."

"It wasn't kind, you're right," Sy admitted. He wasn't promising to stop, but he could see how it hurt her.

"How's Lorraine?" Grey was now puttering around her room.

"She's good." He paused. "Actually...it was kind of her idea I come over."

Grey's head whipped around, eyes blazing. "Oh, really? Because you couldn't even be bothered to think I might need a friend. Is this just a pity call so your girlfriend can brag, *How nice is Sy? He went and saw Grey Shima, the outcast.* That's pathetic."

"Don't call her pathetic." Sy could feel his ire rising. "And an outcast is someone who gets driven away. You're more like a defector." Sy watched as Grey set her jaw and balled her fists. Fairly sure she wouldn't hit him, he stood his ground.

Grey sighed and dropped her hands. "I was actually calling myself pathetic." She paced around the room. "I didn't even want to protest at first, but...there was so much energy. I got swept up. Now everyone, including Mama, thinks I believe she's corrupt—which she isn't. I don't know how to make this right." She flopped down on her bed's edge.

Sy sank down beside her. The silence was warm, familiar. He bumped her shoulder. "How long are you grounded for?"

"Two weeks, maybe more. And she took my comm."

"That's a rough wind." He tried to offer something positive. "Truth be told, it was actually pretty cool to see all those people coming out to support the anti-Glitter movement, and even though I'm not nearly the fan you are of Ed—" He paused to carefully pronounce it. "—*Mund*, he sure can work a crowd."

Grey smiled faintly. "He sure can. For a minute, I felt like I could really make a difference."

A knock at the door startled them. Kat's voice came through. "Hate to break this up but visiting hours in this wing of the Bosch prison are over."

"Visiting hours. That's a good sign," Sy commented.

"Maybe, but she said no Edmund. I don't think I can go two weeks without him." Grey gave a small sigh.

The words evoked a small sting, but not as much as he would have expected. Maybe he wasn't in love with her anymore. Maybe he never was. "You'll get through it. You both will."

They stood, awkward again. Then Grey reached out and hugged him. It felt good to be comfortable with her again. Then she did something she had never done—she kissed his cheek. "That's for being a true best friend."

Sy kept his voice steady as he tried to disregard the burn of emotion that flamed at that kiss. "That's what friends do."

He walked out without looking back. *See you, Grey*, he thought. *I love you. Always have.* He sighed. *Guess I always will.*
***

Grey

After Sy leaves, I lie on my back, a piece of wood in one hand and my knife in the other, making random, angry, rough cuts. Bits of wood fly and ping off my bedroom wall, bouncing to land among my blankets, but I don't care. Two weeks. Might as well be forever. I'll just have disappeared, and Edmund will think I hate him. He may even decide to move on with someone without all the ridiculous complications I have. I contemplate my purple rope, but what am I going to do, walk to campus in the middle of the night? My life is over.

About a minute later, or a couple hours, I really can't tell, there's another knock at my door.

"What?" My tone is defiant, which is what I'm going for because I know it's not Sy this time.

The door opens, but I don't even look over, just stare at the ceiling and continue to carve chunks from the wood block. Mama says gently, "Listen, I think it's only fair that you let Edmund know what's happening. We don't want him worried about you suddenly going silent." She takes a couple steps to my bed, and I feel her set something there. She doesn't wait for a response but just leaves quietly, closing the door behind her.

I finally look. My comm sits on my bed, and I grab it and message Edmund right away:

> There was video of the protest.

> Mama is so mad. I'm grounded.

His response comes through immediately:

> Oh, shit. But I saw the video. I liked it, but I'm not surprised the MC didn't. How long?

I reply, thumbs hitting buttons hard.

> Two weeks. Might as well be forever.

A few seconds later:

> Can you comm me?

Yeah, but only for a bit, then I have to give up my comm for two weeks as well.

I pause a beat, then punch in his number, and he picks up almost before it rings.

"Hey, beautiful."

I almost melt into a weeping mess upon hearing his voice. "Hey. This is awful."

"Well, it's not great, but this is you and me, Grey. We can get through two weeks. You were amazing at the protest. That's why your mom is so mad." I can hear the pride in his voice.

I'm not sure I'd call what I did amazing. That's the damn trouble with being Kat Wallace's daughter. She's right nine times out of ten. "I just feel like a stupid kid getting grounded. And I don't *want* to go two weeks without seeing you."

"You're not a stupid kid. You're an amazing, smart, passionate woman. We'll be okay." His voice is earnest.

Now I am crying. I murmur, "I love you," through my tears.

"I love you too. You're strong. We're even stronger together."

There's a knock on my door. "Time to wrap it up," Mama calls.

I want to scream at her but instead say, "I have to go. I guess I'll talk to you in a couple weeks."

"I'll count the hours. You are my sailheart. Talk soon." The comm clicks off.

Sailheart… I want to melt. Instead, I stand, approach the door, and open it. Mama leans against the far wall a meter from my door. She's trying to show me that she wasn't listening. "Here." I hand the comm to her. I don't feel as murderous after talking to Edmund. I actually look at her. "Thanks."

SY

Sy watched from where he and Lorraine sat as Grey stepped through the big front doors of school. He suspected what was going to happen and, unfortunately, was not disappointed. After the twins veered off to see their friends, Grey began what could only be described as a walk of shame. The closest group of third-years went quiet when she passed, then began whispering together. When the scenario repeated with a group of second-years, he stood, elbowed Leia, and said, "C'mon."

With that the entire friend group followed, Leia calling, "It's Pebble!"

Just as they surrounded her, Sy heard two third-year boys giggle, and one said in a loud whisper intended to be heard, "Glitter has to go, huh? Maybe foreigners ought to go?" At this Sy veered from the group, pivoted, and stepped strategically in front of the offending third-year. "What did you just say?" The kid was a full head shorter than Sy, so he made sure to stand uncomfortably close and look down at him.

The kid set his jaw defiantly for a half a second, then dropped his eyes to the floor. "Nothing," he mumbled.

"I better not hear *nothing* again. We on the same deck, or you swimmin' home?" He watched as the boys scooted away, as silent as a skiff.

"Nice work, Mercer. Didn't know you had a menacing side," Mason commented.

Sy shrugged and felt Lorraine's hand slip into his and squeeze. He glanced over at Grey, who looked paler than usual but gave Sy a grateful smile.

Gemma nudged Grey. "So we have you all to ourselves for two weeks. What kind of mischief shall we get into during school?"

Grey shook her head. "I'm pretty sure Mama expects me to get my grades up in everything and be a good little trooper for the whole fortnight."

"Hey, you have a great singing voice," Lorraine remarked.

"How about you work something up for the February sharing? Then you could rehearse for a bell after school."

Grey looked thoughtful. "I haven't sung on stage since last year." She grinned. "That might be fun. Thanks."

"Hey, Sadie," Anya called, "you could play guitar for her."

And with that, the group began to discuss songs and classes. Sy swept his eyes around the hall and saw several groups quickly look away. They had Grey's back. It would be fine.

♡

GREY

"I didn't know Sadie was so good!" I exclaim as Sy and I walk home. It's a cold, dry day, and the sun is already getting low in the sky. I pull my warm, red coat closer around my neck. "Last time I heard her play was in primary."

Sy nods. "Yeah. I think she's going to focus on music in uni."

"Makes sense," I reply. "I sure would if I was her." We round the corner where our path skirts the woods.

A deep voice comes from behind a big oak: "Hey, Little Red Riding Hood, can I walk with you?"

I almost scream, first from surprise, then from delight. "Edmund!"

He steps out from the oak with a big smile. "Where the hell have you been? I've been freezing my ass off under that tree for almost an hour."

I turn to see Sy looking skeptical. "Please don't say anything," I beg.

His eyes widen, then he looks at me over knitted brows. "You think I'd give up my best friend? Never." Then he looks at Edmund. "Hey, Luminary."

"Sy." Edmund gives him a tight smile before slipping his hand into mine and pulling me close. "I just thought we could steal a few minutes together while you walked. Nothing sordid."

Sy shrugs. "You want me to give you two space?"

This question makes me feel strange for some reason, and I say quickly, "No. You're fine. Let's all just walk."

I begin to rattle off my school day to Edmund, telling him about the score I got in history. "And I only really studied last night." I follow up with my conversation with Mr. Beddle, the post-secondary counselor. "He assumed I was joining the force, so I told him I might just take a year off and sing with a band, just to see him puff up with disapproval."

Sy laughs at that, but Edmund asks, "What about university? We could see each other all the time then."

I love that idea, but somehow, his suggestion makes me uncomfortable. "Well, there's still lots of time to decide," I answer casually. But is there?

When we get to my street, he stops. "This is as far as I go." He pulls me close and looks at Sy, who walks on ahead a couple meters. We kiss, though it's pretty chaste. "See you tomorrow. Same time?"

I nod, my heart full. "Mmm-hmm." Then he slips back the way we came, and I catch up with Sy.

"Not exactly following the letter of the law," he comments.

I sigh. "No. But it's not like we are doing espionage. We're just walking. You okay with it?"

"I think the question is, are *you* okay with it?"

Damn him. I don't like lying to anyone. But lying to Mama is about the worst. "If Mama asks straight out, I'll tell her. Does that work?"

He grins at me. "I don't know. Does that work?"

I give him a shove, and we laugh. "Always with the questions, Sy Mercer."

"Well, I've come to expect that Grey Shima always has the answers," he quips.

I laugh, but inside I think, *I'm not sure what answers I really know anymore.*

GREY

In the kitchen hangs a clock shaped like a sailboat. It used to chime each daylight bell when I was little but stopped years ago. Mama says she's going to get a new one but doesn't—because I love it, and it still tells the time accurately. Seventeen bells, ten minutes— only a minute since the last time I looked. Maybe it's not so accurate after all because clearly time cannot pass this slowly.

With a snort of annoyance, I wander over to the front window again and peer out at the street, trying to will Edmund's vehicle to appear. It doesn't. I'm not mad at him, just at the clock and how long it's taking to get to half-past seventeen.

I flop into one of the soft, gray chairs but pop up again almost immediately. I head back to the kitchen to check the clock.

"Found a glitch in the time continuum yet?" Matt grins, and Mama laughs. They're prepping dinner—meat burgers with all the fixings—in honor of my grounding being over and Edmund finally agreeing to come for dinner. The boys got booted outside to play with Rini because they kept circling and asking for bites.

I grab a crisp from the wooden bowl on the counter and pop it into my mouth. "Not yet," I say through the salty crunch.

"Go see if you can will time to pass in the living room. This food is for dinner. Shoo!" Mama moves the bowl away, but her voice is warm, teasing. I think she and Matt are as relieved as I am to be done with what Mama called my "minimum-security lockup."

I survived two weeks of just going to school, sharing rehearsal, then coming straight home, no comm, no Edmund. Well…actually, only two of those three since Edmund met up with Sy and me for about ten minutes every weekday as we walked home.

We talked about life and school and what comes next. Edmund mentioned there had been another protest while I was grounded.

"The crowd missed your beautiful face, Grey, but it's probably for the best. The whole master commander's daughter thing overshadowed the anti-Glitter message."

I wanted to snap, "So sorry for stealing your thunder—I did get us international coverage," but I'm working on thinking before I speak. So I said, "Yeah, probably for the best." I haven't really decided whether this whole debacle garners me a lifetime's worth of regret or extreme pride.

It was Mama's idea to invite him to dinner on my last night grounded, and I was surprised he accepted. "I think it's a good idea for your family to know me outside of the Glitter issues," he explained. "Besides, I really miss you." I guess I'm a little nervous. Tonight sort of feels like a test—of me and Edmund, of whether we can fit into each other's lives when the stakes aren't just hearts but headlines and parents and dinner with the family.

Back at the front window, I hear the thud of the door opening and then thundering footsteps as Kik, Mac, and Rini come flying inside, with Rummy trotting along.

"Oooh, look, Grey is pining for her boyfriend," Mac needles.

"You bet I am," I reply. "I'm never getting in trouble again. The past two weeks have been so hard."

Kik laughs. "Wasn't exactly easy for us, listening to you stomp around and slam doors."

Two days ago, that would've set me off. But not today. "Not anymore! I am back to my usual sweet self." I laugh.

They groan in unison, but Rini beams. "You all happy now. I glad." She hugs my legs tight.

I scoop her up for a proper hug, and just then, a flash of green catches my eye through the window.

"Ahh!" I squeal and set Rini in a chair. "He's here!" I start for the door but stop and call, "Mama, can I go see him?"

"Yes, you may. Thanks for asking," comes the reply.

And then I'm flying out the door to the sounds of my brothers making kissing noises.

Let them laugh. I don't care. The person I love is standing at the gate, and for the first time in two weeks, it feels like everything is right.

♡

EDMUND

As Edmund turned his small green vehicle down Grey's street, Mr. Bolt's voice echoed in his head: *Yes, that woman is the enemy, but she is the mother of the girl you have chosen, and this invitation is an opportunity. In her home, she may drop her guard. Listen. Observe. Ask. Then we'll discuss how to use what you learn.*

Their conversations had become frequent—daily, sometimes more. Mr. Bolt had even arranged for a new Visicomm unit to be delivered "to better facilitate our talks." The man had praised the first protest, even with the backlash tied to Grey's public presence. "Don't worry, my boy," he had assured. "I think you'll find it will all work out."

And it had. Last weekend, three simultaneous protests took place across Bosch. Five more were scheduled for next weekend. Messages poured in—comm requests, inquiries from students and strangers alike. Momentum was building. And yet, as Grey's little white house came into view, Edmund's mind quieted. The Circle, the cause, even Bolt—all faded. Only Grey remained: her eyes, her fire, her touch.

He had told himself he'd keep his distance during her grounding. He hadn't even lasted one day. Edmund met her after school then, claiming the role of supportive boyfriend—Sy Mercer be damned. That boy's adoring glances and "just friends" closeness grated on Edmund's nerves. He'd imagined several solutions, discarded most, but decided the old adage held true: *Keep your friends close, your enemies closer.* And Sy, for all his dimwitted charm, was definitely the latter.

Now Edmund parked in front of the little white house just as Grey came flying through the gate. Her smile lit up her entire face.

"I've missed you, sweet love." He wrapped her in his arms against the chill of the February day.

Grey giggled. "Of course you have. We haven't seen each other in, what, two whole weeks. Right?" Her pointed glance and guilty smile asked for a promise that their after-school walks would be kept secret.

"Only in my dreams…" he murmured in reassurance, then whispered with a wink, "And let me tell you, they were magnificent dreams."

She blushed but didn't look away. The whisper she returned was throaty with desire. "You'll have to tell me more about them…in detail. Later." She took his hand and said in her normal tone, "Come on. Let's go inside."

As they stepped up the path, Edmund tried to reason with the knots in his stomach. It wasn't like he hadn't been here before—once. But that had been with Grey's brothers and Sy. This was different. The master commander was home. So was her partner. And there was the door.

"Hey, Edmund." One of the twins opened it. Lighter hair. He had to be Mac.

"Hey, Mac." Edmund exhaled through his smile. Then he spotted the other brother—darker hair, sharper features. "Kik, how are you?"

Both boys grinned. "Nice work," applauded Mac. "We look nothing alike, but everyone still mixes us up."

Edmund laughed. "That's crazy." *Check. Good start.*

Then a small voice from near his leg: "Who you?"

He glanced down. Big dark eyes stared up from a solemn little face. "I'm Edmund. You must be Rini." He crouched to her level.

She shook his arm like a grown-up. "I Rini. I have a ponytail." She whipped her braid for emphasis. "You're Grey's friend."

"Yes, ma'am. I am."

Satisfied, she pointed across the room. "That's Rummy. That's Jerome."

The dog wagged her whole body while Mac held her back.

The cat, black and sleek, watched from atop the couch like a skeptical judge.

Animals. Edmund's parents thought pets were unsanitary. But there, in Grey's house, he smiled and crossed to pat the dog, having taken a dose of medicine to counteract the sneezing that dogs brought on for him. "I've met Rummy before, but Jerome's new to me." Rini gave an approving nod and went to pet the cat.

A tall man entered from the hall, scar across his cheek, arm extended. "We haven't met. I'm Matt Warner."

Edmund took his hand. "Edmund Sinclair. Good to meet you, sir. Colonel, right?"

Matt laughed. "Not in this house. Call me Matt. Glad you're here." Then he nodded toward the kitchen as the master commander appeared.

She wore leggings and a loose sweater, sleeves pushed up beneath a red-striped apron. She looked nothing like the stern figure from the Visicomm or even the medal-laden officer he'd met on base. More like...well, a mother. *A vulnerable leader*, Bolt would say.

She extended her arm, voice warm and welcoming. "Nice to have you over, Edmund."

He took it. "Thank you for inviting me, Master Commander."

Her lips quirked. "Call me Kat."

"I'm not sure my folks would like that, ma'am."

She leaned in conspiratorially, loud-whispering, "Well, we just won't tell them then."

Her delivery was so reminiscent of Grey's teasing that Edmund laughed before he could stop himself. The moment echoed through the room as Matt joined in.

"We're not very formal around here," Matt told him. "Dinner in five, troops. Get washed up," he instructed before he and the MC disappeared back into the kitchen.

The younger kids scurried off, leaving Edmund standing with Grey. She slipped her hand into his, and he realized his palm was damp. She looked up at him, her smile soft.

"They're a lot," she said. "But they're glad you're here. So am I."

Her eyes shone with happiness, and Edmund felt a flicker of something real—something dangerous. He needed to focus. Be charming, observant. Be what Mr. Bolt needed him to be.

And if he could also give Grey the night she hoped for? Even better.

CHAPTER 16
GRAFFITI

"Anything more said about Glitter?" Mr. Bolt asked as Edmund watched him move some unseen papers around on his desk, distracted.

Edmund considered his next statement carefully, as he had been doing since the start of the conversation with the archminister. *Balance, Sinclair. Give him enough to stay useful, but there's no need to divulge thoughts you are still making sense of.* Still, without the Chosen's backing, the movement would crumble. Edmund's voice and influence—all of it would vanish like smoke. So he nodded, because what else could he do?

He certainly wasn't going to tell Mr. Bolt that by the time dessert was served at the WWS house, a title that the family said encompassed them all—the Shima kids, MC Wallace, and Colonel Warner—he had felt relaxed, comfortable in a way fully unfamiliar to him.

The MC and Matt had even been surprisingly reasonable about Edmund's position in the anti-Glitter movement.

The MC had said, "Oh, I get it. You're not wrong when you say we are perceived as drug dealers because frankly, that's what we are. And I am sympathetic toward the concept of altering that reputation. But what's also important to keep in mind is you may not have all the information. The Glitter issue is…complicated."

Matt had added, "Indeed it is. Besides aspects that mostly only the R&D troopers understand, trading Glitter gets Bosch into nations and territories that other countries cannot access, giving us a very broad understanding of world conditions and affairs, which, in turn, gives us a leg up for extractions and political negotiations. So…" He had turned both his hands up and raised his heavy brows.

Edmund had finished the sentence. "It's complicated." That comment was rewarded by everyone at the table laughingly agreeing.

The easy conversation and inclusion of the children in the discussion was foreign to him, but he liked it. However, his pleasure was not something that Mr. Bolt needed to be informed about. He calculated the answer that would satisfy his mentor.

"Well, the MC did say that while she understood my position and supported my freedom to voice my views, in light of the kerfuffle—that was the word she used—surrounding Grey's presence at the first protest, she felt it would be best for all involved if Grey's contributions did not include appearances at protests," Edmund reported to Mr. Bolt.

He held back the MC's follow-up comment: "…especially at the ones where I am scheduled to be burnt in effigy, however figuratively." That remark had been presented with a grin and wink in a tone that indicated no hard feelings. Edmund, surprised but gratified, had grinned back. *So this was a family.*

He replied in the same teasing tone, "We'll try to keep the bonfires to a minimum, ma'am," which made the MC laugh.

"Interesting. It is in a woman's nature to put her children's safety before all else. I wonder if we can't use this nugget to our advantage during your next protest," Mr. Bolt mused.

"She won't be on-island during our next protest," Edmund mentioned casually.

Mr. Bolt turned his head to focus fully on Edmund. "Off-island, you say?"

"Yessir, she mentioned flying a mission," Edmund answered, noting Bolt's sudden interest with a tightening in his chest.

The man on the Visicomm screen smiled coldly and looked past Edmund. "The base without its lioness. Delightful." He steepled his fingers. "Grey knows the base well, doesn't she?"

"Yes, very."

"Then she must be involved in the upcoming protest. Her familiarity could be invaluable. Use her insight."

Edmund frowned. "That would go against her mother's wishes."

Mr. Bolt's voice dropped. "Edmund, you are the man in this relationship. You understand the stakes. Leadership demands hard choices. She's no longer a child—she owes you her support. You must guide her."

At the table he'd just left, everyone spoke freely—even the kids. With Bolt, obedience wasn't just expected; it was the only currency that mattered. Could he really speak both languages? Could he straddle warmth and wariness without losing who he was?

"I understand," Edmund said carefully. "I'll speak with her."

"No. You will direct her. She is young, malleable. If she resists, you correct her gently but firmly. Withholding attention is an effective method. It teaches obedience while reinforcing your importance. Women crave structure. And attention. Provide one and utilize the other."

Edmund swallowed his discomfort. These past weeks had seen the anti-Glitter movement push beyond anything he could have imagined back when he was fighting for speaking time on campus. He knew without the Chosen's backing the momentum would stall. "Yes, sir. I'll do what I can."

Mr. Bolt's voice softened again, coaxing. "You want her to be happy, don't you? To find her purpose?"

"Of course."

"Then lead her to it. Now let's move on to planning the next level of protest...."

♡

GREY

"I'm tired of winter," I moan to Edmund as I watch the cold February rain fall. We are warm and cozy, sitting at a tea shop on the university campus, holding hands.

"February is always rough," he agrees, then goes silent. I can tell there's something on his mind.

"So out with it. What are you not saying?" I figure there is no reason not to be direct.

He takes a deep breath in, which he releases in a whoosh. "That obvious, huh?" I nod as he continues, "The next protest is a silent one. We're going to tag different places all over the island."

"That's a great idea. Get the districts involved." I like this plan. "Can I help?"

He looks at me and raises his eyebrows. "As a matter of fact, yes." Eyes locked on mine, he reaches over with his other hand. "I need your expertise."

My eyes narrow but stay with his. "I'm guessing the protest doesn't involve sailing. Or whittling. Or discussing politics. So what?"

"I want you to smuggle two graffiti artists onto the base on Wednesday night. Late."

I balk. "Not a chance, Edmund. Trespassing on base is completely illegal. If we get caught, we'd have to go in front of the council. And that doesn't even compare to what my mom would do to me."

"Then don't get caught." His expression turns mischievous. "Listen, baby, the foray will be done before your mom gets back from her mission. She'll never know. Besides, don't you know all the base secrets?"

I grimace. Even when Mama isn't on Bosch, she still seems to know everything that happens here. And even if she doesn't, she can do the math upon her return. "I know lots. But not everything."

He laughs at that and scoots his chair close so he can wrap me in his arms. "Lots will be enough. Grey, think of the impact it will make—anti-Glitter graffiti appearing overnight on the base. It may just bring some troopers around." He kisses my nose and then adds in his best beguiling voice, "And if enough troopers are against selling Glitter, then the leadership will have to act."

I sigh. That man is so persuasive, I think he could convince me to dive off the peak of Mount Tamrood in a snowstorm. Still, I am wary. "Edmund, we both promised Mama that I wouldn't be part of the protests."

"I know. But you really aren't part of this one. You are simply guiding the artists who will do the protesting."

It's a bit thin, but I grasp onto the reasoning for no other reason than justification. Edmund is right. I am the right person for this task. After years of playing hide and seek all over the base while Mama was working, my brothers and I know close to every inch of the grounds, including weak spots in fencing and patrol schedules.

I blow out a breath. "Fine. I'm in." And I am, because I'm already thinking about the best places on base to tag and what kind of slogan will catch the troopers' attention.

♡

CURTIS

Curtis crossed his arms and looked off to the left as the other Circle members buzzed about the new assignment. Now that he was a supplicant, he found being around these unbelievers diffi-cult, annoying. His Grace, the archminister, had encouraged him to be patient, always reminding him that the moment of redemption was near. That buoyed his spirit.

He and Edmund had created this group, and he had been the one to first call Edmund "the Luminary." His job had been to protect him and to move the crusade forward—to sit at the leader's right hand. He scoffed to himself, *But that position has now been usurped by a mere woman.* Curtis' lips curled in disgust. He didn't trust her or any of the foolish females who thought they were part of the cause.

The Chosen guided his heart and actions now, but still, he was loyal to his luminary—his friend. Standing, he made his way over to where Abeni, Miranda, Rostum, and a few other Circle members were chatting.

"Hey, Curtis." Rostum greeted him. "What's up?"

Curtis glanced at each eager face. "I was just thinking… doesn't it seem strange to you that the master commander's daughter just appeared at a rally in the fall and suddenly was whispering in our luminary's ear—influencing him?"

Miranda shrugged. "I like Grey. But it is weird that someone in uni is dating a secondary kid. Sorta creepy."

Curtis discarded this complaint. His father had told him that on Bosch, it was best to select a very young woman, before she had time to embrace the distorted teachings that would fill her head with the notion that her standing was equal to a man's. Also, a young woman stood a better chance to be pure. "I just wonder if she can really be trusted."

Abeni tipped her head. "That's funny you say that. When the luminary gave me my special assignment, he specifically said not to tell Grey about it."

This comment caused a murmur of surprise to ripple through the assembled.

Interesting. Curtis looked at Rostum. "She is escorting you and Abeni onto base. Maybe that would be an opportunity to test her loyalty. We owe at least that to our luminary."

Rostum grinned. "I'm on it. I know exactly how to test girls like that."

"Good." Curtis nodded, then paused. "And let's keep this among the Circle. No reason to trouble the luminary about our concerns until we know more."

GREY

The late winter night, or rather, early morning, is chill, but at least it's not raining. A good thing on two levels: comfort and, most importantly, reduced detection. No muddy footprints for us. Us being me and two artists I am leading on and off base without detection.

"C'mon," I whisper, motioning to my charges, who look abjectly terrified standing on the base fence's opposite side. "It's easy. Pass me the art supplies first and then scoot on your back under the fence."

Rostum, a tall, broad-shouldered boy with close-cropped black hair, looks at me like I'm crazy. Given that I'm breaking about a hundred Force rules and several pretty significant family ones, he may not be wrong. He points at the narrow opening I just wiggled through. "I cannot fit through there."

I cock an eyebrow and resist the urge to call him a big baby. "Sure, you can." As a sign of good faith, I fall to my knees and dig, deepening the opening a little. The ground's chill seeps through my gloves, but, hey, at least the ground's not frozen.

Next to him, Abeni looks around, clearly expecting some sentry to pass by. She needn't worry. I made sure of the shift timing. Right now, last-shift guards are giving their ten-minute reports to next-shift guards, and besides, I know this area is light on patrols, given that it bumps up next to forested land. "Let's go, Rostum. I don't want to be caught here," she hisses.

Rostum shrugs, sighs, stuffs the bag with his paints and such through the open space, and then lowers himself onto the ground, grousing about the damp, the cold, and the bugs. I make no comment outwardly but think, *Sweet New Earth, he made the right choice to go to uni. He'd never make it through recruitment training.*

He gets hung up briefly, but I give the chain link a lift, and Abeni gives his feet a shove, and he is in, scrambling up and pulling his backpack on. Abeni wiggles her way under, towing her art supplies with her foot. She could make it as a trooper. She's tough, thoughtful, and doesn't bitch about whether bugs are touching her. Bugs… It's February, for Earth's sake.

The Circle identified two targets: the hangar and, at my suggestion, Bosch Hall. Abeni will leave her mark on the hangar, and I'll get Rostum to Bosch Hall. Their job is to paint. Mine is to get them in and out safely, though I came up with a slogan I suggested to Rostum.

Slipping from building to building, we avoid any lights, a trio dressed in all black. I have gloves and a sweatshirt with the hood pulled up and tied snugly so only my eyes are visible. I even pulled black socks over my shoes to not leave shoe prints and brought spare socks so my artists can be just as clandestine. My brothers would say I look like an Old Edo ninja if they got the opportunity to see me, which I guarantee they will not.

A few minutes of silent creeping later, we reach the hangar, one of Mama's favorite places. A wave of guilt-induced nausea hits me. I want the Glitter trade to end, but this? Defacing what she loves? I remind myself I'm the guide, not the protester.

Abeni flicks on her penlight. "Look," she hisses with excitement, "scaffolding!" She points to a wall undergoing maintenance, then climbs up it and whispers down, "Send my bag up." I pull my purple rope out of my own bag and tie one end to her art supplies, tossing the other up to her. She gives me a thumbs-up and starts in, paint hissing out in rhythmic bursts. I lean closer. "I'm taking Rostum to Bosch Hall. If you hear anything or see lights, hole up in that shed." I point to a small outbuilding off to the side. "And be sure I get my rope back." She barely nods, already lost in her work.

"Your turn." I motion to Rostum. His breathing sharpens, but his footsteps stay quiet. A good start.

"Rostum, follow me," I whisper, calm but firm like when Rummy was a pup. He shadows me closely.

The marching green looms ahead. It is wide, open, and moon-lit. We cross fast, staying low. Almost there when—voices. We drop beside Papa T's statue, backs pressed to the base.

"Not as cold tonight."

"Spring's early."

Chimes ring—three bells. The voices drift off. I squeeze Rostum's shoulder and feel him trembling. Definitely not Force material.

"They're gone. Come on."

He grabs my hand. "If I get caught…"

"You won't. I'll make sure of it." I tug him upright, and we hustle to Bosch Hall.

"Okay, here we are." I point to the entrance, where he said he wanted to place his art when we looked at base photos during our prep for this outing.

"Oh, this will be perfect," he whispers, looking up at the brick façade. He unpacks his art supplies, and I watch in wonder as this puppy-cum-child I have been babysitting transforms into a focused, dedicated artist, carefully flicking his penlight onto the wall that has become his canvas and selecting colors to display the chosen message.

He sprays on one color and then another, although to me, they all look deep gray in the dim of night. Watching him work without seeing the results is monotonous, so I make myself comfortable between two bushes and lean against the building. I close my eyes, and before I know it, I am adrift like an unmoored sailboat on the deep, blue sea dreaming of mermaids and sea dragons.

♡

GREY

My eyes snap open. Alarm bells are going off, and lights are coming on all over the base. I'm on my feet in a moment. "Rostum, we have to go to ground." He stands frozen, paint can in hand. I start shoving his supplies into his and my bags. His penlight has dropped to the ground, and I grab it, quickly shining it onto the mostly completed piece that displays a black Jolly Roger wearing an eye patch and reads *The Price of Glitter is Death* with the final *h* trailing off and onto the surrounding bushes as if the artist suddenly spun away as the spray was still in process.

"Impressive, Rostum. We are going to hole up in there." I point to a small, mechanical shed next to Bosch Hall. A small shove and his feet move in the appropriate direction. The shed is never locked, though the boxes that hold electrical and mechanical controls are. I get him inside and show him my favorite hiding spot, back behind a series of pipes, then return to the door.

Grabbing a broom from the corner, I peer out. No one here. The ruckus all seems to be coming from the direction of the hangar. Dammit! I mutter a wish to the universe that Abeni got to the hideout I had pointed out to her. I sprint to the front of Bosch Hall and run back and forth in all directions before walking backward to the shed, brushing away our footprints and covering the path to our bolt-hole with scattered dead leaves.

"We'll stay put here. I'm worried that Abeni might have run into trouble. That's where all the commotion looks to be," I report as I scoot in next to Rostum and consider the situation. We can't contact Abeni because we left our comms in the vehicle at the trailhead a couple kilometers from where we entered the base so they wouldn't get confiscated if we were caught—an eventuality that is looking more likely right now.

"Hope she's okay," he mutters with concern. "How are we going to get out? Won't there be a lockdown?"

"Depends what's going on. If it's us, then no—because who'd lock down a whole pirate base because someone painted on the walls? If there's something else happening…which is unlikely, then maybe?" I shrug and then click on my penlight so we can see each other. His face is contorted in concern. "Listen." I click the light off. "Let's just sit tight for a bell, and then we can see what's happening."

"Okay, but don't leave again." There is a plea in his voice that tells me the artist has retreated, leaving the puppy-child back at my side.

I chuckle inwardly. "I won't." We shift about behind the wide pipes, trying to get comfortable, our shoulders, knees, and the side of our hips pressed together. I tip my head back against the wall and close my eyes, trying to will the dreams of ocean creatures back; instead, I feel Rostum's shoulders quiver. Is he crying? "Hey, it's okay." I slip my arm around his shoulders. "So tell me how you got involved with the Circle."

He pauses and pulls in a shaky breath. "Well, back when I was a kid, my mom was in an exchange program and taught at a school just outside Paris. While we were there, I took a train into the city with my brother, and we got lost and ended up in an area that I guess was sorta rough. Grey, there were so many people on the street just out of it, and the ones that weren't kept asking us for markers. I didn't get it. But once we got back on the train, my brother said they were Glitter-heads. I sorta put the whole thing out of my mind until one day I went with this girl. There's always a girl, right?" He laughs a little, and I give a chuckle because it's expected and nod. "So, I go with this girl to a rally, and suddenly, there's our luminary on stage talking about Glitter, and the whole scene flooded back." He looks at me seriously. "That shit is bad, Grey. We shouldn't be selling it."

He isn't wrong. I look back at him. "That must have been so hard to see as a kid."

"I guess it was. But I shoved it away for a long time. Now… well, I won't shove it away anymore."

Impressed by his passion and commitment, I reach over to squeeze his hand. "Good for you."

Then, to my shock, he leans in and kisses me deeply. I pull away and scramble off to the side. "What are you doing?"

He grasps me by the shoulders, pulling me back. "C'mon, Grey. I can tell you want me." He moves in again, mouth open.

"Like hell I do!" I raise my voice beyond what is prudent for the situation and give him a shove with both hands, causing him to tip heavily away from me and drop one of his hands. *Please don't make me hurt you. Please*, my inner voice begs as my body takes on a defensive posture.

His remaining grip on my arm relaxes, and I hear him sigh, then chuckle. "Oh, well. Nice work. I'll let the Circle know you passed the test." There's no more weeping or pleading. Now he sounds confident, resolute, and a little bit pitiless.

I am confused. "What? What do you mean, test?"

He shrugs. "We wondered if you were really loyal to the luminary. I mean, you just show up one day—MC's daughter, a tasty package of innocence and passion." He gives me a smirk and raises his eyebrows in a disconcerting way. "And lo and behold, you become the luminary's new girlfriend—deep in the inner Circle. We had to be sure, to test you." A pause. "You passed."

I stare at him in the dim. *Who* are *you?* I think of Edmund—how he'd held me, whispered that he loved me, asked me to trust him.

"He asked you to do this?" My voice cracks.

"Not directly," Rostum says easily. "But I know my luminary. He told me to make sure you were okay. He didn't want you knowing about Abeni until after. The test itself was the Circle's idea. I volunteered." He leers a little at his last comment.

I frown, trying to make sense of these words. "What about Abeni?"

In a smug voice, he answers, "Abeni had two assignments— the hangar wall and then at least one vessel."

My brain seems to be slogging through mud; it is so slow. "A vessel?"

"A vessel. She was to tag the wall and then go inside the hangar and deface as many vessels as possible. Extra points if she could paint the pilot windows before one of the Bosch Pathetic Force grabbed her." His voice is matter-of-fact.

"She's *supposed* to get caught?"

Rostum chuckles. "Sure. Otherwise, how would she get our message to the council?"

Everything spins. "And this was the plan all along?"

"From day one as far as I know."

The betrayal slams into me. So Edmund knew. Knew I'd help and that Abeni was set to get caught. Knew I wasn't trusted. Something inside me hardens. Mama's voice echoes in my head: *Get up. Stay sharp. Handle it.* "Well, then, let's go," I say coldly. I shed my black layers, revealing workout gear. "Dump your paints and such in here and get rid of your blacks."

A few grunts and clinks and then, "Okay. I'm ready."

I open the door a crack and look around. No more alarms, but the base is waking up. "Keep your mouth shut and follow my lead." I shove a fake pass onto his chest.

Looking down, he nods, and I slip my arm around his waist. The pre-dawn February morning reveals every breath we exhale. "Put your arm around me," I order.

His eyebrow flicks up and I roll my eyes in response, "Oh, grow up, Rostum. It's our escape plan. Now put your arm around me as if I need help walking."

"Oh, with pleasure, Grey," he smirks and obeys. I really want to hit him, but we need to get off base first.

We begin to walk, me feigning a limp, leaning heavily on Rostum. We are more than halfway to the gate when we meet a trooper—a young woman I have seen on base a couple of times who graduated two years earlier from my secondary school.

"Grey? Is that you?" She clicks on a small light attached to her collar that makes me squint.

I search for her name in my head. "Yeah. Tirzah? Right?"

"Yeah. But I'm more used to Corporal Morrison these days. What are you doing here? And who's this?" She gestures to Rostum.

Pulling all my theater work over the years and banking that the base information flow doesn't include Mama's spontaneous trip up North, I answer, "Oh, this is my boyfriend, Edmund. We came over with Mama for an early morning workout." I slap my forehead and scoff. "But, of course, I pull a muscle and then Mama had to leave to see whatever those alarms were about. So Edmund is walking me home so I can ice my calf." I give my best imitation of a painful grimace.

Now Tirzah is less Corporal Morrison and more sympathetic older sister. "That's awful." She looks at Rostum. "I had heard that our little Grey…" I cringe inside as she describes me this way but keep my smile pasted on. "…had a boyfriend."

Realizing that the anti-Glitter sentiment of my boyfriend will pop up in her head soon, I give a small groan. "It really hurts…"

Rostum gets his first line in. "Oh, man, Grey. Do you want me to carry you?"

The annoyance from his reveal of "the test" floods me, and I'm quick to respond almost eagerly, "Yes. Please."

"Really?" he asks, suddenly looking a bit surprised.

I blink like a baby deer (do they actually blink like this?). "Oh, absolutely." I am fully angry-giggling on the inside.

He scoops me up, and I almost whoop as my feet leave the ground.

Tirzah calls, "Get her home safely, Edmund. See you, Grey."

"Thanks, Tirzah…I mean, Corporal Morrison." I wiggle my fingers and whisper to Rostum. "All the way to the gate, please." The irritated puff of air that escapes his lips delights me. *Be happy you are just pretending to be Edmund Sinclair, Rostum, because I am about to loose the hounds of hell on the real Edmund today.*

You wanted to test my loyalty, Edmund? Great. I passed my test. But you just failed mine.

EDMUND

Edmund flopped over onto his side in his bed, picking up his timepiece for about the twelfth time. Five bells. He groaned. He had gone to bed around two after getting reports from the teams that had drawn out the Circle's anti-Glitter messages across the island, including the central bank in District One and the harbormaster's office in District Four. Those would certainly bring ample attention to the cause. But it was the incursion on the base that was the keystone. Mr. Bolt had said, "Strike at the head of the serpent, Edmund. Demoralize your enemy before you destroy them."

He had just opened his mouth to tell Mr. Bolt that the Circle wasn't looking to destroy the Force when the archminister laid out the most shocking part of the plan. "One of the Circle must sacrifice their freedom. It will serve your cause well. Your people have a curious affinity for letting the accused speak their piece, so your message will be brought to the highest levels. Choose someone well-spoken. A woman is preferable, more expendable."

He had wanted to argue that there was no need to blow up someone's life. But he knew the archminister was not making a suggestion. No, he had passed a decree. And if Edmund wanted to keep the support of the Chosen, well, he clearly had bent the knee weeks ago.

So he deliberated over the women of the Circle. Several came to mind, but after considering various pros and cons, he settled on Abeni. It was a perfect role for her. She was a talented artist and articulate and, most importantly, willing to be reckless and do what was needed to get arrested.

She'd seemed uncertain when he approached her until he mentioned Mr. Bolt would be providing funds "to offset the difficulties your agent may experience" and could guarantee that the university would not expel her.

"How can he guarantee something like that?" she asked.

Edmund had asked the same question of Mr. Bolt. "He says they have connections inside the university."

She looked thoughtful, then nodded. "That's vaguely disturbing, but okay. I'm in. I will be the sacrificial lamb. Can't wait to make a scene at my trial." She laughed.

Edmund then provided a caution. "This is to remain quiet. Only the inner Circle will know the plan to allow for plausible deniability. It is especially important that Grey not be informed."

Abeni frowned. "Why not? Do you not trust her?"

"No, no, nothing like that." He was about to explain that he knew Grey's compassion for her friends would cause her to balk at allowing Abeni to be caught, and any talk of Mr. Bolt with her only precipitated an argument, but he heard his mentor's voice in his head: *Establish a clear hierarchy. You are in charge. Underlings shall not question your directives. Particularly women.* He stood a bit taller and said firmly, "I have my reasons. I expect the instructions to be followed."

Abeni looked as if she was about to say more but then nodded. "Yes, Luminary."

Now, as Edmund checked his timepiece—five and a half bells —he told himself it should be done. Abeni would be in custody. Rostum would have told Grey, and she'd be furious. That part was inevitable. He stepped into the shower, already planning how to manage her reaction.

Mr. Bolt's words came again, low and certain in his mind: *The shepherd does not consult the sheep. He leads them.*

Edmund let the water run hot. He didn't owe anyone an explanation. Especially not Grey.

GREY

Eight bells. At school, Dr. Ahmed's literature class is about to start without me. I am here, staring at Edmund's dorm room door. Doesn't matter. This won't take long. I'll be back in class once I take care of this.

I knock once, twice. The door opens. His face curves into a smile upon seeing me, then his expression drops as my fury flows from my eyes to envelope him.

The first thing out of his mouth is "Good morning."

"Is it?" My eyes narrow. "I don't think so. We have a problem. And that problem is: You are a fucking liar."

His eyes go wide. "You should come in."

"Don't fucking tell me what I should do. No matter what that asshole Bolt says, you are not the boss of me." My voice escalates.

"Stars, Grey. When did you start using language like this?"

"Oh, am I embarrassing you by using the word *fuck*?" I look up and down the halls and note that several doors are now open a crack. "Fuck!" I yell as I kick the wall. "You are a fucking liar. And I hate you!" I hear more doors open, and it delights me.

His arm shoots out and grabs mine as he pulls me into the room, shutting his door. Big mistake. I twist away and then unwind, landing my elbow squarely in his ribs. He cries out, releasing my arm and grasping the space where my blow landed. "Fuck, Grey, what the hell?"

I didn't mean to hit him. Well, maybe I did. Either way, I wasn't going to let him own even one more second of my story. "Oh, now, who is using *language*?" I growl. "Don't you ever touch me without my permission."

His hands lift in an I-give-up pose. "Listen, I did what I had to do."

"You did, huh? You had to test me? After everything we've done, you think I would give you up? Well, let me tell you, ordering Rostum to shove his tongue down my throat was a stupid move. But no more stupid than having Abeni deface vessels. I'm sure he's reported off to you that I passed your stupid loyalty test. You can go to hell. I never want to see you again." Suddenly I'm crying. "I can't believe I loved you. You… You're awful." I pivot and reach for the door. His hand comes down on my arm, and I pause, then slowly turn my head to give him one and only one warning look. His hand drops.

"Grey, what are you talking about? I love you. So I didn't tell you about Abeni…. What are you saying about Rostum?" he stutters.

I have no time to hear him twist the truth. I refuse to look into his gorgeous eyes because they will beckon me to listen and understand. That's not happening. "Goodbye, Luminary. Good luck not turning blue." I yank the door open and march down the hall. I take a breath and calm the fury in my chest. I turn back to Edmund. His face is stricken, and his eyes beg for me to reach out to him. I blow out a breath and look through the hallway—first left, then right. I give a smile, then, at my top volume, yell, "Fuck you!" I turn, satisfied, and see myself out of the dorm as the love of my life stands helplessly alone in his doorway.

CHAPTER 17
A PERFECTLY GOOD HEART

The first period bell sounded, and Sy cast a glance at the empty seat to his right as he stood to leave. The hubbub among his classmates was thicker today, interspersed with hushed comments of "Did you see what the one in District One says?" and "My brother sent me this from base. Can you believe it?"

Where was Grey? She had told him that her mom had made her promise not to be involved in any more protests. He pulled out his own comm and sent a message.

> Where are you? You missed Ahmed's review.

He waited to see the *X's* that showed a message was being written. But none appeared.

> Are you coming in today?

No response. He made his way to study hall. *Maybe she'll be there…* His comm vibrated.

> I just got here. I'm getting a late slip from the office.

Another message followed:

> Can you sign me in for study hall then meet me at our spot in the auditorium?

Sy typed his reply.

> On it. I'll be there in a second.

He took a deep inhale. The auditorium balcony, where they always met for important conversations. He thought back to his talk with Matt. Grey deserved the truth—and maybe today was the day. He wasn't proud of the timing, but some truths couldn't wait. Lorraine would have to come later.

He glanced over his shoulder down the main hallway before taking the steps two at a time to the light booth. The doors to the balcony were always locked during the school day, but he and Grey had discovered that the latch on the right side of the light booth was weak, which meant one wiggle and a shove, and a pathway to a quiet space presented itself. He quietly closed the door behind him. The inner door to the balcony was ajar—Grey must already be there. Sy took a deep breath and inwardly quoted Lady MacBeth: *Screw your courage to the sticking place.* Today was the day. He stepped into the dim, dusty-smelling space. He heard it before his eyes had a chance to adjust to the dark. Grey was here all right, and she was crying.

"Hey, there. What's going on?" Sy asked gently as he knelt in front of the upholstered red seat where his best friend was balled up, knees under her chin, arms wrapped tightly about her legs with her head down, sobbing. He reached out and rubbed Grey's upper arms solicitously.

She lifted her head and unwound, reaching for Sy and almost

toppling him backward as she embraced him, moaning, "Oh, Sy, it was awful. I'm such an idiot."

"No. Grey Shima. You are many things, but you are no idiot," he said into her hair. "Now tell me what happened and why you are crying." He gently pushed her back from him a little as he leaned down to look at her face—it was a mess. Pulling up the hem of his soft shirt, he wiped her eyes, then her cheeks and finally her nose. He didn't care whether it ruined the fabric. That was what friends were for. She snuffled and stuttered as she caught her breath. They sat down in the seats where they had shared so many other secrets and confidences. "Okay, then. Let's hear it."

And Grey told him everything, from the conversation where Edmund had persuaded her to be the base guide, to last night's escapade, to standing in a dorm hallway yelling "fuck."

"I just felt so used," she said, shaking her head. "Like everything I gave him didn't matter." She looked at Sy. "I loved him. And he said he loved me. I was ready to…you know…do it with him." Grey blew out through her lips. "I guess I'm glad I didn't."

Sy had so many emotions flowing through him, he wasn't sure which to prioritize. Should he be furious for Grey? Or jealous? Or shocked that his friend would take such a risk? Or *jealous*? Jealous was good because since the rally, he had been able to get deeply acquainted with that emotion. Honestly, though, he didn't much like how jealous felt and had been both surprised and pleased when the sensation had slowly faded since winter break. Since Lorraine. He shook his head the smallest amount to refocus. Grey needed him. She needed sympathy and support. "You're right. It's probably good you didn't. It would make what you're feeling now even harder."

Grey leaned her head onto Sy's shoulder and sighed. "I was so happy, Sy. And now, I feel like I'll never be happy again." She opened her mouth in an enormous yawn.

Tipping his head onto hers, he resisted the urge to kiss the top of her head. *Watch yourself, Mercer. That way lies madness.* "That's a helluva yawn." He was about to start talking about how she was right to be furious, but something occurred to him. "Grey, did you even sleep last night or this morning?"

"Mm-mm…"

Sy felt her head get heavier and her body lean into his shoulder. Slowly and carefully, he slid his arm from between them and settled it around her, pulling her close. Her breathing, no longer halting from sobs, eased, and she gave a tiny sound of contentment before drifting off completely. This was good. She needed sleep. And since there was nothing else for Sy to do, he leaned onto Grey and closed his eyes. As he drifted off, he thought, *Life feels pretty perfect right now.*

It was almost a full bell later—though it felt like a blink—when Sy startled awake to voices below. The spring play's cast had taken the stage, their lines bouncing around the rafters. He shifted slightly. Grey's head was still tucked into his shoulder, her breath slow and even. Peaceful.

Then behind him, a sharp inhale—so clear it cut through the ambient chatter. He turned.

Lorraine stood in the light booth, hands gripping the edge of the spotlight mount like she might snap it in half. Her mouth hung open. Her eyes, wide with shock, flicked from Grey to Sy and then back to Grey.

Sy opened his mouth. Nothing came out. His brain scrambled for something to say—anything to explain what this wasn't. But Lorraine's expression had already shifted. From hurt to furious.

She shook her head once—just once. Final. Then she turned and vanished.

A heartbeat later, the crash of the booth door echoed behind her. And the rapid-fire slap of retreating footsteps rang out, fading down the hallway.

Sy didn't move. Couldn't. He just stared at the now-empty booth.

"Oh, no," he whispered.

GREY

The dream is lovely. I'm on the sea in a small boat, not *Noelani* but almost. The waves gently rock me, the ocean holding me close, moving me to the rhythm of her breath. I am safe. Utterly safe. But then, seabirds begin to yap and mew, and the sound claws me from the dream.

There's no boat. My eyelids flutter and my brain tries to orient. The auditorium. And Sy. No wonder I feel safe.

"Oh, no," my friend whispers. The arm wrapped around me slips away, and I shiver at its absence. "Listen, Grey, I have to go. Now."

I'm not fully awake and am cranky from being disturbed. "What? Why? Stay here. Put your arm back. I'm cold."

But he's already standing. I squint up. His face is pale, stricken. "Lorraine just saw us. From the booth. Like *this*. She probably thinks... I-I have to find her. I have to explain."

He bolts up the stairs, taking them two at a time. And then he's gone.

I sit up fully, blinking hard. The dream slips away completely, replaced by a rising burn in my chest. My hands clench, tight fists curled in my lap. My shoulders tense; my jaw aches. Sweet New Earth. I'm jealous. The realization lands like a slap—sharp and unwelcome. Why would I be jealous?

It's Sy. Sy, who's always been mine but never really. Sy, who's with Lorraine but held me like something fragile and worth protecting. I can't be jealous of Lorraine. I love Edmund. Don't I?

A flood of images rushes in—Edmund's smile, his voice and hands—but they crash against the memory of last night. The lies and betrayal. The fire in my chest when I screamed in that hallway.

I don't have Edmund anymore.

And now, maybe...I've lost Sy too.

SY

Sy was at a half-run down the main hallway of school. *Where would she go?* He tried to think but had no idea. If it had been Grey, he'd know. Did that mean he loved Grey more than Lorraine or just knew her better? Longer? He halted in his steps. Wait. Did he love Lorraine? *You idiot. Of course you do. Now go look…somewhere.* He started to trot down the hall again.

"Mr. Mercer." Principal Lopez's voice pulled him up short. "We prefer walking to running in the hallways. Where are you supposed to be?"

"Um…study hall." Sy figured the truth may just come in handy.

Dr. Lopez raised an eyebrow. "And why aren't you there?"

"I… I need to find Lorraine Middleton. They need her in the theater." Two truths, unrelated.

"I didn't know you were in the play this year. What part?" Principal Lopez looked ready to settle in for a casual conversation.

"Uh…no part. Helping with lighting. But Lorraine knows way more about it than me." *Okay, now I've moved into two truths and a lie.*

Dr. Lopez nodded. "I think I saw her earlier heading toward the library."

"Great! Thanks. I'll just…walk there."

The school principal smiled. "That's a good choice. Have a good day."

Sy nodded and took off at a brisk walk. He ducked into the library and turned away from the front desk. No more authority figures. No more lying. *Where would she go in the library?* He thought of Grey going to the balcony to cry. Somewhere private. There were two soundproof study rooms in the back. Worth a try.

She was in the second one. He saw her through the windows, sitting at a table, head down on her arms. He couldn't hear anything, but he could see her back quiver. *Shit, Mercer. Looks like you are just another asshole guy.* He thought about every quiet moment with Lorraine—her crooked smile, the way she asked real questions, how she laughed with her whole chest. Not once had he wondered whether she was testing him, or whether he had to prove something. With her, he felt...enough. He eased the door open and knelt next to Lorraine. All the lines he'd rehearsed—"It wasn't what you think," "We just fell asleep"—dissolved like fog. He put a hand gently on Lorraine's back and said, "I'm so sorry I hurt you." And he was. He was gutted to an extent that surprised him.

She lifted her head. Her face was blotchy and tear-streaked, and the look in her eyes knocked the breath from his lungs. "I kept telling myself you and Grey were just friends," she whispered. "Because why else would you go out with me and kiss me and...? Earth, Sy. I thought about having sex with you. And I was touched when you said you weren't ready." Her voice cracked. "Was it because of her? Have you and Grey...?"

"No!" The word escaped him before he could think. "No. Grey and I have never... She is my friend. She had a falling out with Edmund and hadn't slept. She just...needed someone. I listened. She fell asleep. I stayed."

Lorraine sat back, wiping her face. "So I'm just the next crying girl in your arms? That's humiliating."

He reached up and touched her cheek, soft as sea glass. "Lorraine, you're not 'just' anything. You're my first everything—first date, first kiss, first time someone outside my tiny circle of friends made me feel like I might be worth something." His voice caught. "You're the first girl I've ever said, 'I love you' to."

Her eyes widened. "What?"

"It's what hit me when I saw your face in that booth." He took a breath, scared but sure. "I couldn't stay there while the girl I love was hurting. I had to find you." He blinked. Saying it aloud didn't feel reckless. It felt like the truth settling into place.

She stared at him, wary. "But Grey...?"

He gave a lopsided shrug. "You know, I loved her—or thought I did—for a long time. I was so sure. Maybe because she was the first girl to treat me like a person who mattered. But now, I don't think I even knew what love really was." His eyes searched hers. "You show me. Every day. It's not something I need to keep boxed up and hidden. It's meant to be shared, celebrated. And maybe I messed up—hell, I definitely messed up—but I know what's real now. And it's you." He let out a long breath. "But if you want to be done with me, I get it. I deserve that. I just had to be honest with you first."

Lorraine stood and walked slowly to the window overlooking the sports field. Sy sat frozen, heart pounding in his throat. She stayed there, her back to him for so long he thought she might not come back at all. Finally, she turned.

"I can't promise I won't still get jealous sometimes. I mean, it's Grey. She's everywhere. And she's part of your life."

He swallowed. "Yeah. She is."

"But I'm part of your life too. Right?"

He nodded, barely daring to hope. "You are."

She took a slow step toward him. "Then I'll take it. I'll take you. But only if I get to hear you say it again."

Sy blinked. "Say what?"

She grinned through the remnants of her tears. "You know what."

He stood and closed the distance between them. "I love you."

She reached for his face, pulled it down, and kissed him like she was sure.

CHAPTER 18
CONSEQUENCES

EDMUND

Edmund lay on his bed, arm over his eyes, comm in one hand, the other hand bandaged and propped on pillows. He waited for the vibration—the *ding* that would mean Grey hadn't cut him out of her life. She couldn't have.

He'd frozen when she lit into him, stunned by her fury. *You should have gone after her right then, Sinclair.* By the time he came to his senses and ran after her, she was gone—out of the dorms, nowhere in sight. He'd called, messaged fifteen times. He'd stopped after the fifteenth, desperation hitting somewhere around eight.

He couldn't go to her house. The MC was due back anytime. Besides, she had school. He couldn't exactly drag her out of class and demand she listen to him. *That's probably what Mr. Bolt would tell you to do. Be the man, Edmund. Take control.* Well, Mr. Bolt had never met Grey Shima. "Control" and Grey didn't belong in the same sentence.

So he decided to wait. He'd intercept her walking home. Let things cool. In the meantime, what had she said about Rostum?

What exactly had that idiot done? He knew where to find him—one building over, third floor.

"Go away, I'm sleeping," came a groggy voice as he pounded on the door.

"Open up, Rostum. I want to talk to you."

A pause, then a thump. The door creaked open. Rostum stood in boxers and a half-open robe. "Listen, Luminary, I did my job," he said with a lazy smirk. "And I enjoyed myself. Now I need sleep."

That smirk flipped a switch.

Edmund grabbed the robe's lapels and shoved backward until Rostum hit the wall.

"Hey, hey!" Rostum's hands came up. "What's going on?"

"That's what I'd like to know," Edmund snarled. "Why did Grey come at me this morning talking about *you* sticking your tongue in her mouth?"

The smirk widened. "Oh, that. Circle was worried about her loyalty. I was the lucky guy who got to run the test." A shrug. "She passed."

Edmund dropped his grip. Rostum straightened his robe and belted it loosely. "You're a lucky man, Sinclair. Honestly, I was kinda disappointed I didn't get to test her further." He chuckled.

Edmund didn't hear the rest. His fist moved before he could stop it. One punch. A sickening *crack* as Rostum's face jerked sideways, a grunt escaping as he staggered.

"Don't ever go near her again!" Edmund shouted. His hand was already throbbing as he stormed down the stairs. He made his way to the cafeteria, where the ice he found numbed the worst of pain in his hand but did nothing to cool the heat churning in his gut.

She couldn't *really* think he wanted that creep to kiss her. The idea made him sick. But still—she'd passed. She was loyal. It made him feel…proud in some demented way. He hated himself for feeling it. It wasn't a test he'd asked for. So why did it feel like a win? And why did it feel so…dirty?

He wandered campus, skipping class, pausing by graffiti the Circle had left behind. A few students clustered nearby, pointing at the messages. Twice, a group quieted when he passed, then resumed whispering once he'd moved on. He checked his comm. No message from Grey.

His left hand felt stiff, the ice having melted a while back. He couldn't move his index or middle finger. He steered himself to the health center.

A bell and a half later, he walked out with a wrapped hand, six pain pills, an appointment for physical therapy, and a lecture from the nurse about punching people bare-knuckled.

Back in his room, queasy and exhausted, he popped two pills —one looked too small to do the trick—and flopped on his bed, hand elevated, eyes shut.

He was asleep in moments.

♡

EDMUND

It was dark when the knocking started. Edmund groaned. He lifted his head and then let it drop back, cursing himself. He'd overslept—missed his window to find Grey.

His mouth felt full of cotton, and it was hard to open his eyes. The knocking persisted. "I'm coming," he called, dragging himself upright.

A wave of dizziness engulfed him. *Only one pill from now on,* he cautioned himself, then cracked the door, ready for Rostum's revenge.

"Abeni? What the hell are you doing here?"

"Can I come in?" Her face was grim; her clothes covered in paint.

Edmund opened his door. "Of course, come in. What happened?"

She dropped into his desk chair. "I should ask you the same thing." She gestured at his wrapped hand.

Ha waved it off. "Tripped on the stairs. Go on…"

Abeni shrugged. "It went exactly as planned—at first. I found scaffolding and made my piece big. *Glitter Kills*. Then I snuck into the hangar, hit three vessels with the same message, slapped paint on a windshield—and that's when the troopers caught me. Dragged me down, called the Force Police."

Edmund sat. "Well, that was what we expected. And then they charged you?"

She nodded. "They said I'd face a special council session tomorrow."

"So why are you here? Did they let just you go until then?" That made no sense, but perhaps he wasn't thinking clearly after the pills.

"Nope. I told them I wanted a public hearing—it's my right. The lead FP said, 'Whatever,' and locked me in a basement cell with some food and blankets."

"Again, expected," Edmund muttered.

"So, I slept for a bit. Then that same FP showed up and said, 'Come with me.' Took me to the third floor."

Edmund stiffened. He was fully awake now. "Master commander's office?"

"Yep. She was waiting. Told me to clean up in her washroom—super fancy, by the way—then offered me tea. Sat me in the same chair from that January meeting."

"What did she say?"

Abeni laughed—short, sharp, disbelieving. "She *praised* the art. Even mentioned the piece on Bosch Hall—didn't use Rostum's name, just said 'the artist.' Then she told me the FPs would escort me back to campus."

Edmund blinked. "No discipline?"

"I told her I wanted a public hearing. She said, and I quote: 'There's to be no discipline. No need to convene the council. You and your Circle created plenty of your own publicity. There's no need for us to provide more.'"

Edmund exhaled. "She shut it down."

"Then she called for the FP. I tried to ask her for my art bag—she cut me off." Abeni gave him a pointed look. "'Tell Edmund I'm thinking of him,' she said."

Edmund sat back slowly on his bed. *I bet she is…*

GREY

Where did he go? I wonder as I track Sy after he disappears to chase down "poor" Lorraine. Lorraine, bent out of shape over nothing—like we were doing anything wrong. Maybe she needs glasses. Or thicker skin. For the love of… I stop before using that hated expression. I never do, but I'm so tired and drained, I'm not thinking straight. After poking around for a good half-bell in all the usual places we go to avoid the adults of the school and coming up empty, I head back to the balcony to get my bag.

I'm about to open the lighting booth door when I hear a giggle that makes me freeze. I put my ear on the door. Sy's voice as well? Standing on my toes, I peek through the small window. Sy is sitting on a stool holding Lorraine on his lap as she works the spotlight. I drop away, knowing this is a private moment, but something in me compels me to look again, and I watch, hypnotized, as he nuzzles her neck, evoking another giggle. He whispers something to her, and she slaps a hand away that is slipping up her shirt toward a breast. Then she turns to kiss him, and my best friend grasps her neck and hair with his hands as they… I drop from the window. I shouldn't be watching. My stomach churns, and waves of hot and then cold sweep over me. I run for the washroom.

There's almost nothing in my stomach, so my retching only produces green bile. I flush and go to rinse my mouth, staring at my face in the mirror. When did Sy become someone I don't even recognize? When did I? A glance at my comm, which shows over a dozen missed calls and messages. I see one: *Let me explain...* Then I huff in annoyance and stuff the device in my pocket.

I sign myself out of the office, telling the secretary I am sick to my stomach. She gives me a sympathetic look and tells me to get some rest. "That's a good idea. Thanks," I answer, figuring it doesn't hurt to pretend to be nice, though the thoughts bouncing around my brain are anything but.

Mama is due home later today. She'll be upset when she hears about the graffiti and will grill me, but that's okay, as long as she holds me and tells me it'll all work out—because I am not at all sure it will. I sleepwalk home, collapse in my bed, and allow myself the indulgence of another good cry before sleep finally takes me.

♡

GREY

It's dark and quiet when my eyes open again. What time is it? I flip on my light and sit up, looking around my room. My stomach drops when I see my desk. There's a glass of water sitting there next to my neatly coiled purple rope. On top is a note in Mama's hand:

> *There's soup on the stove. I'll heat it when you wake up. We need to talk.*

Am I too big to run away from home?

I creep down the stairs, empty glass in hand. It's nearly twenty-three bells; tomorrow will be here in a moment, but I'm starving. Maybe Mama has gone to bed. But, no, as I step into the kitchen, she already is at the stove, apron on, stirring the soup.

There are two stools at the island. One has her current book and a half-full glass of wine next to it.

"Soup'll be ready in a moment," she says in a voice as calm and steady as if it were just another Friday. Why don't you cut a couple slices of bread and grab the butter?"

"Okay," I say meekly, pulling the bread from its place in the bread box and slicing it. "Are you eating too?'

"I ate earlier. But I'll take a slice of bread." Again, there is no rancor, which honestly is terrifying.

I slap the knife down. "Mama, can you just yell at me and get it over with?" I beg.

She turns her head, spoon still stirring, and meets my eyes. "Nope."

I sigh. "Fine. Can I have a glass of wine too?"

"Not tonight." She sets a steaming bowl of seafood chowder at my place. I bring the bread and butter and refill my water glass.

I eat quickly—first one spoonful, then another, then the next. I hadn't realized how hungry I was. Mama sips her wine, reads a few lines of her book, and nibbles her bread. When I finish, she tops off my bowl with another half-serving. I soak the last of the bread in the broth and eat that too. I wash my dishes while she packs the soup away, and I find a place for it in the icebox.

Softly, Mama declares, "Let's talk on the sofa. I'd like to hear how the rope that I gave you ended up in a graffiti artist's bag in my office. Also, I did recognize the slogan plastered over the entrance to my office."

So, we sit, and I spill the story, leaving nothing out. The plan, the incursion, Rostum's test, Abeni's intentional capture, my fury at Edmund, and Sy. Sy and Lorraine. I do my best not to cry but am only marginally successful.

She listens without a word, occasionally putting a sympathetic hand on my leg or brushing my hair back behind my ear in an old, affectionate manner. When I finish, she concludes, "It seems like a very upsetting day for you."

"Why aren't you mad?" I ask.

"Why would I be?" She sounds genuinely curious.

"Because you told me no more protests."

"Well, this wasn't strictly a protest, was it? It was more like a mission. Not one I would have sent you on, but you executed it quite well. Even that story you gave Corporal Morrison was smart."

"Oh. I forgot to tell you that part."

She smiles. "It was a busy night. I'm sure more will come back to you."

There's a secret curdled in my stomach. One I hadn't planned to tell her. But if Edmund's been lying to me… "Mama," I whisper, "Edmund's been meeting with a Bluie. An archminister. He said they could be allies. He said he could handle them. But I think the graffiti idea came from this Mr. Bolt."

Mama's eyebrows wrinkle the tiniest bit as she looks at me. "It must have been hard to keep that information secret. And to reveal it now. But let me reassure you, I know all about Simon Bolt. He is no fan of mine, nor are any of the Bluies. But then, the feeling is mutual."

My jaw drops open a bit. "You…know?"

Mama chuckles. "It's my job to know these things, darling. I have people watching—not just our enemies but our friends too. Remember, I have an entire intelligence department reporting to me." She puts an arm around me, and I snuggle close. "I don't want to ask you to keep secrets, but when you speak to Edmund again…"

"I'm never speaking to him again," I declare with ferocity.

"Well, then, *if* you speak to Edmund again, don't let him know you told me. The Bluies are dangerous. Your safety is paramount to me." She kisses my hair. "So, do you want my opinion about any of this? Or was talking it out enough?"

I am suddenly very sleepy again. "Can we talk later? I just want you to hold me for a bit."

Mama scoots to the couch corner and pulls me into her lap,

wrapping her arms around me as my head rests on her shoulder. She hums an old Edon lullaby, and right now, I am glad I am *not quite* grown up.

CHAPTER 19
FIX THIS

EDMUND

THE VISICOMM FLICKERED ON, REVEALING MR. BOLT'S FACE. "Edmund, my boy," he started warmly, voice steeped in affection. "How are you? And how did the disruption go?"

All Edmund wanted was to break down and talk to someone —*anyone*—about what he was now calling the third worst day of his life. When he was little, he'd had pneumonia so bad, he was hospitalized for two days, the doctors unsure whether he would live. Today ranked just behind those two days. Of all the people he felt he could talk to, Mr. Bolt was very near the bottom of the list.

But he'd scheduled this comm. He had to report on the graffiti "disruption," as Bolt termed it.

"Overall, the project was a success," Edmund said, reciting the phrasing he'd practiced. "We had artists tag at least one building in each district. The public response has been notable."

Mr. Bolt nodded, pleased. "Excellent work. Tell me about the base disruption."

"Also successful. Two sites were tagged. The member selected for sacrifice managed to deface multiple vessels before being taken into custody."

"And when is her trial scheduled?" Bolt asked, practically gleeful.

This part wasn't rehearsed as carefully. "The master commander returned today and…released her. She said she saw no reason to give the Circle additional publicity."

There was a pause. "So she was released," Bolt repeated.

"Yes, sir."

"Because the master commander decreed it?"

"Yes, sir. That's my understanding."

Bolt stared blankly through the Visicomm. Then he stood and walked away, gazing out of his office window. He remained there for several long minutes before returning to his seat. "I will need to confer with the patrician of Dominion," he said at last, "but his schedule is quite full. The master commander's behavior—like that of all women—is irrational. Which is distressing. It indicates escalation may be required. Let us speak again in a few weeks."

"Weeks, sir?" Edmund asked, startled. They'd been speaking daily. "Is there a problem I could manage?"

"Oh, you will manage the problem," Bolt said calmly. "I want you to track the master commander's movements—mostly off base. We have our own informant on base. You have a unique position—a proximity to her almost like family through the daughter, but wholly unlike family in your allegiance. I expect daily entries starting Monday. I'll be bringing the information to His Holiness."

Edmund's stomach tightened. "That may be…difficult…"

Bolt's eyes sharpened. "Difficult? Let us hope not."

"Grey and I aren't currently… She…" Edmund faltered. He wasn't even sure what was happening between them. Just that it wasn't good.

"I have no interest in the details of your love life, Mr. Sinclair," Bolt told him curtly. "What interests me is a daily record of the master commander's activities. Do whatever is necessary to repair your connection with the girl. If you must appear to renounce your anti-Glitter stance, so be it. I don't care."

Then Bolt's voice and face softened, almost fatherly. "We are talking about the greater good, Edmund. Our words, while meaningful, are tools—useful for misdirection. Go to this Grey and woo her. Women are sentimental creatures. A few sweet words and small gifts will be enough. Have you claimed her body yet?"

Edmund flushed. Embarrassment? Anger? Probably both. "I'd rather not—"

"Rather not discuss it?" Bolt interrupted, still smiling. "I'm only trying to assist. Have you claimed her body?"

"No, sir. She's younger than I am and…"

Bolt grinned. "Ahh. A virgin. How fortunate. You're right to be cautious. But women—well, they crave a man's attention. Their desires are animalistic. You can train her to please you, bind her to you as the one who makes her whole. It's a powerful advantage we men possess as rational sons of the Lord."

Edmund stared at the screen, his skin crawling. *What am I doing here?*

Bolt leaned in slightly, confidential. "And a powerful responsibility. I recommend you use it. If you're blessed, she may even bear your child. That would connect her to you for life."

The thought made Edmund's stomach do a tremendous flip. "That's not something I've considered, sir."

"Children are always a blessing," Bolt said, smiling fondly. "They're the living proof of a man's conquest over a woman's reckless spirit. They calm her. Give her purpose. Help her accept her place. I have twenty-three children, ranging from two to twenty."

Edmund tried very hard not to picture Mr. Bolt conceiving so many, or any, children. "Yes, sir," he managed, voice barely audible. "I do want to reconcile with Grey. But I can't promise—"

"No promises needed," Bolt interrupted again. "Just be a man. Make your Circle proud. Make the Chosen proud. Make your father proud." He paused. "Make *me* proud."

The Visicomm went dark.

Edmund stared at the blank screen, stunned, unsettled…and somehow still motivated. He *did* want Grey back. He *wanted* her, but he wouldn't pursue her for Bolt. He loved her. If that happened to serve Mr. Bolt? So be it.

ARCHMINISTER

INTERNAL MEMORANDUM: LEVEL 7 CLEARANCE REQUIRED

From: Office of the Archminister, Central Continent Division

To: Office of His Holiness, the Patrician of Dominion

Date: 12 February 2372 | Time Stamp: 0100

Subject: Status Update: Operation Dominion Rising (DR-2371)

Subversion Stage Two (SS2): Initiated and Evaluated

In accordance with Strategic Directive 7B, Subversion Stage Two commenced as scheduled, targeting psychological destabilization, inter-peer trust erosion, and preliminary disruption of Bosch public order narratives.

Event Summary: Graffiti Deployment Initiative (GDI-72)

Coordinated Circle affiliate actions executed visual messaging across key civic and military infrastructure. Eight total sites were marked, including walls on Bosch Hall, three Force patrol air ships (known colloquially in Bosch as vessels), and the outer perimeter of the Bosch hangar.

Intended Outcome:

Stoke internal disciplinary responses, prompt narrative fractures within Force chain of command and anti-Glitter youth factions, engineer moral justification and emotional appeal sufficient to frame coming Chosen candidacies for council as both compassionate and necessary for local stability secondary to subject testimony.

Resulting Complication: Executive Override by Master Commander Wallace:

Affiliate "Abeni" voluntarily detained per operational directive but unexpectedly released after direct intervention by Wallace. Rather than pursuing formal disciplinary escalation or public denunciation, Wallace responded with strategic containment and personalized engagement.

Impact Assessment:

This maneuver undermined the anticipated propaganda effect. Instead of appearing weak or fractious, Wallace's behavior reinforced her position as a maternal-commander hybrid figure. Internal data suggests her approval among junior ranks has *increased*.

Wallace's refusal to engage through official channels renders her *unpredictable by traditional authority-response modeling*. As such, her continued survival represents a strategic obstacle to ideological saturation within Bosch.

Recommendation and Request for Stage Three Escalation Authorization:

Due to Wallace's capacity to subvert planned narrative outcomes through informal influence and personal charisma, Subversion Stage Three must transition from *material disruption* to *leadership neutralization*.

The scheduled detonation of newest Whydah airship (2070) may offer an ideal pretext for this outcome. It is therefore requested that Stage Three be reclassified as a sanctioned removal opportunity, with Wallace as a priority-level target, contingent upon situational feasibility and continued narrative cover.

Post-action narrative control will utilize loss of Chosen envoys (included in the casualty perimeter by design) to validate innocence, martyrdom, before moving to occupation under Stage Four (Compassion Doctrine).

Additional details to be provided at meeting scheduled 1 March, 0900.

Prepared in Service of the Divine Order,
    Archminister, Central Continent Division,
    Chosen of New Earth

TEXT THREAD

SY
FRIDAY 1134

Hey, I came back to the balcony, and you were gone.

FRIDAY 1202

Did you go home?

FRIDAY 1300

Are you okay?

FRIDAY 1311

Okay, Ms. Normandy in the front office said you went home sick, so I know you're not dead.

Probably asleep.

Message when you get up.

GREY
SATURDAY 0156

Hey. Yeah, I woke up and my stomach was weird, so I came home and collapsed.

Talk tomorrow?

SY
SATURDAY 0903

You up?

GREY
SATURDAY 0949

> Yep. Went for a run and worked out. You wanna come over?

SY
SATURDAY 1008

Can't. Lorraine and I are going to go winter sailing.

Can you believe she's never gone?

GREY
SATURDAY 1015

> You're taking Lorraine sailing? Cool. Have fun, be safe. Maybe tomorrow?

SY
SATURDAY 1042

Hi Grey! It's Lorraine—Sy is driving.

He says to tell you that we can stop by this evening after we get off the water, if that works?

GREY
SATURDAY 1100

> Um, sure. Just message when you're close. Stay warm.

SY
SATURDAY 1102

Great! Can't wait! And I'll be warm.

Sy told me he'd make sure of it. 😉

♡

EDMUND

"So, are you going to knock or just stare at the door?" Matt leaned on a rake, head tipped to one side.

Edmund turned, startled. How long had the man been standing there? He'd been staring at the doorknob for ten minutes.

"I'm not sure yet," Edmund admitted.

Matt chuckled. "The women of this house are a force to be reckoned with. You didn't ask for advice, so feel free to ignore it—but sincerity, kindness, and respect go a long way." A few slow swipes with the rake. "And the occasional well-placed apology."

"I'm not sure I'll get to say anything. She was really mad."

Matt shrugged. "Well, you'll never know unless you knock."

But if I don't, then I can just pretend…what? That I'm not alone? Just knock, Sinclair. Edmund rapped on the blue door with his unbandaged hand.

Kat opened it, calm and pleasant. "Well, if it isn't our very own luminary, now dabbling in island-wide impromptu art installations."

Edmund gave a shaky smile. "Good afternoon, ma'am."

"Edmund," she corrected gently, "you've shared a meal in my home. I told you to call me Kat. Come in."

He stepped inside.

"I admire your moxie," she remarked. "I assume you're here to apologize to Grey, because I expect *my* apology in my office."

Edmund considered his response. "There's no good way to answer that, is there?"

Kat grinned. "Nope. And good on you for hearing it."

She reached for his coat. "Let me take this. I'll let Grey know you're here." As he handed it over, she leaned in and murmured, "I put away all the knives just to be on the safe side."

Her face remained dead serious. Edmund didn't know whether to laugh or bolt. Matt was right—forces to be reckoned with.

He stood awkwardly, waiting. But before Grey appeared, the front door creaked open.

"Hi, Emmund."

He smiled. "Hi, Rini. Helping your dad outside?"

"Uh-huh. Picking up sticks. Got cold. I'm going back now."

A sudden thought hit him. "Hey, Rini?" He crouched down to eye level.

She turned back.

"I need to say sorry to Grey. I messed up. Do you have any ideas?"

She blinked. Then whispered loudly, "Dragons."

"What?"

"Grey likes dragons. Give her a dragon when you say you're sorry." And she was gone.

From behind him, Grey's voice: "I hope you didn't just lie to her. She's the only girl in this house you haven't pissed off."

Edmund turned fast. She stood with her arms crossed, daring him. He took her in—tunic, leggings, slippers with cat ears and eyes, no makeup, hair in a ponytail. So beautiful.

He had one shot. Spotting a tray of crayons and paper on the living room ottoman, he raised a finger—*wait*—and dropped to the floor. Scribbling fast, ignoring his inner editor, he handed her the finished page.

She stared at the picture, then looked up. "Is this supposed to be…a dragon?" Her voice wasn't mocking, just soft.

He nodded.

"You gave me a picture of a dragon saying, 'I'm sorry?'"

Another nod.

"And that's supposed to make up for you having Rostum *assault* me?" There was an edge of danger in her voice.

His stomach tightened. He thought about what Matt had said. Sincerity. If she didn't believe him, this would be over. "I never knew about that. I just told Abeni not to tell you about her part in the plan. She assumed I didn't trust you. That got twisted into that idiotic 'test.' I just knew if you thought a friend was in danger, you'd intervene. That's all."

Grey said nothing, staring hard. Then she glanced down. "Are those supposed to be wings?"

He stepped closer. "Yeah, wings. Dragons have wings. Don't they?"

"Some of them." Then she added more quietly, "You know… you could have explained. About Abeni."

He sighed. "Yeah. But the plan came from you-know-who. I figured you'd hate it."

To his surprise, she snorted. "You're not wrong. And how'd that work out for you?"

He laughed—just a little. "Not quite how I envisioned." He was close enough now to smell her shampoo—coconut and tropical flowers.

"What happened to your hand?" she asked.

"Rostum," he said simply.

Her eyebrows flicked up for a moment.

He waited a beat, then, "Wanna go somewhere and talk?"

"We can go for a walk. But I have to be around home this evening. Sy and his girlfriend are coming by."

He liked the idea of the Mercer kid having a girlfriend. "I could stay for that."

Grey grabbed both coats. "Oh, you're staying. No way I'm handling that alone. Let's go."

She held out her hand. He took it and gave a small squeeze. She didn't squeeze back. Not yet.

GREY

We walk to the park holding hands. Edmund is quiet, and I'm glad—there are so many thoughts racing through my head, it feels like I'm in a stadium with thousands of people screaming different things. With a deep breath, I slow the noise and pick just one.

"I'm out of the Circle, Edmund. I'm still anti-Glitter, but the Circle—you included—embraced me because I'm the MC's daughter, not because any of you thought I had special gifts to share...." As I say it, I realize it's true.

Edmund interrupts, "You have gifts. You're well-spoken. You're passionate. You made me believe—more than I ever did before. You have ideas about how to bring the cause to the Force."

"Let me finish," I press. "You need to be honest with yourself. Maybe you see those things now, but that wasn't your motivation last fall after the rally when we met." I stop walking and peer up at him, daring him to deny it.

He doesn't, offering a half-shrug instead. "I guess that's sort of true." He catches my expression. "Your passion about the issue drew me." Edmund glances over to my skeptical face. "Okay, fine. My first impression was that your position could help the cause."

"Thank you." We start walking again. "The other thing is the Circle's lack of trust in me. One comment from you, and they turn into a bunch of little old ladies gossiping over the fence and plotting loyalty tests. There's no coming back from that."

"I really had no idea they'd do something like that. And it makes no sense. If you weren't loyal, why'd they trust you to get them onto the base? That asshole Rostum probably manipulated the whole thing just to get his hands on you." Edmund growls. "Listen, I can kick him out. And anyone else who questions your allegiance."

I stop and laugh. "That's not the point, Edmund. I don't want to be protected. I want to be respected. You punched Rostum, fine. But are you going to expel or punch everyone who gives me the side-eye? You won't have much Circle left. Also, pro tip—use your elbow next time." We reach the park, and I head for my favorite bench and sit. Edmund settles beside me, still holding my hand. "So yeah. I'm out. I don't want to know what you're planning. Or hear anything about Mr. Bolt. I'll happily go back to making posters and arguing with my classmates about the dangers of Glitter. That's it."

He sighs. "I don't love that, but I get it. It's going to feel like I'm keeping things from you." He squeezes my hand. "Can I ask you something?"

He's so tentative, so understated, it tugs at my heart. "Sure."

He lifts my hand to his lips and kisses it. "Does this mean I can keep seeing you? Because I really want to."

Feelings are so strange. Yesterday I was so angry at Edmund; my heart felt shattered. Mama ran with me this morning. I was still raging, furious, and she let me vent the whole way. "You have every right to be angry," she told me. "But don't let it be the only thing you let yourself feel. Love, forgiveness, friendship, vulnerability—they all have a place too." I'd laughed and told her Ruth, her therapist, would be proud. She laughed too. It was a good run.

Now, looking at Edmund, the fury is gone. I feel…I guess, love. But my heart is cautious. I touch the spot on my hand where his lips' warmth still lingers. "I want…to start over."

Edmund is quiet for a beat. Then he releases my hand, stands, and walks around the bench. I blink, confused.

"Excuse me, miss, is this seat taken?" He gestures to the now-empty space beside me.

I shake my head, trying not to smile.

He sits, then extends his arm. "Hi, I'm Edmund Sinclair. I'm a second-year at City University. I tell my parents I'm studying business, but I'm actually focusing on history."

My smile breaks free. I reach my own arm out. "I'm Grey Shima. Three months from graduating secondary. Still undecided if I'm enlisting like my mama or going to uni."

He grins. "Nice to meet you, Grey Shima. Mind if I sit and talk with you for a while?"

"I'd like that."

CHAPTER 20
HOME

EDMUND

EDMUND PULLED SEVEN PLATES OUT FROM THE CUPBOARD AND handed them to Kik. "Do we need bowls as well?"

Kik shook his head. "Nope, Matt and Mama are bringing home empanadas with all the fixings."

"I am all for empanada Friday. Fewer dishes to wash," Edmund commented as he grabbed a handful of flatware for the table. As he set them out, he glanced over to one of the big, gray chairs where Grey was reading a book to Rini. "Where's Mac?"

Kik pointed to the music room with the final plate in hand. "Practicing."

Edmund looked at the sailboat clock in the kitchen, then went over and rapped on the door. "Hey, Mac, dinner in, like, fifteen minutes."

The door opened. "Great. I like that you're here all the time, Edmund. Lightens my load, you know?"

Edmund laughed. "You're on clean-up. Grey and I are going out after dinner."

"Ah, man," Mac moaned.

A few minutes later, Matt and Kat came in holding two big

bags, the March wind practically blowing them through the door. Kat's hair was wild, the curls going every which way. Matt exclaimed, "Look at this! A table ready for a Friday meal. Nice work, troops."

Edmund had noted over the past three weeks that Matt noticed everything—and always found a way to praise people's efforts. And he saw how much the people he praised blossomed under it. Edmund had even started doing the same within the Circle, and he thought it might actually be working. He walked over to the bar cart and poured two glasses of wine, setting one at Matt's place and carrying the other to Kat. "Figured you might need this after the quartermaster meeting."

She laughed as she accepted it, though she looked at him curiously. "Thank you. You seem to know my schedule better than I do."

With a nervous laugh, Edmund tried to deflect the comment. "I've learned how to listen from you and Matt and Grey."

Rini was climbing up her mother's legs. "What you learn from me?"

Edmund was glad for the interruption. "I've learned two things from you, Miss Rini: how to have fun and the importance of dragons." He tugged one of the little girl's braids. It was a constant balancing act—enjoying time in a warm and accepting family while still drawing out the information Mr. Bolt required in his reports. Every time Kat smiled at him, or Matt included him in a project, it got harder to pretend he wasn't lying to all of them. He was ready for the relationship with the Chosen to be done, but he was committed to staying through what Bolt called Stage Three. The details hadn't been revealed yet, but Bolt assured him it would be a turning point for ending the Glitter trade as Bosch knew it. A few more weeks and Glitter would be gone, and he could finally breathe—maybe even enjoy this family for real.

He glanced over. Grey caught his eye and smiled faintly. He smiled back. She had said she didn't want to know—so why did he hate the part of himself that hadn't told her everything?

EDMUND

"You have infiltrated the master commander's home quite admirably." Mr. Bolt nodded in approval.

The words dug at Edmund, who was already impatient at having to cut his night short with Grey to keep this Visicomm appointment. "Mr. Bolt, I am not infiltrating. I am visiting my girl-friend's family." He paused, then decided to push a bit more. "I have a question. Given that our master commander is *just a woman*, as you say, why are the Chosen so interested in what she's having for dinner every night and her number of daily meetings?"

Mr. Bolt regarded Edmund quietly for a moment, then began to chuckle. "Well, well, well, our little bear cub is trying out his teeth. How adorable." Then the chuckle disappeared, along with any humor. "Mr. Sinclair, if your amateur conglomeration of privileged university scholars masquerading as the proletariat no longer needs the help and financial support of the Chosen, we are happy to focus our resources elsewhere."

Yes, please... Edmund thought, then with a breath replied, "No, sir, I and the Circle appreciate the Chosen's aid in our anti-Glitter efforts. My apologies for my rudeness. It was out of line."

"Mmm," Bolt murmured. "Perhaps if I inform you of some of our considerations in the early planning of Stage Three as presented by His Holiness the patrician of Dominion, it may satisfy your boyish curiosity."

Edmund refused to take the bait and simply said, "Yessir. That would help. Thank you."

"Details are still being worked out but suffice it to say that it is imperative that your master commander be present when implementation occurs. We want to be sure she...receives the message that the Glitter trade is no longer safe for Bosch to engage in. Hence, the need to track her location and schedule." Mr. Bolt sat back in his chair. "Adequate?"

"Yessir. That makes sense. Though perhaps placing a source that has access to the MC's work calendar would be more beneficial than my mundane descriptions of her homelife." Edmund wanted to be free of this assignment.

A smirk appeared on Bolt's lips. "You assume we don't already have someone inside? We didn't get this far by being blind, Mr. Sinclair."

Edmund had difficulty keeping his face neutral. *If they've really infiltrated the base, why keep using the Circle? Why keep using me? Unless…they want deniability. Or a scapegoat.* "I see. I will continue as you have directed. However…"

A flash of impatience crossed Mr. Bolt's face. "However?"

"It's really a logistical question. The university term ends in late April, and the Circle members will be returning to their homes for the summer. When is the anticipated implementation date of Stage Three?" Edmund hoped that the summer break would allow the Circle's relationship with the Chosen to fade. While the movement had picked up more members, actual Glitter profits did not seem impacted by their efforts.

Now Mr. Bolt returned to his grandfatherly smile. "But of course, a reasonable inquiry. Stage Three will take place next month a bit after the FA elections on April 3rd."

Edmund nodded. "Very good, sir." That was Grey's birthday week. They had already been making plans. So much for cake and sailing and dragons and romance. The Stage Three event worried him. It would be bad enough if it disrupted her day, but if Bolt's message somehow hurt her—Edmund wouldn't be held responsible for his reaction.

♡

SY

"C'mon, you're good with lettering," Grey wheedled. "I want to change out the old posters."

Sy groaned. "Grey, I just sat down."

He was beside Lorraine on the main hall steps, long-estab-lished final-year territory for couples hanging out. And he, finally, was part of a couple. His arm was barely around her before Grey pounced.

But Lorraine popped up. "Okay! I've never made any anti-Glitter posters before." She smiled at Sy. "Let's help."

He let out a breath and held up a hand for her to grab. "Fine." He stood and kissed the tip of her nose. "I can't say no to you."

She giggled.

"Oh, but you can to me?" Grey grumbled, side-eye sharp enough to cut tile.

"I absolutely can. Years of practice." Sy grinned at her.

They followed Grey to the back study room in the library. Sy gave Lorraine's hand a squeeze and leaned in to whisper with a wink, "I like this room."

She grinned. "Me too."

"Leia said she's coming. There's paper and markers on the table, and a list of slogans," Grey said, already setting things up.

Sy and Lorraine sat next to each other, scooting their chairs closer. When Sy glanced up, he saw Grey frowning at them—but the moment their eyes met, her expression flipped into a bright smile. Leia and Mason arrived a few minutes later. Grey gave them instructions, and all five got to work. The room went quiet except for the soft scratch of markers on paper.

Sy was mid-slogan when he noticed Lorraine had stopped drawing. Before he could ask why, she spoke. "So why are we anti-Glitter?"

Sy cringed. Mason snorted, and Grey's head snapped up. She didn't speak right away, but her eyes locked on Lorraine with full firepower.

She's going to kill my girlfriend, Sy thought, heart already climbing up his throat.

"What?" Grey asked, voice tight.

Lorraine seemed not to notice the warning signs. "I just mean

—it's not enough to be against something. We should be able to explain *why*. Posters that scream *Glitter Kills* don't work on people who think it doesn't. Because technically—it doesn't. The drug itself, I mean."

Grey's fists clenched. Sy's stomach dropped.

"I'm not saying people don't die because of the trade," Lorraine added quickly. "But it's mostly the violence around it. From the reading I've done, in the FA, League of States, and African Federation, most deaths linked to Glitter come from weapons. And with addiction, which only seems to occur in 10 to 12 percent of users, the major problem is malnutrition, which some people do die of. But not the drug. Can you pass the green marker?"

Sy stared at her. Mason and Leia looked stunned. Grey's hands loosened, but her brows were pulled tight.

"So, what *are* you saying?" Grey asked, still wary.

"I'm saying facts matter. Education matters. Posters grab attention, sure—but long-term change needs more. We need interweb games for kids. Start early. Teach about Glitter and its copy-cats like Sparkle and Ruby—those get made in labs and *are* linked with overdose deaths. And Bosch doesn't need it as much as the places we *sell* to do. Less than half a percent of the population of Bosch ever even tries Glitter."

Lorraine leaned in, eyes bright. "Imagine a game where kids learn how drugs are made, who profits, how it ruins communities. Something that teaches them *before* they hit secondary." She stopped, looked around, and slumped back. "I'm sorry. I didn't mean to take over."

Sy reached out and rubbed her back. "You're okay."

"Lorraine..." Grey started.

Sy jumped in. "Grey, she's just trying to help. I didn't know all that stuff either and—"

Grey cut him off with a glare. "Sy. Let me talk." They locked eyes. He tried to beg her silently to *be kind* and warn, *don't hurt her*. She looked away and back at Lorraine.

"Yeah, I didn't know that stuff either." She turned to Mason and Leia. "Did you?"

They shook their heads.

Grey let her marker fall. "Okay. Lorraine, tomorrow—can you bring those resources? Show us what you found? I think we—I—need to understand this better." She then leaned back in her chair and thumped her head a few times against it.

"Are you mad at me?" Lorraine asked softly, watching her.

"Mad? Definitely." Grey didn't lift her head. "At you? No. I'm mad because you're right. And because my mom's been saying the same thing for months, and I really don't want her to be right."

Leia laughed. "I hear that."

Lorraine reached across the table and patted Grey's hand. "Don't worry. If I ever meet your mom, I'll deny I ever said anything. We'll keep this between us. Secret educational rebellion among friends."

Grey looked up and smiled. "Among friends, huh? Sounds good."

Under the table, Sy squeezed Lorraine's thigh. She was amazing.

♡

GREY

There's tension as Edmund and I sit at the dining table—me finishing up homework, him attempting to read the book on Glitter I gave him. It's one Lorraine recommended. Normally we'd be in my room—me at my desk, him stretched out on my bed—but Mama and Matt are off in the Eastern Continents for some political thing, so my old nanny, Riki, and his wife, Susan, are staying with us.

Susan is upstairs, tucking Rini in and settling their toddler, Chimon. Riki—who, by all accounts, is still the strongest man I know, with shoulders like a block rig and arms like tree trunks—made it very clear Edmund would not be in my room.

Instead, he's parked himself in a dining chair, arms crossed, face unreadable. Watching us. Well—watching Edmund.

"You know, Riki," I say with my best smile, "I'm only fourteen days from being an adult." Riki has been my friend since I was a baby, and he still thinks of me as the little girl who used to sit on his shoulders, picking lilacs and draping them over his ears. He would kill for me. And has.

His eyes stay fixed on Edmund, but he answers: "Then I will consider altering my position in fourteen days. Finish your homework."

There's no point arguing with Riki. I sigh and glance at Edmund, who looks drawn, distracted. He keeps glancing up like he's waiting for a blow to be struck. His eyes catch mine. I shrug.

He closes the book. "Well, I guess I should head home."

"Good," Riki says flatly.

I giggle. "You know, Riki, someday Chimon's going to have a girlfriend or a boyfriend. Are you still going to be sitting in a chair, watching them?"

The corner of his mouth twitches. "Maybe. You may walk this Edmund out to his vehicle. I will stay in this chair."

I pop up, kiss his cheek, and whisper, "Thank you." His cheeks pink slightly, which is always my secret victory. Then I take Edmund's hand and jerk my head toward the door. "Let's get you on the road."

He follows me but then pauses and walks back to Riki. He holds out his arm. "It was very nice to meet you, Riki. I understand and appreciate you looking out for Grey. I care about her too."

Riki rises, taking Edmund's arm in a shake that dwarfs it. Though shorter, he somehow still manages to tower. "It is an honor to meet any friend of Grey's. It would grieve me to have to damage you."

Edmund nods. "It would grieve me as well. Give my best to Susan."

We step out into the unseasonably warm March night and walk in silence to his vehicle.

"I think he'd actually break me in half if I hurt you. Or touched you," Edmund says.

I slip my hand into his. "Oh, a hundred percent if you hurt me. But he promised to stay 'in this chair'"—I mimic Riki's deep voice. "So we're clear for a good night kiss."

We stop just outside the gate, near his green vehicle, and wrap our arms around each other. When we restarted our relationship, we restarted the physical side too—slow, careful. We only began kissing a few weeks ago. But lately I've been thinking about what I want. What I'm ready for. Something real. Something chosen.

He kisses me—softly, then more deeply. I press in and kiss him back, heat rising under my skin. He pulls me close, and I speak into his shoulder. "I decided what I want for my birthday."

He pulls back, grinning. "Finally. What is it?"

I stand on my toes, lips close to his ear. "I want to spend the night with you. And I want us to…be together."

He freezes. I feel it through every point of contact. He's even holding his breath.

Then, slowly, he exhales. "Grey…are you sure?"

I run a hand along his cheek, fingers brushing the soft stubble there. Even that small touch stirs something deep inside me. "I've never been more sure."

CHAPTER 21
CHOSEN

CURTIS

THE VISICOMM FLICKERED ON IN THE BASEMENT OF THE DISTRICT Four house. Curtis, swathed in a pale blue robe, bowed his head as the archminister's face appeared on screen.

"The Earth Remade, the Path Revealed," the older man intoned.

Curtis responded with crisp reverence. "And the Chosen walk it true."

"You are the newest of the Chosen in Bosch. And I foresee great things from you—and for you," the archminister said, his tone warm with praise.

Curtis's chest swelled. To be seen—truly seen—by the voice of the Chosen was more than he had ever imagined. All his life had led to this moment, in this basement, wearing this robe.

"If it be God's will, I will be Chosen," he recited faithfully.

"Excellent." The archminister gave a nod. "Now, as one of the Bluest and a member of the anti-Glitter Circle, you have an important part to play as we prepare to bring Bosch under the loving protection of our Lord."

"Yessir. Whatever you ask of me, sir," Curtis said, voice bright with purpose.

"After our Chosen candidates are elected next week to the FA presidency and vice presidency," the archminister continued, "we will send envoys to Bosch to peacefully offer them the path forward. But I need you to prepare a contingency in case the woman who claims to lead your island refuses to yield to divine order."

"I am yours to command, Your Grace."

"Very good." The archminister smiled, soft and grandfatherly. "Now—what do you know about explosives?"

CHAPTER 22
THE FINAL COUNTDOWN

ARCHMINISTER

INTERNAL MEMORANDUM: LEVEL 7 CLEARANCE REQUIRED

From: Office of the Archminister, Central Continent Division

To: Office of His Holiness, the Patrician of Dominion

Date: 30 March 2372 | Time Stamp: 09:00 AM

Subject: Pre-Action Authorization: Operation Dominion Rising (DR-2371)

Subversion Stage Three (SS3): Pending Deployment

As authorized under Strategic Directive 9A, Stage Three of Operation Dominion Rising is scheduled for activation 7 April 2372. Deployment to follow the successful election of Chosen-backed FA candidates and subsequent Chosen envoy visit to Bosch.

Planned Event: Critical Infrastructure Strike: Target Airship (Vessel) Whydah 2070

Target:

Public unveiling of newest iteration of Bosch airship—Whydah 2070. Known for speed and altitude achievements.

Objective:

Execute internal explosive detonation timed for launch prep cycle. Outcome to simulate containment failure of hydrogen fuel sources. Narrative goal is to redirect blame toward Force incompetence and/or Circle sabotage.

Primary Goal:

Terminate Master Commander Wallace. Guaranteed presence for ceremonial launch.

Collateral Strategy:

Terminate other high-ranking members of Bosch Pirate Force and civilian guests. Include presence of low-level Chosen envoys aboard airship as apparent victims. Sacrifice acceptable. Enables plausible deniability and positions the Chosen as aggrieved peace-seekers. Funeral ceremonies and outrage campaigns already in early planning to leverage martyr optics.

Subject Involvement: Sinclair (Edmund):

Subject to be informed only of the intent to disrupt Glitter shipment logistics. No intelligence provided regarding airship occupancy, presence of leadership, or tactical payload. Subject remains under moral misdirection parameters and will be monitored for post-event exploitable distress.

Subject Involvement: Moore (Curtis):

Subject will be directed to install the secondary ignition array under the pretense of a non-lethal "signal disruption" charge. He will receive no disclosure regarding blast radius, dual-trigger sequence, or presence of Chosen envoys on board. Subject's recent elevation to Chosen rank ensures maximal zeal and minimal scrutiny; post-detonation, surviving records will attribute device design and placement solely to him, providing a convenient narrative scapegoat if operational deniability is required. Continuous surveillance will capture final communications for martyr-propagation or disavowal, per Contingency File 47-Delta.

Operational Notes:

Ensure explosive load mimics industrial system malfunction to avoid early attribution. Activate rumor-seeding protocols (see

Strategy D5: WhisperNet) within twelve hours post-detonation. Stage Four (Compassion Doctrine) to be implemented forty-eight hours after events of Stage Three. With FA military at the disposal of the Chosen, invasion and occupation of Bosch to prevent further chaos will be implemented across all civic and defense structures. Glitter resources, Bosch national finances, and human capital will then be under Chosen control.

Prepared in Service of the Divine Order,
Archminister, Central Continent Division,
Chosen of New Earth

GREY

It's the first Saturday of April. Edmund, Sy, and Lorraine are over, and the four of us are discussing the books Lorraine assigned us and figuring out what to include in a children's game.

"Definitely what a drug is should be included," Sy says. "I think that's basic. Then we can jump to medic-prescribed versus recreational drugs."

Edmund nods. "Agreed. If the idea is to educate early, we start with the simplest concept and build."

Sy looks briefly surprised to be agreed with, then pleased. I glance away, keeping my face neutral, but inside I'm doing a happy dance. Over the past month and a half, I've watched the two of them move from tolerance to almost-friendship. Sy hasn't called him Ed-Dumb in weeks.

I guess I'm on the same arc with Lorraine. At first, I thought she was a cardboard placeholder—a box Sy checked to say he had a girlfriend. That might've been my ego talking; I didn't want to share him. I'd had Sy to myself for two and a half years, and it was hard to let that go. But Lorraine's sharp. She challenges people to back up their opinions with data, and I respect that.

When I told Mama about her, she said, "Oh, a details person. Bosch Intelligence likes to get their hooks into them."

The conversation shifts to coding, and I immediately take a back seat. I'm pretty good with spoken languages—Bosch, FA, Edoan, plus some Mandarin and Spanish—but I basically peaked in TinkerCode back in primary.

"My friend Flossie was amazing at this stuff. But Mama dumped her in the North Country, so I guess she's out," I huff, mock-annoyed.

From the kitchen, Mama calls, "I didn't dump her. She asked to stay. But if you keep mouthing off, I can arrange for you to join her."

I stick my tongue out at her. She sticks hers out back. We both laugh.

Sy asks, "Isn't there someone in the Circle who does coding? Maybe they could help?"

Edmund and I both go quiet. I say, "After the whole graffiti thing, I'm not involved with the Circle anymore."

Sy's eyebrows lift. "Oh. I didn't realize." The moment lands harder than I expect. We haven't really talked lately. I guess that happens—time, boyfriends, girlfriends. Things shift. He fills the pause. "I'll ask Mason. He's into gaming. I bet he can code it or knows someone who can."

"That should work," Lorraine says. Then she turns to me. "So what are your birthday plans, Grey? Thursday, right?"

Edmund and I glance at each other, and I look away as my face warms. I catch Sy glancing between us, but he doesn't say anything.

"Yep, Thursday," I say. "Dawn breakfast, of course. Then family stuff after school—my dad's coming in—and then I'll meet up at Barton's with friends. You and Sy are obviously invited. Then…I guess I'll see where the night leads until the dawn toast."

It's tradition in Bosch to stay up from dawn to dawn on your seventeenth birthday. Most people sneak a nap, but the champagne at dawn is sacred.

Mama comes in and sets down a tray of crackers and cheese. "Well, I'll be getting real sleep while you're out carousing. I've got a thing Friday, and Phil and Lyss are coming in. Save me a glass of champagne?"

She ruffles my hair, and for a second, I'm a little kid again.

I think she knows what I'm planning. She hasn't pried, just shifted her tone in recent conversations—softer, more deliberate. She's letting me have this on my own.

I smile up at her. "I will."

My eyes find Edmund. His smile is warm, and something inside me stirs at the sight of it. I take a breath and rejoin the conversation, my thoughts a jumble of hope, desire, and apprehension.

♡

EDMUND

The following Monday night, Edmund was preparing for his call with Mr. Bolt when there was a knock on his door. Frustrated by the delay, he opened it. "Curtis? What do you want? I'm sort of busy right now."

"The archminister messaged me a few minutes ago. He asked me to come so he could speak to us both," Curtis said, stepping into the room without waiting for an invitation.

Edmund drew a slow breath. He was so ready to disentangle himself from Bolt and the Bluies. *Just a few more days.* "Okay, fine. I'd say come in, but you already are. Let's get this comm going."

The two young men sat down in front of the Visicomm, and Edmund placed the comm.

Mr. Bolt appeared, his face taut. "Good evening, gentlemen. I assume you've heard the news."

"No, sir," Edmund answered at the same time Curtis said, "Yessir."

Edmund looked at the blond boy, then back at Bolt. "What news?"

"The election results for the FA are not what we hoped," Bolt said. "Our presidential candidate was defeated and will be relegated to the vice presidency. There will be an internal and external review to determine why this happened—and to bring those responsible for this distressing outcome to account."

Edmund frowned. "Those responsible? Aren't the voters responsible, sir?"

Bolt narrowed his eyes. "Mr. Sinclair, surely you don't think we would leave something as important as an election up to the voters."

Edmund blinked. "Are you saying the Chosen fixed the election?"

"I'm saying the Chosen were guided by the Lord to ensure the people of the FA would be led by a moral president, not the vile man the vote tallies suggest was successful." The words were spat from Bolt's mouth.

Something inside Edmund cracked a little. He shouldn't be provoking Bolt, but the arrogance, the hypocrisy—he couldn't hold it in. "You mean, the man who won? What's wrong with him, exactly—other than him not being your Chosen candidate?"

Curtis jumped in, glaring, "He has another man as his spouse."

A laugh escaped Edmund before he could stop it. "So does my cousin. And if I'm not mistaken, your uncle."

Curtis stared, mouth open. "We do not speak to him. He is disgusting."

"Seriously? You actually feel that way?" Edmund asked. "Because it's pretty common here in Bosch—and in Truevale, from what I saw. Isn't your uncle a surgeon? That seems a long way from disgusting."

Bolt rapped his knuckles on the table, pulling their attention. "You two are welcome to continue this discussion later. For now, I must present Stage Three of the anti-Glitter disruption."

Edmund's eyes narrowed. "You've always said these conversations were to remain between us. Why is Curtis here for this?"

"You've been loyal, Mr. Sinclair. But Curtis is one of the Chosen and will play a pivotal role in this stage. I invited him to be present."

Curtis looked positively beatific. Edmund could barely keep from rolling his eyes. "Fine."

Bolt launched into the plan. "On Friday, there will be an explosion on the Bosch Pirate Force base that will destroy one of the newest airships, along with its cargo of Glitter. Curtis has been trained to set the charge. Edmund, you will assign Circle members—those from the graffiti operation—to escort him. It is essential that the blast occur between 0810 and 0820 hours."

Edmund's stomach turned. "An explosion? No, sir. We agreed to peaceful protest."

"If you want to evoke change..." Bolt's eyebrow flicked up. "...you must be heard." Then he smiled. "But not to worry. The ship is stationed well away from Force activity. Its placement meets all requirements."

"So just the vessel and the Glitter will blow? No one will be hurt?" Edmund asked, already fearing the answer.

"No one will be hurt. Unless they're in the airship. And why would they be?" Bolt gave his grandfatherly smile.

Edmund wasn't convinced. "If—for some reason—someone is on board, can the explosion be aborted?"

"You are right to value human life, Edmund. Of course. Both you and Curtis will be provided with remotes to abort the detonation."

Edmund exhaled and sat back. "Very well. I'll talk to Rostum and Abeni. But if anything goes wrong..." He left the sentence hanging.

CHAPTER 23
I LEARNED THE TRUTH AT SEVENTEEN

GREY

I'm seventeen! Mama wakes me at five bells, settling herself next to me in my bed and wrapping me in her arms as she tells me the familiar story of my birth.

"There was still snow in the shaded patches of the woods around the cabin where your papa and I lived. Mama M and Papa T had been there for a couple weeks, and on April 5th I had gone to bed, huge and uncomfortable. I got up to pee in the middle of the night and felt crampy, and when I wiped, there was a little blood. So I went to ask Mama M if it was okay, and she smiled and cupped her hand on my cheek and said, 'You'll meet this baby soon.' Then she asked if you were wiggling, and I said yes, so she told me, 'Go back to bed and try to sleep until you can't.'"

"What does it feel like when a baby moves inside you?" I ask.

She thinks for a moment, then says, "Early on it's like someone is just brushing against you but from the inside. But by the time you are ready to birth, it is strong and hard, like when Rini was a baby and would kick until her blankets were off."

My eyes get big, remembering holding my sister as an infant. "Doesn't that hurt?"

She shrugs. "Sort of, up in the ribs, but mostly it is lovely because it tells a mama her baby is safe."

I squeeze her hand because I know she still grieves for my littlest brother. She squeezes back. "Go on," I prompt.

"Well, I slept fitfully for a few hours, rousing up a bit when the tightenings would happen and then falling back to sleep until I needed to pee again. That's when I woke your papa. He was all sorts of nervous. I sent him to toast me a piece of bread and felt the tightenings coming stronger. I was on my knees leaning on the bed, moaning with one, when he came in with the toast and coffee." She giggled. "He dropped the coffee cup."

I laugh as I do every year. "Papa is so silly."

"He was worried. He had never seen a woman bringing forth before. Mama M came in and told him not to worry about the coffee and showed him how to press on my back during tightenings. She listened to your heartbeat with her special stethoscope and then went and made food for the day.

"I walked around the house in my night shift. That made your Papa T very uncomfortable, something my brain said was funny, but I was so focused on you and what my body was doing, I couldn't address it until later when I teased him about it. Your Papa sent for Aiko from the temple because he knew I wanted her there, and she and Papa T sat talking and drinking Warner Wine. Isn't that funny?"

I giggle and snuggle closer, imagining her, hair wild and big-bellied, pacing the cabin in her night shift.

"Then around noon, the tightenings shifted and began to press you down. Mama M laid a birthing blanket in front of the fireplace, and I began to push you out. It didn't take long since you were the second baby I had birthed, but I still remember your papa's face as he held his hands out to receive you, Mama M's hands under his. He cried with joy when you arrived, a full head of hair and howling because you wanted to tell the world your story. I cried as well and was so filled with love, I felt there was no possible way I could love anything any more than I loved you at that moment. But of course, I was wrong because I loved you more each day and still do." She kisses my forehead. "How did seventeen years slip by so quickly?"

I sigh. "When I am truly, fully grown and living in my own house, will you come over on my birthday before dawn to tell me this story?"

She laughs. "Only if you want me to."

"Oh, I do," I say with conviction.

She pushes herself onto her elbow and looks at me. "Seventeen. An official adult. I am so pleased to know the young woman you have become. And as you celebrate today, in all the ways you have planned, give yourself grace. Being grown up is wonderful, but it is also challenging. Just know your papa and I and Matty and your brothers and sister and Mama M and all those uncles and aunts will always be here for you, no matter what."

"No matter what," I sigh.

"Oh, I almost forgot to ask you—Phil and Lyss are coming in tonight because they're attending the official maiden flight of those damn, expensive new vessels Matty loves so much tomorrow morning..." Mama begins.

"Are they both glad her term is about to be finally over?" I interrupt. Alyssa Russell has been FA president for not just her six-year term but for an extra six months as well because of the decision to shift elections from fall to spring.

"I imagine they are ready for some peace and quiet. But anyway, can we pop over to Barton's later so they can wish you happy birthday?"

I grin. "That'd be nice, unless they have to bring all their security."

"They don't need security—they've got me." Mama laughs. *She's half-joking, but I know she's more than capable of defending them.* "But I will make sure they keep it minimal. No armed guards at your party."

"Thank you, Mama. You are the best mama I know."

She kisses my nose and then climbs out of bed. "You stay cozy until just before dawn. Matty and I will make breakfast."

Then she slips out of my room, and I hear the voices in the kitchen and sigh. It's wonderful to be grown up and to think about what's to come. But in this moment, wrapped in memory and clattering pans, I don't want to be anywhere else. Not yet.

SY

"What did you get her?" Lorraine asked, her voice incredulous.

Sy held up each item as he repeated, "Cherry woodblock for carving, the newest Robbie Glass novel—*The Fire Beneath the Sea*—sharp cheddar from District Six, and a scarf that my mom picked out."

He watched as his girlfriend grinned and asked, "And what did you get her last year?"

"Lorraine Roberts, what are you trying to say?" Sy tried to keep a straight face, but he couldn't help laughing at her expression.

"Answer the question, Mercer."

He sighed. "Basswood for carving, *The Deepest Song* by Hugo Reyes, and some brie, and my mom picked out a sweater." Sy winced. He could hear it now. He looked at Lorraine. "Shut up."

She laughed. "Okay, I'll give her the best gift today. You don't have any big classes or tests today, right?"

"No, it's a pretty easy schedule." He narrowed his eyes. "Why?"

"Great, then c'mon." She slipped her hand into his and gave it a tug.

He grabbed the gift bag and let her lead him across the quad, heart thumping. He had no idea what she was doing, but he trusted her.

They crossed to where several other already-seventeen final-years were laughing and telling Grey stories about their birthday rites of passage. The conversation paused as Sy and Lorraine approached.

Grey looked up with a smile. "Hi, Sy. Lorraine…"

"So Sy has his bag of gifts for you, but I wanted to give you my gift first," Lorraine began.

"Lorraine, you don't need to get me anything," Grey objected.

"Oh, hush. You'll love this." She pulled Sy in front of her and gave him a little push toward Grey. "You get Sy for the day—all day. Just you two. You can hang out and talk and have friend time without sharing him with me."

Sy saw the stunned look on Grey's face and turned to Lorraine. She winked up at him like she'd just checkmated the entire emotional board.

He leaned in and whispered, "You are not only the smartest person I know but also the nicest." Then he kissed the side of her head, careful to glance around for teachers first.

She gave his arm a quick squeeze. "He can also carry your stuff to all your classes."

Grey laughed. "What a great gift! Lorraine, you are a genius!" Then she handed her bag to Sy. "Here, hold this."

"Hey, now. Thralldom is illegal in Bosch," Sy protested, lifting the bag with a grin.

Lorraine ignored him. "He's all yours, Grey. I'll collect him this evening at Barton's." She flashed the smile she wore when she wanted to be kissed, turned, and walked off.

Sy watched her go, appreciating the way she moved—then blinked back to Grey as her voice snapped him out of it.

"Hey. Eyes over here, Mercer. You're my gift for the next few hours."

He smiled. Just her and him. Like before. "Fine," he said. "Just you and me, like old times." It felt good—and maybe a little bit dangerous.

♡

GREY

Sy boosts me up onto the almost-meter-high pole vault mat that recently appeared on the sports pitch, a sure sign that spring is truly here. He clambers up and flops next to me. The sky is so blue with just a few wispy clouds, and the sun is very warm here, where the breeze can't get to us.

"It was very cool of Ms. Rajan to tell us to 'go study' somewhere," Sy comments.

I nod. "I'm getting such special treatment today. I wish I could turn seventeen every day."

Sy laughs. "Yeah, the teachers treated me well on my birthday too, but January isn't exactly the time to lie around outside."

I cringe. "Hey, I'm sorry I missed your birthday. I still owe you a dawn champagne." Sy turned seventeen while we were in the middle of our longest fight.

"I'm just glad we aren't fighting anymore. We can toast both our adulthoods tomorrow morning," he replies.

Now I chuckle. "You know, I can barely remember what we were arguing about."

Sy goes quiet for a few moments, so I just lie still and look up at the sky, watching a few birds up high.

"So, I need to tell you something." I can hear the hesitation in his voice.

I glance over but he's looking straight ahead into the sky. I shift my head back to do the same. "Go for it," I say. "You know, you can tell me anything."

Sy takes a long inhale. "I love Lorraine. I want to say that up front."

I nod and wonder where this is going. "Okay…"

"But before Lorraine…" Sy pauses for so long I'm about to prompt him. But then he adds, "I was in love with you, pretty much from the first week I knew you."

I freeze. I should be stunned. But somewhere deep down— past the jokes, past all the times he showed up for me—something says, *You've always known.* I open my mouth to respond, and the only thing that comes out is "Oh."

Now Sy starts to talk a little faster. "I mean, at first, I just figured it was a crush because you were so nice to me. Then, as we got to know each other, I thought it would pass, but it didn't. I just loved you. A little more every day, but I also knew neither of us wanted to deal with all the dumb dating stuff, so I kept it to myself." He gives a self-effacing snort. "I also figured, who was I kidding? A girl like you would never go for a guy like me…"

Now I am up on my elbow, protesting. "Silas Mercer, don't say something like that. You are amazing. You are smart and handsome and kind and sweet, and any girl would be lucky for you to give her the time of day."

He looks at me, and his voice sounds sad when he tells me, "I'm no Edmund Sinclair."

I fall back down on my back, remembering the rally, Sy on the patio, me going off with Edmund that first poster night. "Oh, Sy… that must have hurt you." I feel tears well and run down my temples as I realize how cruel I have been to someone I claimed was my best friend. "*I* must have hurt you."

"Well, you didn't know," he says reasonably.

The damn voice inside pushes at me. *He's being honest with you. Shouldn't you be honest as well?* In a small voice I reply, "I think maybe I did know, but I took it for granted because I knew you'd always be there for me."

Another extended silence, then, "Well, that's kinda shitty." But he doesn't sound angry, just a little tired.

"I can't disagree." I close my eyes and shake my head. "So does Lorraine know?"

"We've talked about it." Now he pushes up on his elbow and looks at me. "The thing is I should be thanking you for acting like you did. I was so jealous and angry about Edmund, and even though I hadn't said anything straight out, Leia and Mason sort of knew what was going on, which is why Leia arranged the date with Lorraine." He grins. "I would have never really gotten to know Lorraine and gotten to love her if you hadn't been so gaga over Ed-Dumb." He says the old epithet in a goofy voice and winks at me.

I push up on my elbow as well, so we are face to face. "So… you're happy? You really love her?"

"I really do," he says in earnest. "And I'm no longer pining away for you. You are my best friend. That's a lot." Then he tips his head. "And what about you? Are you happy? You really love Edmund?"

I nod. "I really do…. In fact, we have sort of a special night planned tonight." I feel the blush come into my face.

"Wow, that's a big step."

"I know. I'm nervous. Have you and Lorraine…?"

"Not yet."

We both lie back down, lost in our own thoughts as the breeze pushes a couple of clouds across the sky. Our hands are right next to each other, and without either of us saying a word, we slip them together.

I give a squeeze. "I'm glad to have my best friend back."

He squeezes in return. "We'll always be there for each other."

We will always be there for each other. That's not something I'll ever take for granted again.

EDMUND

There was too much going on. Edmund could barely keep up in his classes; his mind ricocheted between the looming Stage Three explosion and the night he had planned with Grey.

He had to slip out of Barton's after dinner during Grey's celebration to make sure Abeni got Curtis onto the base and herself safely back out. Curtis seemed unconcerned about the danger associated with his task, and it unnerved Edmund.

"Listen, you need to be careful and be willing to pull the plug if it looks like anyone will get hurt," Edmund cautioned his friend.

Curtis simply smiled. "All will be well. I put my trust in the Lord. My task comes from the patrician of Dominion through whom our Lord speaks to us."

Abeni and Edmund looked at each other, concerned, but said nothing more.

They reached the fence line where Grey had directed the last incursion. "Do you have what you need? Where's your gear?" Edmund asked, seeing that Curtis carried nothing with him.

"I need nothing. There is a man I will meet near the vessel that will provide the essentials," Curtis responded and then slipped under the fence. Abeni would escort him to the hangar and then return.

Edmund waited in the tree line back from the fence, tapping his foot and biting at a fingernail. *A man inside? Then why was Curtis needed?* His nerves were taut to the point of breaking. He would relax a bit once Abeni returned safely. Curtis would hole up until after the explosion, slipping out during the aftermath created by all the confusion.

Abeni returned and slid under the fence, kicking at the dirt and dried leaves to conceal the entryway. "Let's go," she hissed, her face grim.

"Everything went okay?" Edmund asked once they were back in his vehicle.

Abeni shrugged. "I got him to the hangar and showed him where to hole up. But he was still acting weird. I don't know if he actually knows what he's doing."

Edmund blew out a breath. "I don't like this. I'll be just as happy if we have to abort and replan something else in the fall."

Once he dropped Abeni at her dorm, he went to his room to contact Mr. Bolt. A package was at the door. He opened it—the remote. He wondered what would happen if he pushed the single red button immediately. He slipped it into his jacket pocket.

"I received the package and Curtis is in place," he said shortly.

"Excellent. Tomorrow will be glorious," Mr. Bolt practically crowed.

"Mr. Bolt, do you really think it's wise to have a college student setting charges? Curtis is studying music, not explosives engineering."

Mr. Bolt waved off the concern. "Edmund, my boy, I commend your concern for your friend, but he's been thoroughly trained by our experts. He'll set a moderate charge triggered remotely—nothing dangerous for him. That charge will ignite the hydrogen engines, creating a major explosion. And sending a major message."

"I don't like this," Edmund decided, jaw tight. "It feels too dangerous.

Bolt peered through the screen. "It's not uncommon for amateurs to develop cold feet as an operation escalates. But we are in this together. The Circle wants Bosch out of the Glitter trade, and the steps the Chosen are recommending will ensure that. Only another day or so, Edmund. The payoff will be tremendous."

Edmund exhaled slowly. "And no one will be hurt?"

"Our Lord protects the innocent and rewards the daring." Bolt sounded like he was preaching a sermon. Then his tone shifted. "I have another comm. We'll speak after the event." The screen went black.

"Damn you, Bolt. Does that mean yes or no?" Edmund shouted, kicking over a pile of books beside his desk. All he could picture was Grey, smiling at him tonight—and what he might have to tell her tomorrow.

GREY

"Another glass of wine here?" the server asks.

I shake my head. "Not yet. I have to stay up until dawn."

She laughs. "Oh, you're the birthday girl, then? Well, welcome to adulthood."

"Thanks." I grin, watching her take orders from the dozen or so friends around the table.

Dinner was delicious, but I do feel a little tipsy from the two glasses of wine I had with it. Edmund had to leave for a little while on Circle business, so we are waiting for his return to start on the cake.

A few minutes after he left, Mama and Matt stopped by with Phil and Lyss to wish me happy birthday. Mama said, "Well, you don't need us around. Be safe. We'll have some bubbly tomorrow evening after you nap." Then she gave me a kiss on the cheek, murmured one of her usual partings, "Remember the love," and they left. It was nice because I hadn't seen Mama or Matt since breakfast because Papa and his wife were in town, and my brothers, Rini, and I went to their Bosch house after school.

I head to the washroom to relieve myself, and when I return, I pause at a distance to look at all the laughing faces around the table telling stories and making jokes. There's a pang as I realize how much is about to change with graduation. It's exciting but bittersweet. I look at Sy and Lorraine in particular and watch as Sy tells some story, his face going through all the expressions and his hands accenting his tale. He has really grown this year, and I think a lot of it has to do with Lorraine. I am happy that we talked about our feelings today. I will always treasure him as my best friend.

I go to sit down and hear from Sy, "The luminary's back," and Edmund is suddenly right beside me, wrapping his arm about my shoulders and kissing my hair.

"We can have cake now!" I exclaim as I hug him, and a cheer goes up from around the table.

Edmund comments, "You waited for me?" His eyes hold a worried look, but he smiles warmly at me.

"Of course we did," I reply.

"She wanted to have it without you, but I insisted we wait," Sy teases with a wink.

The easy atmosphere seems to relax Edmund, and he laughs. "Good to know someone has my back here."

The cake is delicious—moist and chocolatey. I blow out all my candles in one breath, provoking applause from everyone. After we have finished, people slowly start to head home, first Gemma and Sadie, followed by Anya and Paolo; Jonah and his new girl, Beth; and Paige, who has been solo for a bit. Leia and Mason are next, saying they have to study, but Mason waggles his eyebrows in a way that makes Leia giggle and slap his arm, and I doubt much studying will happen. Once they are out the door, I see Lorraine nudge Sy.

He stretches and leans back in his seat with a smile. "Well, why don't we get a deck of cards and start an all-night pirates poker game?"

I give him a reproving look while Lorraine squeaks, "Sy-y."

"What? Aren't we all hanging out together until dawn?" He laughs.

"No, we are not. Go home, Silas. Or go somewhere and kiss Lorraine," I state firmly, the last part nudging a giggle from Lorraine.

Now Edmund finally chimes in, "Because that's what we are going to do."

Sy is up and getting his and Lorraine's jackets. "No way, Luminary. You aren't going to be kissing my Lorraine."

This makes us all laugh. We say goodbye, and first Lorraine gives me a hug, then Sy does, whispering, "I'll always be there for you, friend."

"And me for you," I whisper back, and then they are gone, and Edmund and I are alone.

Standing there, in the quiet left by everyone's departure, wave after wave of nervousness sweeps over me. I want this—I really do. But that doesn't mean I'm not scared. "So, I guess we should go…" I pause, not daring to look at him. "…to your dorm room?" I hadn't even thought about where this was going to happen.

"Oh, no," he says with an air of mystery. "We're going to take a little drive." He stands up, and we gather my things into various bags. He offers me his arm, and I take it as the server and the bartender call out, "Happy birthday!" on our way out.

We drive for about half a bell, chatting about my day. My stomach still flip-flops, but the conversation is calming. Edmund turns off the main road and down a small drive until we come to a tiny cottage tucked next to a stream. "My aunt owns this and lets it out for visitors. It's really quite charming," Edmund remarks.

"It looks like something out of a fairy tale," I breathe. "Are you sure there aren't magical creatures inside?"

He touches my cheek softly. "There will be, once you step over the threshold."

My nervousness begins to melt away, anticipation rushing in. We walk to the door, and he opens it with a flourish. I gasp—fairy lights are strung throughout the cottage, and a bottle of champagne chills on the table next to out-of-season berries. In the far corner is a big bed covered with colorful quilts and squishy pillows. Two robes lay across the foot of it.

"Oh, Edmund, you did all this for me?"

"You deserve all this—and more. I love you, Grey Shima."

"I love you, Edmund Sinclair. And I can't wait to show you just how much." I tip my head up, and he kisses me so very softly.

"Let's get rid of these coats," he murmurs, taking off his, then slipping mine off me and hanging both carefully on a hook.

He returns with a gold-foil square box and holds it out like a shy schoolboy. "This is for you. Happy seventeenth, my beautiful Grey."

My cheeks feel almost sore, I am smiling so much. I take the box and remove the black and red ribbon. I lift the golden top and gasp. It's an armband—thin, gold filigree in a double loop. Three charms hang from it. As I inspect the first one, he narrates.

"That's you, the sun. Because you burn so brightly, Grey, and you have it in you to power the world."

Then, I lift the second.

"That one is me. I'm the moon. I think I am more lunar-ary than luminary. I may provide light in the darkness, but it's the light reflected from you."

And finally, I see…

"It's a dragon. Because there will always be reasons we need to apologize, and I've been taught that dragons are a big part of that."

My heart is so large right now, it chokes my voice. "Oh, Edmund," I croak like the bullfrogs in May.

I take the armband from the box and gaze at it again, then hold it out. "Put it on my arm, please."

He grins and starts to roll up my sleeve, but I pull my arm back. "Not that way." I hold my arms out, offering myself to him.

His eyes are connected to mine and seem to gaze into my soul. "Are you sure?"

I nod. "I'm sure."

His hands fumble with the buttons of my blouse for just a moment, then undo them smoothly. I deliberately wore nothing underneath, and the heat of his hands brushing my bare breasts sends shocks of need through me. He pauses, rolling a nipple between his fingers, and I gasp. Since our restart, we've only kissed—it's been so long since he's touched me like this.

Then he takes my left arm and slips the gold armband on, pushing it up past my elbow to circle my upper arm. The metal is cool and smooth, yet it feels like where his fingers pass is on fire.

He pulls off his shirt, tossing it onto the sofa *and* exposing his strong torso. I reach up, running my hand from his shoulder to his belly button, then grasp the waistband of his pants and pull him to me, kissing him.

I want more. I wrap my arms around his neck, sighing as I pull him close. His body is hard and warm, even between his legs, and

I trace my hands over his chest, then down to the swelling beneath his pants. I reach for it, instinctively stroking.

"Oh, Grey. I want you so much," he groans.

I kiss his neck and cheek, whispering, "I want you. I'm yours." A nervous laugh slips out. "But I don't really know what to do. Will you show me?"

"With pleasure." He locks his eyes on mine as he slides my shirt off my shoulders and drops to his knees. Slowly, he slips off my leggings, taking my undergarment with them. I stand naked in front of him.

"Sweet New Earth," he breathes, reverent. "You're beautiful." He runs his hands along my sides, then cups my bottom, kissing my belly. His mouth trails lower until it meets the soft thatch of hair between my legs. He rests his cheek there, inhaling, then rises. "Let me look at you," he says—part request, part command.

I lift my arms and do a little spin. He chuckles, a sound full of wonder. "You are absolutely magnificent."

Then his trousers are on the floor, and the swelling I'd felt pressed against me springs free. My eyes widen, and I smile. Nervousness and anticipation surge inside me, but there's more now—a deep, aching want that escapes me in a small moan.

His eyes meet mine, dancing. He steps forward and scoops me into his arms, kissing me deeply. The cottage is truly tiny—he carries me to the bed in three steps.

My life feels like it's about to begin.

CHAPTER 24
EVERYTHING HAS CHANGED

EDMUND

It was the birdsong outside the window that stirred his consciousness. Edmund was on his back, one foot outside the pile of blankets and quilts. For a split-second, he wondered about the unfamiliar pressure on his shoulder. Then his brain registered: Grey. His hand came up and touched her hair. She was tucked under his arm, her arm draped across his chest, legs tangled with his, taking the secret nap all seventeen-year-olds take. He slow-blinked his eyes open, and as full awareness returned, so did the memories of the night before—and a slow, wide grin spread across his face.

Making love to her had been every bit as extraordinary as he had imagined. And he had imagined it often, almost from the first moment they met.

She'd been curious, open, and a little unsure. She followed his gentle instructions, let him guide her hands, her body. He could still see her eyes—wide and glimmering with apprehension—as he entered her. But he'd made sure she was ready, bringing her to ecstasy twice before seeking his own release. He'd watched the anxiety melt from her features, replaced by something he would never forget: raw, reverent wonder.

Afterward, curled in each other's arms, she had asked about what he liked and didn't.

He'd laughed. "I liked every single thing we did—because I'm with you."

She sat up, gazing down at him. Her hair was tousled, spilling across her bare shoulders. He never wanted to look at anything else again. She bit her lower lip. "Well, I enjoyed it—quite a lot, but…"

"But?" he asked, suddenly worried. Had he messed something up? "Was there a problem?"

"No problem," she assured. "It's just…the first time you do anything, there's always room for improvement. So now I want to practice." Her grin was wicked. "Let's do it again."

For a beat, he was stunned. Then he burst out laughing. "I may need a moment or two."

She laughed with him, then kissed his palm, then his wrist and began trailing kisses up his arm to his shoulder. When she reached his chest, she glanced up at him, eyes dancing. "Up or down? It's quite a decision." Wearing that wicked little grin of hers, she began moving downward.

He sighed at the memory. The second time had been different —hotter, wilder. Grey had gone from cautious to bold, touching him with a growing confidence, whispering, "How's this? What about that?" They had rolled and writhed, their breath and bodies merged, until they came undone together, gripping one another and calling out each other's names.

He checked his timepiece—almost half-past five bells. He exhaled, wishing he could make time stop for just a while, then brushed her hair from her face and lifted her chin to place a soft kiss on her lips. "Grey, wake up. We need to get to the hill for your dawn champagne toast."

She made a low, contented sound, not opening her eyes. "Mmmm… Do we have to? I'm so happy right here."

"I could go tell your friends I wore you out making love to you." He grinned. "Think they'd understand?"

Her eyes popped open. "Oh, Leia would dine out on that for months. So no, I'm getting up."

She rolled over and stretched, arms reaching long as her back arched. The covers slipped off. Edmund took a beat to admire her. The soft light from the fairy lights across her skin, the bare curve of her spine—it was all he could do to remember that dawn was less than a half-bell away.

Later, he promised himself.

But the word jabbed at him. Because *later*, after the champagne and smiles, would come the explosion. Unless... He remembered the remote in his jacket pocket.

♡

GREY

We scramble up the hill and spread a blanket under the blossoming cherry tree. I love this place. The first time I was ever here was when I was Rini's age and Mama brought me. It reminds me a little of the mountain I was born on in Edo. When it came time to decide where to have my dawn toast, there was no question—here.

I stand on a rock and look in every direction through the fading pre-dawn gray. If I squint, I can see the silver line of the Tamrood River off to the south. Neighborhood homes' roofs cluster below the hill, and I can just make out the base hangar where a fresh coat of paint has erased the graffiti that once marked it. Everything looks so peaceful.

I'd wondered whether I'd feel different after last night. I do. The world's sharp edges feel...softened.

Edmund climbs up behind me and wraps his arms around me. His warmth shields me from the morning chill. "What are you thinking about?"

"How the world looks more peaceful and charming after sleeping in your arms." I lace my fingers with his. "Is it possible nothing bad will ever happen again, now that we're together?"

He doesn't answer.

I twist to look up at him—his eyes are closed, his face drawn tight. Before I can say anything, voices rise from the path laughing, calling.

"Your friends are here," he says, hopping down. As he steps away, I notice him slip a hand into his jacket pocket.

A beat lingers in my chest. I'll ask him about it later. Right now, I go to greet my friends—armed with breakfast, blankets, and extra bottles of bubbly to toast a new day—as the sky turns pink.

CURTIS

From his hiding place inside the small cargo hold, Curtis checked his timepiece: 0758. His lips moved in silent prayer. The vessel shuddered—just as the archminister said it would —signaling the arrival of those he was to escort into the afterlife.

He listened.

First, a man's voice: "Look at this airship, Lyss."

Then a woman's, firm and commanding. The master commander: "Vessel, Phil. You know the nomenclature."

"Okay, fine, vessel. Either way, it's impressive."

Another woman asked, "And you say it can fly above twenty thousand kilometers?"

The master commander again: "It can. And it cruises around 2,500 kilometers per bell, which means global circumnavigation in five."

A low whistle. "Impressive."

Then: "Deacon Miller, Elder Turner, you can sit there." The

master commander addressed the two Chosen envoys the archminister had informed him would be present.

Another vibration—doors sealing.

"We're all set, Colonel. Take off when ready."

The vessel engines roared to life. Curtis checked the time again: 0806. Four minutes to glory. He could almost feel the fire, the holy cleansing to come. He intensified his prayers, picturing paradise, the accolades, the moment when God Himself would lift his spirit skyward.

Then—an interruption.

"Deacon, is that your robe?"

Curtis' eyes flew open. His robe. He'd meant to slip it on before the hold sealed. The archminister had forbidden it.

"Leave it off," the explosives man had said. "This can't trace back to the Chosen. The Lord's plan."

But Curtis had sneered inwardly. That man was just a janitor—lowest caste. Barely above thralls. He, Curtis, was a Chosen among Chosen. His name would be spoken with reverence. His robe would rise with him to Heaven.

"No, Master Commander. I wear mine," came a new voice—one of the envoys.

A beat.

"Matty—cut the engines! Deploy the escapeway!" the MC barked.

"On it."

Her voice was sharper now: "Not you two. Everyone else first. You'll go just before me."

0811. Curtis kicked open the cargo door. "The Earth Remade, the Path Revealed!" he cried, detonator in hand.

"Curtis? Curtis Moore? Stop. Don't do this."

He paused as his earthly name was called.

The master commander. She was walking toward him, calm, composed. The envoys behind her were panicked, scrambling, blocked by a tall, dark-skinned man at the escape window.

"The Chosen walk it true," Curtis intoned, raising the device.

"Listen to me," she said gently. "You don't have to do this. You still have a life ahead of you. Just hand me the detonator."

The tall man barked, "Kat—we need you off. Now."

She waved him off. "One moment." Her voice softened. "We can make this right."

Curtis hesitated. Her tone—it reminded him at first of his mother singing to him back when he was still a boy at first.

But then she ended with "right."

And he remembered: He was right. The Chosen were right. She must be obliterated. Bosch must burn to be cleansed.

"The Flame will claim me," he cried, eyes shining. "And I shall rise in His glory!"

The last thing he saw was the tall man lunging toward the master commander—then light. Then nothing.

♡

EDMUND

Pop! One of Grey's friends had opened yet another bottle of champagne. Edmund stood on the rock overlooking the base. He had just had one of the best nights of his life, but now the explosion loomed, and his stomach knotted. He checked his timepiece: 0748.

He, Grey, and the others had been up here for almost two hours, eating bagels with creamed cheese, sipping bubbly, chatting. But at 0630, he'd grown restless. The whole plan gnawed at him. How could Curtis guarantee no one else would be nearby? Why the hell had he agreed to this? *Maybe it wouldn't have mattered whether you did or not. Bolt seemed determined to get his way.* His fingers curled around the remote in his pocket. *Lifeline,* he thought.

At 0700, he stood and faked a stretch. Glancing down at the base, he spotted a large vessel being towed to an open space east of the hangar. That had to be the Glitter vessel. It was well away from other activity. The twist in his gut loosened—just a little—and he settled back to enjoy the morning.

Around a quarter to eight, he heard faint music drifting up the hill. He stood to check again—and his breath caught. Now bleachers had been set up. Dozens of people were seated. He walked over to the rock to get a better look.

Mason joined him. "What are you peering at, Sinclair?"

Edmund pointed. "There's something happening down there."

Mason squinted in that direction. "Oh, yeah. Grey's mom said they were unveiling some new vessel today. She mentioned she had to make a speech."

An unveiling. Okay. Maybe that was what Bolt wanted—an explosion in front of a crowd to humiliate the MC. Warped but not deadly. "So, what, they're going to pull off a giant sheet and say, 'Look, we have a new vessel?'"

Mason shrugged. "I dunno. Maybe." He wandered back to the breakfast spread.

Edmund pulled out the remote. *Don't push it,* part of him whispered. *Bolt's steered you right so far. He promised this would end Glitter.* He slipped the device back into his pocket. It felt like it weighed a hundred kilos.

But…people were around that vessel. Someone could get hurt. He pulled the remote out again, stared at it for what felt like an entire season. *Decide, Sinclair. Do the right thing.* He pressed the button.

Nothing happened.

Of course nothing happened. That was the point. He exhaled shakily, checked his timepiece, and felt his body begin to relax.

He returned to the group and bent to kiss Grey.

"What were you doing?" she asked, flashing that glowing smile.

Edmund shook his head. "Nothing much. Just watching something going on near the hangar."

"Oh, yeah—Mama said she and Matt were taking Phil and Lyss up in the new vessel this morning. Some kind of ceremony."

He froze. "Wait. What?" He shoved his hand into his pocket and pressed the button again—once, twice, three times. Those names tugged at his memory, but he couldn't place them, so he asked, "Who are Phil and Lyss?"

"Lyss—you know, Alyssa Russell? Outgoing president of the FA? And her husband, Phil," Grey answered casually, licking a smear of cream cheese off her finger.

The ground tilted under Edmund. His breath caught. Bolt had lied. Why did that surprise him?

The Chosen were going to blow up the vessel—with the master commander and the FA president aboard. And they were going to blame it on the Circle. A voice down deep whispered, *You aren't somebody. You're nothing but a pawn.*

He pulled out the remote and stared at it. Had it worked? Had he actually stopped anything? Was it even real?

"What's that?" Grey asked.

He looked at her, frozen for a heartbeat. Then: "What time is it?"

She frowned and glanced at her comm. "A little after eight bells. Why?"

"We have to get to the base. They're going to blow it up!"

Grey stared at him. "What are you talking about?"

Edmund was already running. "Bolt planned it. Call the FPs on base! There's a bomb on the vessel!" he shouted over his shoulder.

The picnic exploded into chaos—yelling, crying, everyone in motion.

And Edmund ran.

♡

GREY

One word escapes my lips as the reality crashes down.

"Mama."

Edmund has taken off running. I see Mason and Gemma on their comms, trying to reach the FPs. I want to run. To throw up. A hand closes on my arm—gentle but firm. "C'mon. We'll take the shortcut."

I look up. It's Sy, his face grim with anger. Lorraine stands beside him. Together, they hustle me down the hill and into Sy's father's vehicle. Instead of turning toward the road, Sy drives straight into the woods that border the base.

Lorraine is in the passenger seat, gripping the edges of her chair. Her face—usually a deep brown—is pale. Almost as pale as mine. I must look like a ghost. There's a two-track path here that Sy and I found last year, and he follows it, winding down the slope. In minutes, we reach the chain-link fence surrounding the base.

Sy slows. I'm about to tell him to turn left toward the nearest guard house when the air explodes.

A blast—deafening, bone-rattling—rips through the air.

I scream. Not words. Just pain and fear.

Sirens wail to life.

"Fuck it," Sy mutters, and the vehicle surges forward, crashing through the fence and barreling toward the hangar. Behind us, whistles. Then an armored vehicle tears ahead, skidding to block our path. Sy slams the brakes.

He looks back at me. "Go, Grey. Get to your mom."

An image of my mama, white and still, swims in my mind's eye and paralyzes me. Lorraine reaches back, grabs my arm, and shakes me. Her grip is fierce. "Go!" she yells.

So I open the door, and I run.

♡

GREY

I'm panting as I sprint full-tilt. Troopers rush everywhere. A couple pause when they see me, then recognize my face and let me pass. People are shouting orders, and sirens are blaring all around me. I veer past the hangar—and then stop short, heart seizing.

A hundred meters ahead, a massive, gleaming vessel sits in the field. The back half is mangled—twisted metal, scorched edges, smoke still curling. A gaping wound.

Emergency vehicles screech in. Several troopers are escorting spectators away to the safety of the hangar, and other, armed troopers tighten a perimeter around the wreck.

To my left are the bleachers—mostly empty now. But two people sit, surrounded by guards. I race toward them. Phil is cradling Lyss, who's openly weeping. He looks up.

"What are you doing here, Grey?" Phil asks, voice tight. "It isn't safe."

A guard steps toward me. "Miss, I need to get you to the hangar."

I thrust a finger at him. "Don't you dare. What would you do if it were your mother?"

He takes a step back but keeps his eyes on me.

My attention returns to Phil. "Where is she?"

Lyss rises and grabs my shoulder. "Oh, honey.... She was on board when—"

"No!" I scream. It can't be. I can't lose her. I feel the bottom drop out of my entire world, and I am falling, falling into nothingness. *Get ahold of yourself, Grey Shima. Do what needs to be done.*

I feel my feet on the ground and pivot, bolting toward the vessel, dodging past troopers. Stretchers are being pulled from the wreck. Someone tries to stop me—hand gripping my arm—but I throw an elbow and hear a grunt that allows me to break free and reach the stretchers just as they're loaded into the med vehicle.

"Kid, you can't—" one of the medics begins.

"I'm family. I'm staying." I slam my hand on the stretcher carrying my mother.

The medic shrugs and gets to work, threading a needle into her arm. She's pale—face bloodless. Her left shoulder is impaled by something jagged, blood soaking her shirt. I don't know where to touch, so I grab her leg and lean close.

"I'm here, Mama. I love you."

"Grey?" moans a voice.

I turn—Matt. He's on the other stretcher, prone. His back—burnt, raw, pink, and seared—is like a slab of meat.

"How's your mom?" he asks, voice bubbling through pain.

The medic beside him gives me a quick nod. "Her shoulder's bad. And a concussion. But she'll live. We all will make sure of it."

I nearly collapse with relief. I move to Matt's side. "Did you hear? She's going to be okay."

The medic working on Matt says, "Because of him. He threw himself on her when the blast hit."

"Oh, Matt," I whisper.

He chuckles weakly. "She's the MC, had to keep her safe. Think I'll get a shiny medal?"

"You're incorrigible, Matt Warner," I manage, laughing through tears.

Then another voice—quiet, raspy. Mama. "No medal. You did your duty."

Matt gives a groggy chuckle.

I spin back to Mama. Her lips move. "Curtis?"

A chill runs through me. "Curtis?" I repeat.

She blinks. "Where is he?"

The medics shake their heads.

Gone. My thoughts flash to Edmund, the Circle, that bastard Bolt. Fury ignites in my chest, lighting a bonfire. I bank it—for now. First things first.

"Just rest, Mama," I whisper. "Just rest."

I slip one hand into hers, the other into Matt's, then I bring their hands together as the vehicle races toward the hospital.

CHAPTER 25
WE WEREN'T PERFECT, BUT...

"GREY." SOMEONE SHAKES MY SHOULDER. "GREY, WAKE UP."

I blink open my eyes to see Papa looking down at me, his expression serious. Panic rises in me, and I whip around—Mama is still in her bed, Matt in his. Both are sleeping.

"What?" I snap, now annoyed.

"You've been here for three days straight. You need to go home," Papa says.

My answer is short. "No."

"Sweetheart, they're well cared for. The doctor said your mama might be discharged tomorrow or the day after. Matt has another week of burn treatments, but then he'll be home." His tone shifts toward wheedling.

I repeat, "No."

He sighs. "Okay, I didn't want to pull this card, Grey, but—honestly—you stink."

"Papa!" I exclaim, horrified. "How can you say that?"

"Three days. No shower. Easy."

I groan. "Fine. I'll go home and shower."

"And contact your teachers for homework—"

"Papa-a…" My voice sharpens with warning.

"Grey-ey," he mimics, matching my tone perfectly. "You've worked hard for years. You need to graduate. I will not be the one who tells Kat Wallace her daughter must attend summer school for truancy."

He's not wrong. "I'll contact them," I mutter.

"I'll keep an eye on our patients." He slides into my chair as I rise. I lean down to kiss Mama and Matt, then slip quietly out the door.

Mama told me Curtis had acted out of some twisted Chosen belief. "It wasn't anti-Glitter, baby," she said. "It was some kind of religious zeal." Still, I haven't answered any of the dozens of messages and comms from Edmund. I just…can't.

Once home, I shower. I eat. The house feels hollow—Rini and the boys are at school, and Mama M must have taken Rummy and Jerome to her place. I climb into my bed and fall asleep in seconds.

Sy's ringtone chirps, waking me. I answer groggily, "Hey. What's going on?"

"I stopped by the hospital—your dad said you went home. I grabbed your schoolwork. It's not much; the teachers are super sympathetic."

"Oh." I blink. "Where are you?"

"Outside," he says, and then adds, "Um, so you know. Edmund's here too." There's no emotion in his tone, but I can picture Sy's face, bracing for me to come unglued.

I don't. I sigh. "I guess I have to talk to him eventually."

I head to the washroom, pee, and splash my face with water. I pull on an undershirt and underpants, then a fresh pair of leggings. I start to reach for my tunic, and there on the table in my room is Edmund's gift, shining up from where I'd placed it before I showered. I pause and shut my eyes. I'm unsure whether I want it to disappear when I open them again or if that would add a fresh break to my heart. I open my eyes, and the band is right there.

I consider turning away, but instead I slide the golden armband back where it was before all this happened. Then I slip my long-sleeved deep-green tunic on, not even bothering to belt it.

Checking myself in the mirror, I don't see the girl who left home for her birthday. Nor the woman I thought I'd become that night with Edmund either. I'm something in between. Sharper. Less trusting. Wiser.

Outside the door that my mama painted so lovingly years ago, Sy and Lorraine wait. Sy hands over a slim folder. I flip through it. *Easy-peasy,* I look up and hug him tightly. "Nice driving."

He laughs. "Anytime."

I turn to Lorraine and embrace her too. "Thank you for giving me your brave when I was scared."

She practically glows. "I'm glad we're friends, Grey."

"Me too."

They head to Sy's vehicle. Edmund stands leaning against his little green one. My heart leaps—and aches. He walks slowly toward me as I stand on the stoop.

"Grey, I am so, so sorry." His eyes search mine.

I am all out of tears. I nod. "I know. Thank you."

He doesn't deflect or explain. Doesn't try to plead.

"May I hold you?" he asks.

I pause a beat. Then nod. We step into each other's arms, and everything—grief, love, history—wraps around us like a fairy mist.

I don't want to break the spell, yet I know what I have to do. "Edmund..." I whisper into his chest, breathing him in one last time.

"Yes, Grey?"

"I love you, Edmund Sinclair."

I hear him pull in ragged breath as he kisses the top of my head. "I love you, Grey Shima."

It's time. I pull back and meet his eyes. Red-rimmed. Hollowed. Still beautiful. Still captivating.

"I love you," I say again. "And I never want to see you again."

Tears well in his eyes. He touches my cheek. "I completely understand."

He leans in to kiss me, but I turn my face so it lands on my cheek.

"Goodbye, Grey."

"Goodbye, Edmund."

I watch him walk the path, through the gate, into his vehicle. He drives away. No tears, but my heart is crushed to bits.

I stay where I am for several long moments, staring down the empty road, wondering where to turn next. Then Sy's car pulls back up.

He leans out the window. "Need a ride?"

My sadness makes just enough space for a smile. I reach up and feel the band Edmund gave me on my arm, and one of Mama's saying echoes in my mind. *Remember the love.*

"Yeah," I call to my best friend. "I'll be right there."

EPILOGUE

GREY

T̲ʜᴇ ʟᴀᴛᴇ Mᴀʏ ꜱᴜɴ ɪꜱ ᴡᴀʀᴍ ᴀꜱ I ᴡᴀʟᴋ ʜᴏᴍᴇ ꜰʀᴏᴍ ᴛʜᴇ ʙᴀꜱᴇ. I'ᴠᴇ done it. I just signed my enlistment papers: Come late summer, I'll be a Bosch Pirate Force trooper.

It wasn't an easy decision. No matter what's happened, I still have serious issues with the Glitter trade. But the way the whole base pulled together after the explosion. How they all rallied for Mama—oops, sorry—for the MC and all the people in the vicinity, reminded me that the primary job of the BPF is to ensure the safety of Bosch's citizenry. And that's what I want to do. I want to be safe and keep others safe.

And I've realized: If I have a problem with Glitter, I should work to create change from the inside. Also? I'm really looking forward to the flying, fighting, and shooting part of training, just like when I was little.

"I'm home," I call, stepping through the door. Rummy trots up, and I scratch her ears. The house is weirdly quiet. "Kik? Mac? Rini?"

Footsteps sound on the stairs, and Mama rounds the corner with a folder in her hand, smiling.

"There's my trooper," she greets affectionately. "How was it?"

I shrug. "Kinda…anticlimactic?"

She laughs, then winces and rubs her shoulder. It's mostly healed, but the range of motion's not great, and I know the pain is still with her.

"Well," she says, "after your spring, that tracks." She holds out the folder. "I want you to read this."

I eye her warily. "Why? What is it?"

"Read it," she says, her voice edging toward command.

I click my heels together and bring my right fist to my chest, then snap it smartly down. My first official BPF salute. "Ma'am, yes, ma'am."

Mama grins. "See to it, troop."

I plop onto the sofa and open the folder. Some of it is dry report-speak—but the meat of it…

"Mama…" I call out.

She leans in from the kitchen. "Yes?"

"BPF vessel engines and Bosch power… They run on *fusion*? Using *Glitter*?" I blink. "Seriously?"

She nods. "Yes, ma'am." She starts to step away again.

"Wait—so no hydrogen engines?" My assumption—hell, everyone's assumption—has always been that Bosch vessels are powered like any other intercontinental airships on New Earth: by hydrogen.

Her head pops back, looking expectant. "Nope."

"Wait again. Why are you telling me this now?"

She walks back into the room and stands straight, hands behind her back, commander mode engaged. "Trooper Shima, the contents of that folder are classified. All enlistees are briefed. You are permitted to discuss this only with active members of the Force. Not with family. Not outside Bosch borders. The rest of the world, particularly those allied with those little Blue folk, can keep thinking our vessels run on hydrogen."

She pauses, then lowers her voice conspiratorially and puts a hand to her mouth. "Well, the admin suspects China knows. But since they're usually jerks and no one believes them anyway, I'm not too worried."

She winks like a cartoon character and disappears into the kitchen.

I am laughing when something occurs to me.

Curtis.

He thought he would be igniting hydrogen. If that had been true, the fireball would've consumed everything—bleachers, the hangar…hell, probably half the base. But there was no hydrogen. No Glitter either except what was already sealed inside the engines.

He died believing he was a martyr.

And he was…for a lie.

I refocus on the next section, so I don't have to feel my anger. But I'll be sure to share it with Emily, my therapist.

I return to the folder. And I'm once again stunned. I flip back and forth, reading and rereading. It takes me almost a bell to understand it all. There is more to all of this than the love of Glitter and profits and pirates. Something bigger. Something Mama knew but couldn't tell. Once finished, I sit for moment on the sofa, shaking my head. Then I head to the bar cart and pour two glasses of Warner Wine—yep, that Warner. Matt's family. Which means kinda mine too.

I bring one into the kitchen and slide it toward Mama, who's reading.

She looks up and smiles. "Well?"

I raise my glass. "You always had a plan. No more Glitter sales in thirty years."

She lifts hers. "I always had a hope. *You*, Grey Shima, are why I made it a plan."

We clink.

A new day. A new mission.

Here's to what comes next.

ACKNOWLEDGMENTS

Writing *For the Love of Glitter* has been a joy-filled challenge—a return to the world of Bosch through younger eyes, where first love, radical ideas, and personal identity collide. Grey's journey surprised me more than once, and I am so grateful for the village that helped bring her voice, and this story, to life.

To my phenomenal book coach and dear friend, Martha Bullen, thank you for your steady guidance, gentle nudges, and ever-encouraging belief in this story—and in me. Your presence in my writing life is a gift.

Deep appreciation to Dave Aretha and Andrea Vanryken, whose editorial acumen continues to sharpen my prose. And heartfelt thanks to Rebecca Maizel, whose thoughtful developmental feedback helped shape this manuscript into a stronger, more emotionally resonant story.

A special shoutout to Maggie McLaughlin, my formatting and tech wizard. From troubleshooting metadata glitches to ensuring a smooth launch, you are an unsung hero behind every book release.

I'm forever grateful to my beta readers and early reviewers—especially those who shared such thoughtful insights about love, activism, friendship, and growing up under pressure. Your reflections helped me polish Grey, Sy, and Edmund into the complicated teens they are meant to be.

Thanks to the ever-talented Alan Hebel and Ian Koviak of The Book Designers for once again creating a breathtaking cover that captures the fire and heart of this story.

To my incredible street team and social media supporters:

thank you for helping *Glitter* sparkle across platforms. Your word-of-mouth magic is the reason new readers find their way to Bosch.

To the educators, book clubs, and podcast hosts who invite me into conversations about stories, thank you for making space for speculative fiction with soul.

To my amazing children—David and Jana, Megan and Josh, Daniel and Jansu—thank you for being constant cheerleaders and creators in your own right. To my grands—Jude, Will, Ezra, Desmond, Julian, and Dilara—your curiosity and imagination remind me why storytelling matters.

And always, always to Rick, my partner, anchor, and sounding board. Thank you for believing in me and for being my truest compass.

ABOUT THE AUTHOR

Award-winning author **Sarah Branson** spent nearly thirty years as a midwife before pivoting to write feminist speculative fiction filled with action, adventure, romance, and resilience. Her debut, *A Merry Life*, won the 2022 Connecticut Adult Fiction Award from the Indie Author Project and launched her four-book *Pirates of New Earth* series. She has since expanded her universe with books for young adult, middle grade, and adult readers, including the YA novel *For the Love of Glitter* and the adult standalone *North Country*. Learn more at www.sarahbranson.com

ALSO BY SARAH BRANSON

Pirates of New Earth Series

Book One: A Merry Life

Book Two: Navigating the Storm

Book Three: Burn the Ship

Book Four: Blow the Man Down

The Legacy of Bosch

Unfurling the Sails: A Grey Shima Adventure

A Pirates' Pact: A Kik & Mac Adventure

The Adventure Continues

North Country: A Kat Wallace Adventure

www.ingramcontent.com/pod-product-compliance
Lightning Source LLC
Chambersburg PA
CBHW061807190726
48289CB00007B/2102